LIBERTY
BAZAAR

Published in the UK by Aurora Metro Books in 2015
67 Grove Avenue, Twickenham TW1 4HX
www.aurorametro.com   info@aurorametro.com

Liberty Bazaar © copyright 2015 David Chadwick
Cover Design: Arianna Osti © 2015
Editor: Cheryl Robson

Aurora Metro Books would like to thank Simon Smith, Neil Gregory,
Richard Turk, Suzanne Mooney, Grace Thiele, Lucia Vornicu.

Printed by Berforts Information Press, UK.
ISBN 978-1-906582-92-0

LIBERTY BAZAAR

BY

DAVID CHADWICK

AURORA METRO BOOKS

ACKNOWLEDGEMENTS

I am deeply grateful to the academic staff and my alumni group at Manchester Metropolitan University Writing School, where this novel began its journey, as well as to Cheryl Robson, my editor at Aurora Metro, for valued insights and input.

I am also enormously indebted to Stephen Gallagher, Dallas Hackett and Shirley Morgan, for encouragement, belief and kindness over more years than I care to remember.

For Sharon with love

1

EXPERIENCES IN THE LIFE OF A SLAVE GIRL BY TRINITY GIDDINGS

Society Hill, South Carolina, September 1863

Slipping out of the Big House before first fowl crow, I found a gap in the peach orchard fence and went east. My plan, such as it was, meant finding the landing stage at Society Hill then hiding on a steamboat to take me down the Great Pee Dee River to Georgetown on the coast. From there I'd take my chances: the railroad north, or a ship to Havana. I was young – twenty-four that June gone – and paid no mind to what I would do with my freedom.

Long time ago. But I recall the moment of that decision so clearly. Two occurrences colliding: my mother's death but twelve hours gone; and the stripes applied not much earlier by my owner's wife, Mistress Honoria Giddings. My beating had been light – no unsightly scars to drive down my value on the auction block – and without witness, though this was less about my dignity than hers. The whipping was Missy Honoria's way of telling me privately to quit tempting her husband.

No matter that he was the wrong-doer and I the victim. See, this was South Carolina. This state, more than any, lived out the small print in the Declaration of Independence that said: *Nigger want justice, he don't get it here.*

Same afternoon I got beat, the Lord took my mother. She passed away quietly on the straw mattress where she'd lain these two months gone. Physician said she hadn't suffered greatly and I believed him.

Last of my family done gone.

It was like this: my father died sometime past in an accident repairing the big cotton gin. Brother Benjamin lately drowned in the river. Everybody said this was by tragic accident, but we all knew otherwise. No other living relatives, least not that I knew of. Missy Honoria and my owner, Master Zebulon Giddings, perceived these things all too well. After my mother's burial they would watch close, suspecting I'd run. No family – what's to lose? But they wouldn't watch me *before* my mother's burial. Now, tonight, was my brief and only opportunity.

Anger and regret aplenty bundled in my head. Guilt, too. Girl leaves her mother unburied, she's got a powerful price to pay. But right now, no room for sentiment, no time for tears.

It seemed so simple – until those patrollers stepped out from behind a big old tree. With their lanterns shining in my face, the confidence that spurred me to quit the plantation began to wilt.

"Where you going in such haste, girl, before sunrise?" In the cone of yellow radiance, the older patroller's pinched and stubble-shaded face, smelled of whiskey when he breathed.

"My mama took down poorly, sir, and the Massa sent me out for the doctor." I could speak properly, even in those days – or at least reasonably well – but pretended a slouchy rural accent for these patrollers. They looked like poor whites, people with a special dislike for black folk with any hint of schooling so I took care to give them no excuse to turn nasty. Not that they needed one.

There was a sly glint in the second patroller's eye. He was much younger than his companion – young enough to fight with the Rebels against the Yankees. So why was he here? My belly agitated. Were they deserters? Robbers? "Where you from, girl?"

"Giddings' plantation, sir. Small piece on from Society Hill."

"Let's see your pass."

Fumbling in my dress, I found the note, apparently from my master, that I'd written a few hours earlier, giving permission to go to Society Hill for the physician.

Younger patroller placed his lantern on the ground and took the pass from me using the same hand, and I realised he'd lost an arm. Then, as he leaned into the lamplight, I saw the flesh on one side of his face was missing, from an eyeless socket to the shattered jawbone. This boy done finished fighting, I could tell that much.

They studied on my counterfeit pass a long while, tilting the notepaper this way and that. Perhaps they couldn't read so well; perhaps they suspected me. At last they seemed to grow tired of their inspection and let me on my way.

I walked quickly for a spell to get away from those patrollers, then stopped and sat by the roadside, head in hands, quivering. Not three miles from the plantation and already thinking about turning tail. If I hurried, I'd be back in the Big House before Missy Honoria awoke.

Yet this was my one chance for freedom. I made myself consider the consequences of failure: Massa Zebulon's unwelcome attention; the burrowing fear that sooner or later he would wear me down. All the while, Missy Honoria, already suspicious, would continue to chastise me.

I had another motive. My previous owner and benefactress, Missy Antonia Giddings done schooled me in arts and sciences, excited my mind with rich tangs of knowledge. But my education was hotchpotch, half-done. I spied bright rays in the dark, but nothing to join the one to the next. Missy Antonia had a mind to free me, but took poorly and died before she could make things legal. So I passed into the ownership of her son, Zebulon. He stopped my lessons and started chasing me. Kinder if I'd learned nothing at all. See, this unfinished schooling meant I belonged nowhere: not the scullery, nor the library. Only by escaping could I finish what Missy Antonia begun.

Fortified by these notions, I pressed on, reaching Society Hill without further hindrance soon after sun-up.

A big paddle steamer named *Stonewall Jackson* was moored to the landing stage. Outside the warehouse, four rib-thin mules hitched to a wagon, but no sign of the teamster. Small piece downstream, I saw a ferry converted into a Confederate gunboat. Two rebel soldiers in ragged butternut blouses sat in the shade, sipping from tin mugs. Prospects better than I could have hoped for.

Finding a private spot among some willow trees, I took off my linsey-woolsey dress. Missy Honoria insisted all her house girls wear garments of this coarse wool and linen twill, which I regarded as a symbol of servitude. Soft chains, maybe; chains nonetheless and removing them was powerful uplifting.

Next, I pulled on the mariner's costume I'd put together using various garments from the Big House – woollen shirt, sturdy trousers, short blue coat and straw hat with enough of a brim to disguise the upper part of my face. Adopting my hastily practised sailor's gait, I set off toward the landii

Greasy black weaves of smoke were rising up fr twin stacks of the paddleboat. Clearly, the captain was i steam and, please Lord, would be casting off very soon. Front of the boat was stacked with cotton bales that almost came up to the wheelhouse – any higher and the captain couldn't see where he was going. There was another stack of bales at the back and two wooden gangplanks ran from each end of the boat to the landing stage.

I headed for the one at the rear – less going on there. I reached the junction of the gangplank and the landing stage when two sounds sent my heart into a crazy scamper: bloodhounds baying; and shrill piping of the boat's whistle. Massa Zebulon coming; steamboat going east.

Next few minutes would see me gone from the plantation one way or the other. If this child couldn't escape on the steamer, I'd jump in that river and drown myself for sure. Mind made up. Swear to God.

Quick glance around. Some men up front uncoiling mooring ropes, no one at the back. Three figures high in the wheelhouse, looking forward.

Placing one foot on the wooden laths of the gangplank, I started forward, slowly, quietly. Already the sun was melting the tar seams between the timbers. Bare feet fizzed with pain and I had to ward myself against rushing: noise or sudden movement certain to get me caught.

Half way there. Giddy with tension. Few seconds more, I'd be across.

"You, there!"

The shout froze me.

"Yes – you!"

Dizzily, I looked down at the band of water between boat

and shore, scummy-brown and choked with trash: half-sunk whiskey bottle, boxwood fragments, rotted coal-sack. Dead rat too, floating on his back. Not a pleasant place to drown. If there was such a place.

I looked up to the deck above. Captain leaning over the rail making angry gestures with his arms. "Where's that damned river pilot?"

Pause. Somewhere, bloodhounds yowling. Somewhere, my unburied mother.

Another voice shouted backed to the captain: "I seed him in the store, sir, not ten minutes gone. Reeked of rum."

Now I realised this conversation had nothing to do with me.

"Fetch him this very instant, Corporal, before he gets even drunker." The captain was clearly furious with this errant river pilot. "We can't move without him."

Needing no more encouragement, I stepped the few remaining paces onto the deck of the *Stonewall Jackson* and quickly made my way to the stacked cotton bales at the back.

Each bale was perhaps five feet long by three feet deep and bound in a coarse jute jacket that was fastened by a half-dozen hemp belts. Using the gaps between the bales for hand and foot holds, I began to climb. At last, sweating and panting, I found myself sitting atop a big flat cushion of cotton some twenty feet above the deck. Behind me was a sheer drop from the back of the boat into the water. Ahead, the wooden bulk of the steamer's balconied cabins and saloons concealed the wheel house and on either side were the big paddle wheels.

Peeking over the edge of my cotton mountain, I saw crewmen heaving the gangplank on board the boat, while another group unfastened mooring ropes at the back.

Again, the baying of bloodhounds carried on the baked air. I looked across to the far bank and saw the tawny hounds busily sniffing among the willows and reeds, while a horseman rode back and forth along the bank.

Then, very slowly at first, the front of the boat began to swing away from the landing stage. Peering over the side, I saw a widening arrowhead of water below. A hysterical exultation brimmed up in me. The *Stonewall Jackson* shivered into motion, powerful paddle wheels threshing the water, driving us forward into the broad elbow of the river.

Society Hill quickly passed out of sight.

*

Jubilation was soon replaced by fresh concerns. I presumed the *Stonewall Jackson* was bound for Georgetown, but what to do when I got there?

I would not be recognised beyond the vicinity of Society Hill. Yet I was sure my owners would spare no effort to recover me for reasons of principle and, in Massa Zebulon's case, sexual appetite. Just as compelling was the incentive of finance. As a young healthy female mulatto, I represented expensive property, although the inclination to run away would reduce my value. All the same, advertisements would be placed in the 'Escaped Negroes' columns of newspapers throughout South Carolina, alerting folk to the particulars of my appearance and the substantial cash reward for my return.

In the meantime, I was confined to my perch on the stack of cotton bales. Georgetown was a good fifty or sixty miles down the river and the boat would take the whole day to get there, maybe more. Nor was my position as comfortable as I'd expected. Sun hoisted himself high into the unclouded sky and beat down on me without pause. No shade. No wind. Vinegary stink and itch of cheap jute covering the cotton. And the warm cotton itself making my journey hotter and drier and dustier.

Afternoon dragged. Sun seemed to hang, unmoving, directly above. Small towns, uncannily similar to Society Hill, stole by so slow that I had a sensation of the boat not moving and all the towns and villages in South Carolina parading by, as if they were leaving, and I was being left behind.

Late afternoon and two crewmen sauntered to the back of the boat, sat by the guard rail chewing tobacco. Like the patrollers who accosted me in the night, they were long-shanked country boys with dusty faces and hayrick hair. At first their arrival made me anxious, but they had no cause to suspect I was up there and soon I found their banter pleasantly diverting.

That was until one named Nate explained to the other – fellow named Jimmy – that the *Stonewall Jackson* was not bound for Georgetown, but a concealed anchorage in Winyah Bay. There, they would transfer the cotton to a British blockade runner that would slip in and out under a quarter moon before the blockading Yankee warships were any the wiser.

Up there on my spongy perch, my head was fitten to burst. Everyone in the South knew the only Rebel currency that done kept any value was cotton, sold to British textile merchants for huge monies. Much as this child wanted the North to win, a small Southern success in this far-flung corner of the country would suit my purposes. North Island was the gateway to the Atlantic. Stowed away on a blockade runner, I would be on my way to Britain that very next morning.

*

Yankees had a different plan.

The *Stonewall Jackson* had crossed Winyah Bay at dusk and

now lay at anchor near a stretch of low-lying land I presumed was North Island. Not much to see in the gathering darkness: makeshift jetty and wooden buildings hunkered on a bleak foreshore.

They started unloading the cotton from the front of the boat and I seized the opportunity to get off at the back. Clambering down the jute sacking, I dropped the last six feet to the deck with a thump.

Sensed the man's presence immediately.

"What you been doing up there?" The voice was vaguely familiar.

Turning slowly, I was confronted by the crewman named Nate. Close to, he seemed much more formidable than from twenty feet up. Twitchy eyes, ratty face, crumpled skin inlaid with grime. Stench of tobacco spittle and sour sweat as he came still closer, knife tucked in the front of his belt.

He raised his voice. "You deaf, boy?"

Dazed by the suddenness of his appearance, I done forgotten I was in my mariner's clothes. Whatever he suspected, it was not that I was a runaway slave girl. Not yet anyhow. I had to exploit my advantage before it disappeared. "They sent me from the jetty, sir. Said to climb up and check them bales on top ain't got damaged coming down the river."

"You mean they sent you by way of making sure they ain't getting short-changed."

I shrugged, played like I didn't know anything except to do what I was ordered.

"All right, boy, you done your checking. Now do something that's useful."

Grabbing my shoulder, he pushed me to the guard rail, pointing to a bar of rocks protruding from the seaward side of the anchorage. "See that spit of land?"

He leaned in close and I looked in the direction indicated by his outstretched finger.

"There's a dinghy tied onto the port side. Take it out there so you're just off that spit and holler when you see the runner coming in. Understand?"

I started across the boat towards the side, but he stepped across my path so we almost collided.

"Whereabouts you from, boy?"

"Georgetown, sir."

"You know the Royal Hotel in Johnson Street?"

I nodded, eyes fixed on a point someplace between his jaw and chest.

"Now that's powerful peculiar, boy, seeing that there ain't no Royal Hotel in Georgetown and even if there were, it wouldn't be on Johnson Street 'cause that don't exist neither."

Tried to speak. Failed.

"You surely do come from the damnedest place ..." His eyes were fixed on the swell of my breast where the mariner's jacket done come open. "All the boys there have tits, do they?"

Tried to move. He was too fast. Caught my arm, jarred me up against him.

Then I did move. Pulled the knife from his belt, pushed it inside his belly. Blood, oozing warm and thick and slow over my fingers, like spilled gravy, slopping on the wooden deck.

"Why'd you do that?" His narrow face made a smile, almost wistful. "Won't going to hurt you none." Then he collapsed on the deck.

"I couldn't know that," I told him, though he didn't hear me.

I let go the knife, backed off to the guard rail. Dinghy tied on below, as he said. I climbed over the side and slid into the boat. Last thing I recalled of him was that same, gently offended smile. I hoped they found him before he bled out.

The oars were stowed in the bottom of the dinghy. Using one to push off from the side of the steamboat, I pulled away hard as I could into the gloom. Had to master the art of rowing fast; pulled like the devil till I had to stop, arms numb with exertion. When I glanced back, I saw I'd turned a full circle and was headed back toward the *Stonewall Jackson*. Tried again, this time minding to pull on those oars together. Next time I looked, I'd put a good hundred yards between me and the steamer. The rocky strand Nate had indicated was perhaps a further hundred yards off. When my arms regained a little strength, I headed for it, thinking to round the headland and make my way up the coast of North Island.

Shout from the land and I thought they'd found Nate and were raising the alarm. I expected gunfire. Heard it, too. But then I realised this was heavy stuff – cannon, not muskets.

I saw the two ships at once in the faint light of the quarter-moon: sleek blockade runner and a tall-masted Yankee frigate. From my little dinghy, they seemed almost to be touching. How far out, hard to tell, but they seemed powerful close to the shore. Blink of light from the frigate as she fired again. Great column of water rose up by the runner, but still she steered for the coast. I sensed she was in striking distance. The Yankee ship turned, maybe fearing to run onto the rocky shoals. Blockade runners could sail shallow waters, I knew that much.

Another flicker from the frigate. Louder boom. Flash of light. Whole shoreline lit up, just for an instant. My dinghy dipped into a trough of sea and when it rose up again, the runner was transformed into a blazing wreck. Shattered wood and metal went spinning up into the orange glow.

Hard to believe such complete destruction could happen so fast. All those souls gone in that fierce sheet of flame. Surely no survivors, not that I could imagine. These runners carried munitions and this would account for the powerful detonation.

Thoughts returned to my own situation. What to do now? Obviously, there was no going back to the *Stonewall Jackson*. They'd find poor Nate soon, then start combing the island. I could see the Yankee frigate; guessed she was about two or three hundred yards out to sea.

My idea seemed sound enough: if I could catch up with her while she searched for survivors, I'd be taken on board.

With fresh vigour, this child pulled towards the burning wreckage, glancing eagerly over my shoulder to measure progress. Again, I had to rest, boating the oars, panting and sweating, waiting for strength to return.

But when I looked again, the blazing debris had somehow come between me and the land. Frantic, I tried to row back. My efforts were futile. Even as I watched, the flames dimmed and disappeared. That was the moment I realised I was being carried into the ocean by the tide. I shouted for help, succeeding only in hurting my throat. I railed at my own stupidity. But there was no use in any of it and I sank back, gazed at the faint lace of cloud in the almost black sky.

I thought of how far and how little I had travelled. Absent-mindedly, I realised I was going to die.

*

Some time on.

Rich smell of ocean brine, darkness replaced by light. Another bright September day. Probably my last.

Drowsed in the rising heat.

I awoke to shouting.

Opened my eyes, then shut them tight closed, dazzled by

daylight. Loud voices again. They were speaking English yet somehow it sounded foreign. Raising myself on my elbows, I looked over the side of the dinghy. The Yankee frigate's stout wooden sides towered high above me, and above them, great masts and yards.

Something not right about the flag. Not the Stars and Stripes; not the Southern Cross neither. Too confused to be scared.

Boat full of mariners bumped into my dinghy. Black man gazing down at me – but wearing the peaked cap and gilt lace of an officer. Stranger still, a white sailor next to him, saying: "Seems to be alive, sir."

I'd be lying if I didn't say I was much less surprised at being pronounced alive than by a white fellow calling a Negro 'sir'.

2

RECOLLECTIONS OF A CONFEDERATE GENERAL BY JUBAL DE BROOKE

Chickamauga Creek, Georgia; and Charleston, South Carolina, September, 1863.

The Union infantry was waiting behind its entrenchments across a picket-fenced meadow where corn once grew.

"General de Brooke, sir!"

Glancing across my shoulder, I saw Lieutenant Fickling, one of my commanding officer's aides, rein in his frantic horse dangerously close to our front line.

I called out to him. "It would please me greatly, Mr Fickling, if you would come down from your saddle. You will present less of a target and I shouldn't want you shot before you relay your message." A poor joke, but it would help to calm the lieutenant whose agitated state was having an unsettling effect on my boys.

Hurriedly dismounting, and leading his horse away from the forward position, Fickling made an extravagant salute.

"General Longstreet's compliments, sir, and he would be greatly obliged if you would attack immediately."

"Thank you, Mr Fickling," I said. "Please return my compliments and inform General Longstreet that I will advance at once."

Fickling made another windmill-like salute and remounted his horse.

My brigade of nearly three thousand men was drawn up directly before the Federal entrenchments. If we had attacked early that morning, as planned, the enemy would not have had so much time to arrange its defences. But the sloppy issuing of orders delayed the attack until midday.

We went forward with fixed bayonets across open ground towards the Federal breastworks, perhaps two hundred yards distant.

Initially, we moved slowly, at common time – seventy yards per minute. The Federals opened fire almost immediately, but, at this range, the accuracy of their shooting was poor and we pressed on, accelerating our advance to quick time. Another ripple of enfilade fire depleted our line, then another. Men were skittled and scattered and smashed, some crying out, others strangely silent – perhaps not believing that after beating the odds so many times, fortune had deserted them.

At less than one hundred yards, I ordered double quick time. A further volley thinned our line, yet didn't break it.

Half a dozen paces to my left, Sergeant Major Laws took a bullet in the throat and keeled sideways, taking our battle flag with him. Another member of the colour guard picked it up, became an instant target, and was struck down within seconds. A third man – Sergeant Papajohn – snatched up the flag, this time prevailing, at least while a cloud of scorched gunpowder obscured him from enemy rifles.

Our respite was brief. The next volley raked our entire line. The attack stalled.

Men looked groggily to their sergeants; and they to their officers. But so many had fallen that leaderless gaggles loitered like confused children amid the field of human wreckage.

Our colours remained clearly visible in Papajohn's hands. But, for the first time since I had known them, these veterans of the Army of Northern Virginia needed more than a flag.

I was not given to showmanship, yet I had to concede there were times when it was effective. So I stuck my hat on the tip of my sword and held it high to show them their general was still there – that we would go on together.

"Virginians! To me!" My voice sounded curiously dislocated, as if projected from some other's throat.

There was a long pause. Men wavered, looking about themselves.

"You heard the general, boys!" Papajohn waved our flag, oblivious to the hail of minié balls that reduced it to a rag. "Surely, you ain't gonna keep him waiting?"

A ripple of shouts, even the odd cheer, transmitted along the ranks. Slowly at first, the brigade resumed its advance, gathering pace on the hard dirt furrows.

At last, we charged full tilt and I felt the familiar embrace of wild yet remote madness.

The Federals were hastily reloading their Springfields, knowing they had time only for one more volley.

Nearer we came, nearer still, until we could see their teeth flashing white as they bit off the ends of their paper-wrapped cartridges, then poured the powder into their muzzles.

My hat had slid down my sword half way to the hilt, yet it could still be seen; and although I could hardly be heard, I shouted again in that other voice: "Over we go, boys!

For Virginia!"

The Yankees fired at point blank range. More of us fell, torn and split. Yet we were upon them now, streaming over their breastworks. They fought bravely, but were overwhelmed in the close-quarter fighting. These were the moments that haunted me most: looking into the enemy's eyes; smelling his breath; feeling his blood warm and thick between my fingers – fearing it might not be his but mine. The only mercy of these encounters was their brevity. They were simply too frenzied to last. The Yankees not directly engaged began to throw down their weapons. Others withdrew towards Missionary Ridge and Snodgrass Hill.

As the shooting began to stop, a faint draft licked my cheek – a minié ball fizzing by, not two inches from my face. Sergeant Papajohn was less fortunate. He was hit above the elbow. Mashed bone gleamed white in ripped flesh.

"Damn." He spoke softly, as if inconvenienced by a trifling mishap.

I turned to the soldier next to him. "Get a tourniquet on that arm right away, then take the sergeant directly to the surgeon."

Papajohn looked at me and we exchanged grim nods as a jean-cloth strip was lashed in place and tightened to stop the bleeding. We both knew he would lose the arm.

*

The Confederacy won the battle of Chickamauga. But our losses – eighteen thousand casualties – prevented the capture of our main objective, the city of Chattanooga, eight miles to the north.

Nowhere was the human cost more evident than in the field hospitals where my duties oftener involved attending dying men than recovering souls. In all honesty, I didn't know how many more times I could look another hopeless man in his eyes. It would have been easier – and perhaps kinder – to stay away. Yet these were my people. I had brought them to this. How could I leave them now?

Sergeant Papajohn had lost his arm as we had feared. Yet there was worse. Infection claimed more lives than bullets and my friend was not expected to survive the morning. The surgeon, Major Crisp, met me at the entrance to one of the hospital tents. He wore a crimson-streaked apron and a weary mien.

"Sergeant Papajohn is waiting for you, sir."

"Thank you, Mr Crisp." I paused, about to exchange pleasantries, but his look forestalled me.

"I advise haste, General."

Inside the tent, the unmoving air held an ill-suited weave of odours: damp canvas; human waste; suppurating wounds; chlorine. Flies circled and weaved over the maggots being used to cleanse open wounds.

Papajohn was lying alone in a corner, his complexion waxen but his expression unconcerned. I had seen this aspect of resignation before, but it only became harder with each passing life.

"Doc's give up on me, ain't he, sir?"

"I'm sorry. There's nothing to be done."

"How long?"

"Not long."

Not a trace of doubt or fear. How I envied his peace.

Placing his hand over his face, he smoothed his eyes closed with his fingers, then stretched himself straight, crossing his arm over his chest.

"I'd be obliged if you'd fix me, sir."

I completed the procedure by using a brass safety pin to fasten the toes of his stockings together. Boys often arranged themselves for burial in this way before letting go, content that they were in good order for the grave as they had been for the line of battle.

Papajohn died a few minutes later and part of me died with him. I'd lost more people than I cared to recall, but none had given as much of himself as this man. He never quit, never shirked the smallest duty, and never complained. He'd been at my side at Mechanicsville and Fredericksburg, Chancellorsville and Gettysburg and a string of smaller engagements; some nameless, all bloody. I didn't know if I could go on without him. I said a prayer and walked out into the thickening dusk.

*

Some time later, in my bivouac, I removed my coat and took a glass of whiskey into which I poured a few drops of laudanum tincture. These substances were no cure, but they did help me to sleep that little bit deeper, blinded me to those visions of exaggerated reality that could not have been real at all. If my mind played tricks, the tincture helped still them.

Sitting back in my canvas chair, I took from my breast pocket the small leather-bound bible handed down to me by my grandfather. When he gave it to me some thirty years ago I believed I had received a token of my birthright. Inside the fly-cover, there was an inscription in pale ink: "To Robert de Brooke, from his good and loyal friend Lazarus Hotchkiss". My Grandfather Robert had never mentioned Lazarus Hotchkiss, although he died when I was still a child so that wasn't so surprising. All the same, I was always impressed by this simple affirmation of one man's loyalty to another in those equally bloody days when my grandfather cut his ties with Britain and enlisted in Washington's army.

Sipping more of the whiskey and tincture mix, I glanced at the small portrait of my grandfather that I kept in my mess chest. He would have been about my age – thirty-eight – when it had been painted, and there was a marked resemblance in the sharp cheekbones either side of a narrow nose, the broad mouth and large deep blue eyes. A clear difference was evident, though, in his almost bald head which contrasted sharply with my dense, dark hair perhaps inherited from my grandmother's side of the family.

Absently, I pondered where he would have been in all this … Like me, he'd taken up arms against central authority, but not without deep contemplation. The truth was that I'd never know whether he'd have fought for the Confederacy or the Union.

I must have fallen asleep, for I was roused by attacking Yankee cavalry.

I heard the beat of hooves, a screeching bugle, ragged gunfire. Seizing my sword, I ran from the bivouac and saw the Federal horsemen with impossible clarity: faces masked by wide-brimmed slouch hats; scarlet guidons vivid against dusty tunics; sabres glinting; carbines raised.

They were almost upon Lieutenant Fickling. Incredibly, he wasn't aware of them.

"Fickling! Get out of the way!"

Scurrying forwards, I knocked over a pail of milk and barged though a line of laundry before hurling myself at the lieutenant. We tumbled to the ground together and I rolled sideways, ready to parry a sabre thrust.

But the Yankee riders had vanished; and Fickling, his head wrapped in a turban of undergarments from the toppled laundry line, was not looking at me with the expression of a man whose life I had just saved. His expression was more like pity.

*

"Join me for a little refreshment, de Brooke."

My commanding officer, General James Longstreet, indicated a chair by his desk. His headquarters was located in a semi-derelict farmhouse, two miles behind the front lines.

Longstreet ladled some brandy peaches into two bowls, then handed one to me.

"Nice manufacture," he said, between mouthfuls, examining the back of his fork. "Sheffield, England. You have family over there, don't you?"

"There has been no correspondence since the Revolution, sir."

Longstreet feigned surprise. He was an imposing man with square features and a full bush beard. Dark hair was swept back from a wide brow and his eyes were shrewdly expressive. "I was given to understand your grandfather was an English nobleman and your ancestors fought in their civil war."

"That is true, sir. But as far as I'm aware, there has never been any attempt to resume relations with our English cousins."

Through the window, I could see a column of field artillery labouring along the hard clay road that ran north to Chatanooga. Above the clatter of hooves and grind of wheels, heavy guns squealed and groaned in wooden limbers hauled by teams of six horses. Men cursed and whips snapped in the hot, dusty air.

"All the same, General, I guess you'd like to visit England, given your professional background and all." He was studying me with a peculiar curiosity that I found mildly irritating.

"I don't follow you, sir." It seemed unpleasantly warm in this upstairs room and I set about unfastening the uppermost buttons on my double-breasted tunic. One became entangled in some loose thread in the buttonhole. I tugged, frustrated, but couldn't pull it free.

After carefully dissecting a peach with his little fork, Longstreet eventually glanced up at me. "You were a newspaper editor before the war, weren't you?"

"Yes, I was, but my paper reported news in southern Pennsylvania, sir. Its circulation area, although growing, didn't quite extend to the other side of the Atlantic."

Longstreet indulged my mild sarcasm with a good-humoured chuckle and downed his last portion of brandy peach.

Unable to contain my impatience any longer, I decided to press him. "Sir, this conversation about my family is very pleasant, but I'm anxious to know why you wanted to see me. Are we to move on Chatanooga?"

Longstreet gave me a long, studied look. "How is your health?"

"Good, thank you, sir. Holding up …" Again I started to fiddle with my loose tunic button, but I tugged too hard: the thread snapped. The gilded metal button slipped between my fingers and went skittering noisily across the wooden floorboards.

Longstreet searched a stack of documents on his desk and retrieved a copy of the *Richmond Examiner*. "I've been reading your letter to the editor." His expression became lugubrious. "It isn't every day that a Confederate general argues that slaves should be freed in return for fighting for the South. What sort of reaction did you think you would provoke?"

"My comments were entirely reasonable," I said, perhaps

too quickly. "You once said yourself that we should have abolished slavery and then fired on Fort Sumter."

"That was a speculative remark made in private – not in one of the most influential newspapers in the South. You have provoked uproar among some extremely powerful people." He was clearly annoyed.

"Where is this leading, sir?"

Longstreet started to smile, but seemed to think better of it. "England. You will take ship to Liverpool where you are to revive your family connections to bolster support for the Confederacy. We have many wealthy and influential friends among the British ruling classes and their support could be critical to our success in this war."

I felt as though I'd taken a minié ball in the chest that had driven the air from my lungs. Earlier that week I'd seen Papajohn buried, along with hundreds of others. Now it seemed the rest of my boys were being taken from me. I was going to lose everything I lived for ... "But I belong here, sir, with my brigade."

Longstreet's voice acquired a compassionate softness. "You no longer have a brigade. You lost half your strength at Chickamauga Creek."

The memory of the slaughter was hard to bear, and I struggled to respond.

"But we won that day, sir. I implore you to reconsider."

"It's out of my hands, now." Longstreet picked up an official-looking letter. "This arrived this morning, direct from Richmond. The War Department has decided that you will go to England as our envoy."

"But my boys – "

Longstreet held up a flat hand to halt my protest. "You can still help your boys, Jubal. Liverpool is to hold a Grand Liberty

Bazaar in aid of the families of Confederate prisoners held in the North. The organisers are confident they can raise as much as twenty thousand pounds – that's more than one hundred thousand dollars. Imagine what that amount of money could do to relieve the destitution among the wives and children of our boys penned up in those prison camps."

"General Longstreet, sir, I am a soldier not a diplomat – "

"Please, Jubal. Sit down."

I hadn't realised that I had come to my feet, and returned to my seat, muttering an apology.

"As a friend, I hope you won't mind me saying you haven't been yourself of late. It's come to my attention that there have been a number of … episodes." He raised one eyebrow. "Only this morning you bowled over Lieutenant Fickling for your whole camp to see, hollering about an ambush by Yankee cavalry."

With great force of will, I kept my hands away from those damned buttons and looked at him directly. "Are you telling me I am unfit for command, sir?"

Longstreet made a fatigued sigh. "I am telling you that you are one of the finest brigadiers in the Confederacy; that you have been identified by the War Department as being uniquely capable of carrying out an important diplomatic mission in Great Britain. But more than any of these, I am telling you that you have pushed yourself too far, too hard, for too long and must take this opportunity to recuperate."

"I see." The grim set of my commanding officer's face told me that it would be futile to object. Suddenly, I felt too tired to argue further ...

Reaching forward across the desk, Longstreet picked up an envelope, sealed in red wax with the stamp of the War Department, and handed it to me. "These are your orders.

There is a ship waiting for you at Charleston."

*

The waterfront at Charleston, where the Ashley and Cooper rivers emptied into the Atlantic, was the most lucrative location in the South for profiteers and shysters, shady dealers and reckless captains with fast ships.

So I decided to stay clear of the thronging jetties and quaysides until my ship was ready to sail on the next tide. She was a blockade runner called the *Owl*, a powerful paddle steamer that could outrun any Yankee warship and she was bound for Liverpool in England.

Away from the waterfront, Charleston presented a pleasantly distracting maze of thin streets crowded by antique buildings.

I visited a bookshop where I bought some reading matter for the sea passage – The *Southern Literary Messenger* and some novels by British authors – William Makepeace Thackeray's *Vanity Fair* which I hadn't read since I was up at Harvard Yard, together with Dickens' recently published *Great Expectations*, in three volumes. In addition, I obtained a copy of *Redburn* by Herman Melville, in which the city of Liverpool figured prominently.

Because of the shortages, there was little fare of any worth to be had in the restaurants of Charleston, so I made my way back to the quayside and was drawn to a small workshop where an elderly potter sat at his wheel, fashioning shapeless fists of clay into the most astonishing artefacts. In that moment, I felt deeply envious of this modest craftsman and his ability to create form and grace, for it seemed my talents lay only in violence and destruction.

I chose two dishes and a small vase for my mess chest, which came to just fifteen cents. I handed him a Confederate five dollar bill, but he shook his head with a look of embarrassed apology.

"Mighty sorry, sir, but I don't have that much cash in the shop."

"Please, General de Brooke, let me help." A lissom young woman stepped from behind me, opening her purse as she came.

"You have me at a disadvantage, ma'am."

"Sarah McConville." She extended a hand. "You and I are to sail aboard the same ship – the *Owl*. I know we haven't been properly introduced, but that would have happened very shortly in any event." She spoke with an English accent, but the vowel sounds were elongated and there was a brusqueness to the cadence of her words that I'd heard before the war when I met a fellow editor from Manchester, in the north of England.

"Miss McConville, I must thank you for your kindness but politely decline. I can't accept charity from a lady on the foundation of an acquaintance made but moments ago."

"Nonsense. You may call it a short-term loan, General." She gave me a penetrating look and I noticed that, although attractive, her face had a harsh aspect – slightly rough-edged, like the accent.

She handed the potter a Bank of South Carolina one dollar bill which he cut in two with scissors, handing one half back and making up the rest of the change in silver.

The walk back to the ship was a short one and as we prepared to part company on the quarterdeck, a generous smile dispelled the aspect of frostiness that seemed to linger on her countenance. "I shall look forward to seeing you again at dinner, General. And, of course, discussing business

34

with you."

"Which business would that be, Miss McConville?"

"The Grand Liberty Bazaar, of course, General. I understand you are to play a substantial part in recruiting support for the event, while I am a member of the organising committee." The smile had briefly vanished, but now it returned and I sensed a note of mischief in her tone. "And of course I shall pursue you relentlessly with regard to the repayment of your debt."

I went to my cramped cabin and set about finding places to stow the items I – or rather, Sarah McConville – had bought. Something about this young woman perturbed me and I was not altogether happy to be in her debt.

A place for everything, and everything in its place. That, I had been led to believe, was a maxim much vaunted in Britain. Yet I was no longer certain where my place was. Instead of charging Federal entrenchments, I was to support what the Confederate government considered to be a strategically important biscuit party directed by the British well-to-do.

3

EXPERIENCES IN THE LIFE OF A SLAVE GIRL BY TRINITY GIDDINGS

North Atlantic and London, England,
September & October, 1863.

In the South they called absconded slaves missing property; in the North, contrabands; here, on board Her Majesty's Ship *Vigilant*, they called me ma'am. Yes, they did!

Yet despite the joy of freedom, my new surroundings brought on an unsettling edge of hysteria. That may sound downright peculiar, but it was like this: all my life in bondage; only place I knew, the plantation; only foreigner I ever saw, some Bohemian fire-eater at a circus Missy Antonia took me to some years gone. Of course, I'd read books about people in other lands. But reading is one thing; experience, that's a lot different.

So here I was in this crazy world where all I'd known got stood on its head. And although these British folk were devilish polite, and although I was extremely grateful for their concern,

I couldn't throw off the feeling that I really done died in that boat and was now in some crazy afterlife.

They gave me the first lieutenant's cabin, a pleasant room with a cot suspended from the deck above so you always stayed level. Never once seasick, though sometimes, when the ship rolled in those big Atlantic swells, I was certain she'd go on rolling and rolling until she capsized and went spinning down to the bottom of the ocean.

Now, here's a strange thing: this first lieutenant's accommodation was stacked with potted plants and dried herbs; infused flowers and oily tinctures. There was even an alembic still with a long-necked glass bottle. And everywhere an earthy smack of damp peat and dry dung; tangs of wood betony and meadowsweet; Joe Pye weed and Solomon's seal – rich aromas that minded me of childhood and my mother's herbal brews.

But strangest of all – strangest by a country mile – was that this first lieutenant was a Negro. Swear to God.

Called 'sir' by everybody on the ship but the captain.

This first lieutenant was named Josiah Mill and it was his face I'd first seen when they lowered that boat to rescue me. It was a handsome countenance with wide-set eyes and a firm jaw underlined by a neatly trimmed beard. I could tell by the score marks on his brow and at the corners of his mouth that he was in his middle years, although I would never have guessed he was fifty-five, which I discovered some time later.

A rap on the door announced his arrival. Since I was brought on board, three days ago, I'd been confined at first to the sick bay and then to this cabin to recover a little strength. Today, I was to be escorted by the first lieutenant for a short walk around the upper deck before supper.

I opened the door to find Lieutenant Mill waiting in

the corridor and he raised his peaked cap in a gesture of awkward courtesy.

"Please come inside a moment, Lieutenant," I said. "After all, this really is your cabin. Perhaps you'd like to make sure your plants are still thriving?"

"I'm sure they haven't come to the remotest harm." That voice, elegant and smooth as polished marble, sounded powerful strange coming from the mouth of a coloured man.

He stepped into the cabin and inspected its contents somewhat apprehensively, rubbing the leaves of certain plants between two fingers, tamping down peat in clay pots, peering closely into murky vials of tincture.

"Some of your plants are familiar to me," I said. "My late mother dabbled with herbs and suchlike when I was a little girl."

He regarded me with a kind expression. "You must have had an interesting childhood."

One way to describe it. Nigh on twenty years past and I could still taste those bitter-brewed remedies.

I looked at Lieutenant Mill and pretended a blasé expression. "All we had was a hotchpotch patch behind our cabin. Nothing scientific like this. You're no dabbler, are you, Lieutenant?"

"Nor am I a qualified apothecary." He indicated the room with a waft of his hand. "I do what I can to keep abreast of the latest developments, but what you see here is the work of an enthusiastic amateur."

"May I ask how you came by so much knowledge?"

His smile wasn't reflected in his slightly sad tone. "My father was an apothecary. He trained me in the fundamentals before I joined the navy. The interest, though, has never left me."

Eager to learn more, I followed him from the cabin, up to the quarterdeck at the rear of the *Vigilant*, where the officers managed the sailing of the ship.

This was an exhilarating experience: rich whiff of coal-smoke and tar on a salt wind. Plump canvas sails and rhythmic thump of steam engines driving us east. Blue sea crumpling and bulging. Sky sparkling clear. Never seen the ocean before this Sunday gone. Now it was my route to freedom.

Sailor glanced at me as we walked by, nudging a companion, who also took a sly peep.

Cold shiver of dread. I was out of Master Zebulon's frying pan – but had I landed in the British navy's fire? More than two hundred men on this ship, I'd been told. Most of them young and no doubt suppressing powerful desires for the several months they'd been at sea. Suddenly I'd been plunged right there among them.

"You must forgive the men." Lieutenant Mill must have read the anxiety on my face. "It is very rare to have a woman aboard, but they mean no offence."

Somewhat comforted by the calm authority of his manner, I felt the tension in my chest begin to subside.

As we walked, he complimented me on the dress I'd fashioned from a silk dressing gown given to me by the surgeon. It was certainly more comfortable than my mariner's attire, and more stylish than the cotton nightshirt that had replaced it in the sick bay.

Thanking him for his kindness I took the opportunity to ask how Negroes such as him could rise so highly in British society.

He laughed at that. "I beg your pardon, Miss Giddings, but I don't perceive myself as having risen to an especially elevated position. And whatever advancement I have achieved is down to the good fortune of having been born into a family with rich patrons."

"Your story sounds intriguing."

With a small shrug, he moved a piece down the deck towards the stern. "My grandfather was a Connecticut slave who won his freedom by fighting for the British in the War of Independence. He saved the life of his commanding officer at Yorktown. The officer came from an influential abolitionist family and after the war he took my grandfather to England, where he was educated and became an apothecary."

He paused by a bottle-shaped cannon, adding in an unexpectedly wistful tone: "It was my father's wish that I should follow this family tradition into the medical profession, but as you can see I chose a different path."

This brought to mind another question I'd been keen to ask. "Are you the first coloured officer in the Royal Navy?"

He shook his head. "A mulatto by the name of John Perkins was commissioned in Nelson's day and went on to become a captain." Smiling thinly, he added: "I do, however, have the distinction of being the oldest lieutenant in the service."

This child was determined not to be browbeaten by his sour humour. "Yet a lieutenant you are – and a very senior one at that. Surely Britain's attitude of enlightenment should be applauded."

I saw conflicting thoughts skittering every which way across his face. His words came stiffly, in carefully measured doses, as if he was restraining some profound frustration. "No doubt applause is due. But it is important to recognise that there are not four million coloured people in Great Britain, as there are in America. So we are not considered a threat."

I'd be lying if I said his ungracious manner didn't stoke me right up.

Turning away, I was surprised when he caught my elbow.

His voice was softer. "Miss Giddings, you are an intelligent young woman with an exciting new life ahead of you, and I don't mean to stifle your enthusiasm. Yet you should remember that you remain coloured whether you are in rural South Carolina or the most fashionable quarters of London."

At that precise moment, I considered him an ungrateful nigger. Some time later, I saw he had a point.

*

HMS *Vigilant* took sixteen days to cross the Atlantic.

As she sailed into the Thames estuary, I became more and more anxious about quitting my cabin with its reassuring aromas of plants and fertile earth. Only natural, I suppose, to cling to familiar things, even if they are very recently familiar. As I stood on the quarterdeck, cold autumn wind scraped the slate estuary, sending a rheumy chill deep inside my bones. British climate, like the folk, would take some getting used to, I guessed.

Banks of the Thames appeared on either side of the *Vigilant*, as if she was a minnow swimming further into the jaws of some huge predator. Ships everywhere, buff sails rising high above us like sheer cliff faces; sleek black hulls shining in the watery light. So many and so close I was sure we must collide, but our pilot was skilled in his trade, threading us safely through the maze of buoys and sandbars.

At last, we closed with the shore. Dead ahead, the Tower of London minded me of a pale molar surrounded by a wall of flat incisors. Oldest building I ever saw, and I pondered awhile on all that history locked tight in its flanks. Some of it mine, for I was a mulatto with Anglo-Saxon blood in my veins as well as African.

Further into the distance, the great city of London was a

hazy sweep of brick and stone. Biggest place I ever been. What did it hold for me? How would I manage there? Tried not to study on such questions, since I plainly had not the remotest inkling as to the answers.

We moored near the tower. Sailors laboured at the capstans and anchors splashed into the muddy water while I prepared to depart.

I was powerful sorry to say goodbye, for all the officers and men had treated me considerately, especially Lieutenant Mill.

Sometimes I thought this was because we were both coloured folk; at others, he appeared quite irritated when his colleagues presumed any sort of natural kinship between us. For sure, he could be a grouchy fellow, yet I later discovered this was due in some part to his poor health.

All anxieties about leaving the ship vanished in a flood of excitement as I followed Lieutenant Mill into a taxicab and its two horses hauled us away into the thronging streets of the metropolis.

You want to see the future, go to London. Every place I looked, grand constructions in progress: excavations the size of cornfields; marble buildings climbing heavenward in vests of scaffolding; marvels of engineering on every street corner. Before we'd arrived, Lieutenant Mill explained that these vast works were part of the world's first underground railway that had started running trains just a few months gone.

Never did get to see too much of London during that visit. Framed in the taxicab window, I glimpsed long stampedes of double-decked omnibuses and broughams, heavy dray wagons and shabby donkey carts. And people – so many and so busy and so unmannerly! Lord, how they bustled and shoved, and not a soul among them giving his or her neighbour so much as the time of day.

We quickly arrived at the United States legation, an elegant town house in Portland Place, a little to the south of Regent's Park.

Parting company with Lieutenant Mill was powerful difficult. Regrets and apprehensions tussled in my head. Here I was, about to lose the only friend I had on God's earth.

Josiah Mill seemed to appreciate my anxiety and took my hands in his, squeezing reassuringly tight. "You're a United States subject, Miss Giddings. A free citizen. They will look after you, I guarantee it."

"Where will you go?"

"Wherever they send me."

"Can I not find you?"

He smiled winsomely and produced a small, sealed envelope. "The address of my family home. If you need to contact me, they will know my whereabouts."

Clutching the little envelope as a drowner might hold on to a rope cast from the shore, I turned and walked up the steps to the United States legation.

*

I was shown into the office of Charles Francis Adams, the US minister to Great Britain, who shook my hand and bade me take a seat by a low walnut table laid out with a china tea service.

Old boy had a distinguished, if studious, countenance: intense eyes, closely set under a formidable bald dome, snowy beard fringing a bold jaw.

When the tea had been served, he congratulated me on my successful escape and asked what I wanted to do, now that I was free.

Using some dainty silver tongs, I picked up a sugar-lump from the little porcelain bowl and dropped it in my tea. "That depends on what possibilities are open to me, Mr Adams."

He was watching me with peculiar interest. "As a former slave, emancipated by President Lincoln's proclamation, you are entitled to safe passage to the United States where provision will be made for your welfare."

Leaning forward, without taking those narrow-spaced eyes off me, he set down his cup and saucer so that the silver teaspoon tinkled against the china. Sounded like the little bell Missy Honoria used to summon us house slaves. Old boy continued in a quieter voice. "However, your arrival in Britain has aroused much public sympathy and I believe this has created an unusual opportunity for you to assist the Union – if that is your wish."

I sipped my tea. Lord, it tasted good. Minded me of the brews Missy Antonia and I would take together during the good times. "How might I perform this service, Mr Adams?"

Old boy's gaze never left me; probing, assessing, evaluating. Despite what he told me about obtaining freedom, I felt more than ever like a slave under examination on the auction block. "The Confederacy has powerful friends in Britain," he said. "People with vested interests in aiding the rebellion by supplying war materials. They use a narrow interpretation of British laws intended to prohibit such activity, while the government turns a blind eye."

He made the wintriest smile I ever done seen – I pictured pulleys and cogs and ratchets straining to haul that reluctant mouth just a smidgeon wider. "Support for the Union among working people is encouraging, but sadly they are yet to be enfranchised and we must therefore challenge the Confederacy's supporters in the ruling classes. I want you to take the argument of moral obligation to the most formidable Confederate bastion outside Dixie: the city of Liverpool."

I sipped the last remnants of that delicious tea from my cup and looked directly at him. "I'm but a former chattel slave, Mr Adams. Surely no match for clever richcrats."

"It is precisely because you are a former slave that you will be more than a match for these people. I gather you have some education and it's abundantly clear that you are quick-witted and articulate."

I sensed this old boy's flattery had a deeper purpose.

Another ratcheted smile confirmed this suspicion. "I'm sure you will be glad to learn that we have a small battalion of 'richcrats' of our own," he said. "One of them, Lady Alice Featherfax, is waiting downstairs."

The name minded me of an article I read on board the *Vigilant*. This Lady Featherfax was a glamorous socialite with a reputation for radical ideas and a husband famous for his work as an engineer with the late Isambard Kingdom Brunel.

"Might I introduce you to Lady Featherfax?" Old boy was a schemer, sure enough, but by no measure the only one to cross my path. No, not in Great Britain.

Nonetheless, this child was fascinated by the prospect of meeting Lady Featherfax, while at the same time helping the cause of President Lincoln.

Glanced at the shoal of tea leaves in my empty cup. Some folk reckoned fortunes could be discerned in such patterns, but for me the future was a blind maze. That was just as well, otherwise I'd never have accepted his offer.

4

RECOLLECTIONS OF A CONFEDERATE GENERAL BY JUBAL DE BROOKE

Liverpool and East Lancashire, England,
October, 1863.

"Welcome to Liverpool." Sarah McConville appeared at my side near the quarterdeck guardrail as the *Owl* nudged towards the Albert Dock.

The blockade runner's arrival had created something of a stir on the waterfront. Though no mariner, I knew she was strikingly different to the other vessels thronging the Mersey. No sails to help her steam engine, just a sleek hull with two big paddle wheels and three slim smokestacks. As her name suggested, the *Owl* was built for speed and stealth, which had enabled her to pass unnoticed through the cordon of Federal warships blockading Charleston harbour. The rest of the voyage had passed in the same uneventful vein.

"Which church is that?" I indicated an elegant lantern-shaped spire, close to the foreshore.

"Our Lady and St Nicholas. And to the right" – her outstretched hand indicated a taller landmark with graceful lines and the opulent texture of carved ivory – "you can see the Tower Buildings. That's where the United States Consulate is situated."

"Useful to know where the Yankees are – knowing thine enemy is a first rule of war." The joke was feeble and I wasn't surprised when she ignored it. During the two week voyage from Charleston, to Liverpool I had learned much about Sarah McConville and grown to admire her candour. I knew she wouldn't pretend laughter if she wasn't amused, in much the same way as she wouldn't say something she didn't mean. "Over there" – she pointed to a mass of red-brick buildings, just visible through a fine reticulation of masts and rigging – "is George's Dock and the warehouses of the Goree. Beyond that is a hive of gin palaces and concert halls and sporting venues for any aspect of the fancy you care to name."

"The fancy?"

She gave me a sideways look. "Sounds quaint, doesn't it? Sadly, its meaning is entirely the reverse – rat pits and cock pits, dog fights and bare-knuckle boxing. Any 'entertainment' that is cruel or bloody, that's the fancy."

There was asperity in her voice, bitterness even, that made me curious. "You don't seem especially pleased to be home."

"Liverpool is a queer city. It delights and angers me in equal measure. Grand marble mansions, cheek by jowl with filthy courts where people live worse than hogs."

"The cotton famine?"

She shook her head. "Look around you, General."

I didn't need to, for the Mersey was congested with ocean-going ships waiting for berths, while the waterfront bustled with commercial energy.

"The cotton famine has struck down great swathes of Lancashire," she said. "But not Liverpool. Skilled men can earn handsome wages then spend every penny in a single evening, tossing for whisky. And all the while, wives and children go cold and hungry."

Not for the first time, I discerned a hint of nonconformist, even radical opinion. This puzzled me, since these sentiments normally went hand in glove with abolitionism – and therefore support for Lincoln's Union. Yet all of this was at odds with her position in society. During the voyage she explained how she'd been managing the affairs of her father's shipbuilding company since he became ill with consumption. So Sarah, not her ailing father, had been responsible for the construction of the *Owl* and other blockade-runners – a business venture that actively aided the slaveholding South.

"Do you have a solution for these social ills?" I asked.

"Moral improvement, education and enfranchisement." She tapped her forefinger on the guardrail as she spelled out her remedy. "But of course that is far easier said than done, and you don't want to listen to a lecture on social reform, do you, General?" She gave me an ambivalent smile that transformed her severe countenance into a startlingly attractive one. Some time later, I mused that Liverpool could be similarly mercurial: austere under a cloudy mantle, then fugitively romantic when the light was right, casting off the river and catching graceful aspects.

"I might," I said, without really thinking, "If you were giving it."

She turned away, ostensibly to watch the *Owl* glide through the lock gates, and I sensed that I had surprised her with my directness.

In truth, I'd surprised myself.

*

It was impossible not to be impressed by Dunstead Manor. Its half-timbered walls and mullioned windows rose up amid a cluster of sycamore, scorched ochre and vermilion by the first forays of autumn.

Not thirty minutes after disembarking from the *Owl*, I had been brought to this secluded estate, a few miles south of Liverpool. My host had insisted on offering me accommodation here.

As the brougham crunched and squeaked over the gravel driveway, I noticed a line of pale marble statues along the front of the manor: elegant works depicting classical heroes and great men of the modern age.

It was not until my carriage came to a halt that I realised that the figure closest to me was no statue, but my host. Even as I stepped from the carriage, he stayed quite still, observing me without expression. Attired in plain white breeches and a loose-necked shirt, his abundant silver hair appeared meticulously dishevelled. Nor was this windblown aspect lost in the smooth-boned pallor of his face, which seemed more artfully crafted that any of the statues.

Then Lord Arthur Harrowby's mouth stretched in a luminous smile, like the opening of a theatre curtain, and the long-lashed eyes became vividly alive, animating the rest of his countenance as if by a transmission of electricity. Although I knew him to be in his early sixties, he could have passed for a man fifteen years younger.

"My dear fellow, how very much I have savoured this moment of your arrival." He spoke in a calibrated drawl, each syllable painstakingly modulated..

"You're too kind, my Lord."

"Oh, that sumptuous, sumptuous Dixieland accent!" He laughed delightedly, then gave me a cool look. "But this won't do. Damned if it will. You must call me Arthur. And I – if you permit – shall call you Jubal. We are cousins, are we not? Born of the same bloodline, possessed of the same instincts that bid us ride, *ride* to the sound of the guns?"

Reluctant though I was to dampen his enthusiasm, I didn't want him to entertain a false impression. "I'm afraid I don't ride," I said. "At least, not very well. And certainly not anywhere hazardous, such as a battlefield."

His crestfallen look made me feel guilty. "Of course, you're an infantry commander," he said. "Nor are we cousins – not in the strictest sense." He rolled his head from side to side, as if arranging a fresh pattern in a kaleidoscope. Instantly, the laddish grin returned. "But we are both soldiers. And we are both revolutionists. And, whether we choose it or not, the bluest, *bluest* of blood pumps through both our hearts." My host's habit of repeating certain words gave him a theatrical air which, like his drawl, was undoubtedly a fashionable affectation.

Placing his hand firmly on my shoulder, he urged me towards a heavy timber portal. "And in any event, my dear Jubal, if you will indulge my wordplay, are we not lords of our own manners?"

Of course, I couldn't refuse his request for the two of us to use first-names without giving offence.

Yet I was also flattered by this unqualified friendship extended by one of the most famous men in European society. Despite his reputation as Britain's oldest dandy, Harrowby was said to be a man of considerable charm and intellect. He had been a friend of the celebrated dilettante Count Alfred D'Orsay, as well as the romantic poet Lord George Byron. And it was true that Harrowby had been a real soldier and a real rebel. He had fought alongside Byron in Italy's revolutionary Carbonari, and for the Greek nationalists against the Ottoman Turks.

He removed his hand from my shoulder as we moved into the manor house, where the sour smell of the dinted stone floor mingled with an ancient fustiness from thin rugs and faded drapes.

Leading me into his drawing room, he picked up a black neck tie and set about fastening it. "Over the years, I have welcomed many friends here. Among the most illustrious of them was Kossuth – yes, the great man himself." He stopped fussing with his tie and gave me a solemn look. "I rank you his equal, Jubal. I think you should know that."

I had forgotten that Harrowby had also served with Louis Kossuth, leader of the Hungarian patriots, in their struggle for independence from Austrian rule. Wherever there had been a popular rebellion, it seemed, Harrowby was close by. Nonetheless, being compared with a man of Kossuth's stature was an immense compliment, and I said so.

"Of course, Kossuth spoke English in a rather peculiar Shakespearean style." He finished knotting his tie, then pulled on a white waistcoat and Wedgwood-blue frock coat. "Learned our language while in prison, you see, where his only sources of English literature were the bard and the bible."

"Light conversation must have been quite a challenge," I said.

"It certainly was – but also huge, *huge* fun."

With scarcely a pause, he switched subject. "Do you fish?"

"I cast a line somewhat better than I ride a horse," I said.

"Marvellous, *marvellous*. And which method do you favour? The wet fly or the dry? You're a dry fellow, aren't you? You must say 'yes'!"

One of the passengers on the *Owl* had told me that in Britain, there was some snobbery attached to dry fly-fishing in preference to wet. It didn't matter one jot to me whether the fly was 'dry' and floated on the surface of the water, or was submerged and deemed 'wet'. But since I was familiar with both techniques, I said: "You're quite correct, Arthur, I'm a dry fellow."

*

Next day, we went fishing. The trout stream was broad and shallow, meandering the parkland of Dunstead Manor with relaxing languor. In the clear autumn light, fierce dazzles played on the surface, but Harrowby found a spot in the shade of a big elm whose yellow leaves absorbed the sun's rays and glowed like miniature oriflammes.

"I vehemently, *vehemently* disapprove of slavery, of course."

My host had an unsettling habit of going to the nerve of an issue without pretext or preamble. Over dinner, the previous evening, he had remarked on nothing more significant than the special flies he crafted himself for the trout in this very spot, while breakfast had been occupied by a short debate on the best material for flylines – horsehair or silk.

"I have no fondness for that particular institution either," I said.

"I know, Jubal. Your letter to the *Richmond Examiner* was reprinted by *The Times* in London. And I respect you all the more, given the unpopularity of such principles in certain quarters. Like you, I am a friend of the South, but not an uncritical one."

I knew from my briefing at the War Department in Richmond that Harrowby supported the Confederacy more because he was a habitual revolutionist than a deep political thinker. Nonetheless, there was an uncomplicated charm to what he referred to as his 'underdogism'.

As we prepared our rods for casting, he cleared his throat as if preparing to broach a difficult subject. "There's a chap coming to Liverpool."

A brisk whisk of his rod sent his line looping into the air. I watched his fly veer across the water, like something vivid and vital.

"Slaveholder," he said. "Big plantation, I'm afraid. Member of your senate. Name of Rankin. States Rights Rankin. Odd name – not a nickname either. I have it on proper authority that it's his real one."

Flicking my rod, I watched my line follow a similar trajectory to Harrowby's, then commenced the business of casting and recasting to keep the fly active. I didn't know this senator, but had heard of him. "He has a reputation as a political firebrand. What brings him to Liverpool?"

My host's tone became subdued. "Senator Rankin is investing in one of my companies – an engineering firm that makes steam engines. They are built mainly for textile mills but also for steam ships, including blockade runners, which is Rankin's line of business."

He made a downcast expression. "Like you, I support the South but abhor slavery and therefore have no wish to do business with a slaveholder. But the cotton famine means textile mills are no longer buying steam engines and I must sell them where I can."

He was clearly looking for my reaction. "You need to turn a profit to keep your people in work. And any munitions taken through the Yankee blockade will help my boys."

My host's incandescent smile returned. "We are cousins indeed, Jubal. More – we are the firmest of friends, the very firmest."

A sudden, deft flick of his wrist brought a corresponding splash across the stream. I caught a glimpse of a trout's silver belly as it took the fly before plunging back below the surface. Yet there could be no escape. Harrowby palmed his reel and began to play his line, tiring the hooked fish until he was ready to land it.

*

I met States Rights Rankin, two days later, at the McConville's country residence on a grouse moor on the Lancashire-Yorkshire border.

Harrowby and I travelled by coach and he remained uncharacteristically quiet throughout the uncomfortable three-hour journey.

The previous evening we had played faro, a gambling card game, at his club in Liverpool. While I had concluded the evening with modest success, my host had lost almost twenty guineas. This was a substantial sum and I ascribed his taciturn mood to this turn of bad luck.

The McConville estate was much larger than Harrowby's, while the mansion dwarfed the modest Elizabethan proportions of Dunstead Manor.

After a long period of silence, my companion stirred and peered through the carriage window, frowning. "What an ungainly mongrel of a building, Jubal. Look at the hotchpotch of styles: neo-Gothic, mock-Tudor, simulated-classical. Even red-brick baroque."

I had to agree that it appeared to be three or four very different buildings cobbled into one.

"One hates to harp on about the qualities of good breeding,

Jubal," Harrowby said. "But all too often these *nouveau riche* types are their own worst enemy. Thomas McConville builds fine ships, though I can't imagine what made him believe he could also design a house."

When I was presented to Thomas McConville, not five minutes later, I saw a slender, slightly stooped man in his late middle years, with excavated features and sallow skin, darkly mottled and faintly cracked, like old drum-skin. The smile on his purple lips failed to register in the milky grey eyes. I knew he suffered from consumption – this was why Sarah, his only offspring, was running the family business. All the same, I was somewhat shocked by the extent of his illness.

"Glad to meet you, General." McConville's voice was barely above a murmur. Like his face, it lacked any sort of energy. But at least he was making an effort. "My daughter speaks highly of you. I'm sure the Liberty Bazaar will be a great success with you to, ah, lead the charge."

I gathered this was intended as a small witticism, and responded with a modest chuckle.

As he led us across his chandeliered lobby, two small white dogs – Jack Russell terriers – pelted through a doorway and came to greet me, skidding comically on the smooth tiled floor at my feet. I had a fondness for these industrious little creatures and stooped to return their welcome.

"I presume these ruffians belong to your daughter, Mr McConville," I said.

"No, General de Brooke, they belong to me."

I glanced up to see a man of similar age to my own thirty-eight years. His powerful constitution virtually filled the door-frame as he entered the lobby. As he gripped my hand, I took in rough-hewn features and great bushy side-whiskers that would have been better tended by a topiarist than a barber.

This could be none other than Senator States Rights Rankin.

When the introductions were done, Harrowby and I went to our rooms to change for dinner. On entering the dining room, I was especially pleased to see Sarah McConville seated near me at the table. Her décolletage revealed a glimpse of ivory shoulders and her expression, capable of so many nuances, appeared to radiate exuberance.

"Are your beaters set for tomorrow, Thomas?" Harrowby asked McConville.

"They will put up the grouse, have no fear, Arthur." McConville coughed feebly into his napkin.

"How many do you estimate we will bag?" Rankin's voice thundered across the dinner table. "One hundred? Two, maybe?" A side-glance at me. "And most of those downed by the General, here, I'd wager."

I set down my wine glass. "I don't shoot, Senator."

"A general of the Confederacy who doesn't shoot?" Rankin sounded aghast.

"Not wild animals – unless I mean to eat them."

"But these game birds will be eaten." Rankin was being annoyingly persistent.

"This party will not eat one hundred birds, Senator, still less two hundred."

"Others will eat them!"

"Then let others shoot them."

The truth was that I had become unhealthily obsessed with the preservation of life having so often witnessed the wanton carnage of battle. When I caught a trout, while fishing with Harrowby, I returned it to the stream because he had already landed two for our supper. Lately, I had taken to examining the sidewalk ahead to avoid stepping on insects; picking up stranded worms and slugs and placing them safely in deep grass. All my life, I had never destroyed life cruelly or carelessly. Yet this new-found preoccupation with averting death was certainly related to the apparent disorder of my mind.

Obviously I couldn't explain that to these people, who would probably consider me insane.

*

The next day, I was walking along the garden terrace with Sarah McConville. The shooting party had departed earlier that morning. States Rights Rankin was clearly disappointed that I had not gone along. I sensed he wanted to show me off as a great warrior of the Confederacy, capable of vanquishing not only Yankees, but grouse too.

Near the greenhouse was a gardener's wooden barrow, stacked with pale clay plant pots. Propped against it at various odd angles were shovels, hoes and rakes. A large Hessian sack had been split open. Grey powder – fertiliser, I presumed – spilled out.

Up on the moor, the shooting started. A couple of shotgun blasts at first, then more and more until the noise of gunfire became a deafening roar. I tried to block out the noise by covering my ears with my hands and then I fell to my knees, as the ground seemed to tilt …

The barrow was now a stretcher; the plant pots, boys' skulls; shovels and rakes and hoes had become their bones. Where the Hessian sack had been, I saw fragments of butternut jackets, one with a corporal's stripes on the sleeve. I noticed a muddy ribcage amid the ripped sackcloth. And a pair of boots, cracked leather caked in clay. In one boot, I could make out a shin-bone, splintered below the knee.

Manassas, on the Bull Run River, a year after the

Confederacy's first victory there.

We were preparing for a second battle on the same ground, but had returned to find many of the fallen boys had not been buried properly after the previous engagement. Scavenging animals had dug them up and scattered their bones, so I'd ordered all the bodies to be disinterred to allow proper burial. Trouble was that a large number couldn't be identified.

This was my fault. Before First Manassas, I'd seen boys scribbling their names and next-of-kin on paper tags, which they'd pinned to the backs of their coats. I'd considered this anticipation of death to be bad for morale and forbade the practice.

Now I was being held to account.

The dead boys were reassembling themselves. The snarl of bone and cloth on the stretcher began to heave and shift. Splintered limbs re-articulated, skulls found torsos, uniforms knitted back together.

Three boys stood before me, still blasted to damnation, but essentially whole. The corporal spoke. Even though his face was only half there, I recalled his name – Turnbull, a liveryman from Harrisonburg.

"You should've let us fix them tags, sir." He was respectful, but angry. "Now we ain't never gonna get home. My Janie, she don't even know for sure I'm dead. Ain't right, sir."

"Sorry, boys," I said. "Sorry – " I mumbled, feeling light-headed, sick.

"General de Brooke? Are you well?"

Sarah McConville's concerned features filled my vision. Suddenly, the ragged boys were gone and I saw how shamefully I had behaved in this lady's presence, almost taking leave of my senses.

No, I was not well.

5

EXPERIENCES IN THE LIFE OF A SLAVE GIRL BY TRINITY GIDDINGS
Liverpool, England, October, 1863.

Like all else to do with Lady Alice Featherfax, breakfast was lavish and elaborate. Just the two of us sitting at that dining table, comfortably large enough to accommodate a dozen people, while the butler and a footman busied themselves offering up silver dishes of dressed fish, kidneys, cutlets and roast partridge.

Since I was accustomed to Missy Honoria's extravagances, I wasn't surprised by the scale of this banquet so much as my position in relation to it: no longer the servant, but the served.

Lady Alice set about her breakfast with gusto while animated chatter came bustling through mouthfuls of chewed pheasant. "I have the most astonishing news for you, Trinity! Received only this morning from my dear friend, Mrs Marjoribanks. It appears we have a Confederate general in our midst. Yes – here in Liverpool! *Quelle horreur!*"

"Surely the Rebels haven't invaded Britain?"

Of course, I was joking but Lady Alice took me at my word. She stopped eating and regarded me over a hillock of muffins with a look some place between affection and condescension. "My, what an amazing imagination you have, Trinity, but it wouldn't be a practicable military operation. No, this is a diplomatic offensive by a fellow from Virginia named de Brooke. Brigadier General Jubal de Brooke."

I ground a little black pepper on my omelette. "Name means nothing to me, Lady Alice."

"Alice, please." She gave me a hard stare.

Lady Alice was a strikingly attractive woman, though a little on the plump side, which was probably to do with her fondness for good living. She was attired in an elaborate crinoline dress. Skin like ivory and wide azure eyes set in dainty features, with fair hair done up in intricate plaits. I guessed she'd be in her early or middle thirties. She did not speak of any offspring, nor of her husband, the eminent engineer Lord Cecil Featherfax. Only person in the affairs of Lady Alice appeared to be Lady Alice.

Nonetheless, she was a generous and attentive hostess. Advanced me fifty pounds cash, insisting it was a loan against the monies I would make from writing my memoirs. Also, she'd assembled a wardrobe for me, which she said was essential for a lady in British society.

"It would seem this General de Brooke is a hero of many great battles, a dashing cavalier of Dixie." Sip of tea, acid smile. "And no doubt a slaveholding devil, up from the bowels of hell! Why else would he be here but to join forces with the Ladies' Forum?"

I explained that this organisation wasn't known to me.

"The Ladies' Forum of the Liverpool Southern Club is a veritable Satan's nest of ne'er-do-wells, organising what is being called a Grand Liberty Bazaar for the Southern Prisoners' Relief Fund. Mrs Marjoribanks' intelligence suggests that this General de Brooke fellow is here to bolster support for the infernal event."

Despite the fury in her voice, Lady Alice did not stop eating once – no, not even for a heartbeat. Had to admire her for that.

Yet I didn't see why she got so stoked up and asked why the organising of a fête should be so vexing.

"We are combatants in a pitiless war against slavery, Trinity – a battle to enlist the hearts and souls of the British public in President Lincoln's valiant struggle!" As ever with Lady Alice, words hurried out in a dramatic tumble, but then abruptly stopped – as if a different part of her mind done become aware of her histrionic outpouring.

Dabbing one corner of her mouth with a napkin, she gave me a somewhat embarrassed smile. "You must think me a frightful exhibitionist."

"Not for one moment, Lady Alice – *Alice*."

"You see, my dear, the cause of abolitionism means everything to me."

"Surely there's no cause more noble."

"If I were fighting in General Grant's army, or perhaps nursing wounded Union soldiers in a hospital, I might agree." There was a sarcastic, self-mocking edge to her tone. "But my silly campaign to stymie the Ladies Forum of the Liverpool Southern Club is rather less heroic."

"It isn't silly."

"It's all I have." She seemed to be only partly aware of my presence. "With no husband to care for, no children to love, what else is there?"

I frowned. "Surely you have Lord Featherfax?"

First time I ever seen Lady Alice appear fragile. All that

bluster fell away and before me I saw a vulnerable woman. "Cecil does what society demands. He is currently building a great viaduct in India and I do not know when he will return."

She looked down at her lap, as if in shame. "We have not been husband and wife, not in the proper sense, since …"

Leaned forward, eyes skewering my friend's. "What happened?"

Her voice quavered. "It's not uncommon, you know for infants to just stop breathing … for no apparent reason.'

"You had a child?" I asked.

She nodded but could barely speak of it. "He would have been nearly eight years old, had he lived."

Across the table I could see her cheeks were latticed with tears. "He was approaching his first birthday when it happened. The nurse took him away and never brought him back."

I went round the table and sat in the chair beside her, laying my hand on her arm. "That's a truly tragic story, Alice, and it makes me so sad to hear it. But surely there can be more children?"

Taking out a dainty handkerchief, she dabbed the moistness from her face. "Cecil so wanted an heir, you see … it was hard on him when the physicians told me I could have no more."

I couldn't keep a note of accusation from my voice. "Surely your husband can't blame you for what happened?"

"He doesn't. Cecil is a good man, a kind man. He did try. We both did. But a marriage without children – without any possibility of children – is simply too great a burden. And so we do not speak of it. We rarely speak of anything. He builds his engineering wonders and I do what I may to help the cause of abolition."

I felt deep sorrow for my friend and we sat quietly awhile.

Then some iron shutter seemed to come down across that

enormous wound in her mind, sealing it off completely. She tinkled a little hand-bell to summon the servants and, in a voice now drained of all emotion, instructed them to side the table.

Turning to me, she made a gentle smile. "Now, my dear Trinity, let us be about our work. We must first turn our attention to that wardrobe of yours. We shall be walking out this morning and you will be the subject of much scrutiny – by friend and foe. So we must ensure your ensemble is not a jot less than immaculate."

This business of my attire proved more of a challenge than I could ever have imagined. Although I'd been employed in the Big House for some years, my duties confined me to the kitchen and dining room. So when Missy Antonia and Missy Honoria appeared in their lavish gowns, or lady guests arrived from other plantations, I had no inkling as to how long they'd spent preparing.

Now my education was beginning. Under the directions of Lady Alice, two maids named Daisy and Myrtle busied themselves with the intricacies of dressing me in a crinoline of crimson *poult de soie* silk that my hostess had picked out.

My main function in this complicated process was to stand as still as possible before a tall mirror while various items were placed, arranged and fixed upon me. In a curious way, I felt like a medieval knight being decked out in a suit of armour for some grand tournament.

First came the corset, a formidable garment with long laces at the back and a whalebone busk to stiffen the front. When Daisy and Myrtle had done heaving and tying the laces, they set about tugging the steel hooks that fastened the busk up tight. The effect took my breath away – for real. Belly and waist got pulled in so tight my lungs felt cramped and my bosom was pushed up and out. Yet despite the discomfort I was astounded by the way the shape of my body switched in a trice. Peering at my image in the mirror, I thought I was looking at some other woman. Up until that moment I'd thought black women were different underneath to white women, with their tiny waists and feminine curves.

Next came a contraption of steel hoops that got bigger and bigger as they went from top to bottom, forming a structure that minded me of a beehive. After I'd stepped into the centre of it, Myrtle buckled up various leather straps that secured the uppermost hoop around my waist. Over this they placed bulky linen underskirts. Then came the crinoline itself – first the skirt, then the bodice.

The *poult de soie* was like warm breath on my skin – and how that fine silk contrasted with the coarse garments I'd worn as a house girl.

As the maids set a matching pillbox hat on my head, I continued to gaze at my new self in the mirror – not in vanity but amazement at the transformation that done happened right there, right then. From chattel slave to the equal of any richcrat missy in the Confederacy. That was some special moment.

The crinoline silk rippled in sumptuous cascades as I smoothed it with my fingers. Not so long ago I could not have looked more different, disguised in my mariner's clothes. I felt a tremendous sense of control: for the first time, I realised I could decide what I looked like.

"You look entrancing, my dear." Lady Alice appeared at my shoulder. Her smile was generous, her voice excited. "Tell me: how do you feel?"

"A little cramped and a little restricted." I took a few steps forward and it was as if a big top circus tent was moving with me. Then I saw my silhouette shifting in the mirror: the elegant swishing motion of the skirt combining with the eye-catching V of my waist and chest. "But when it makes you look as grand as this, it doesn't matter so much."

Lady Alice chuckled. She was enjoying this for sure. "Now we can see what those she-devils of the Ladies Forum have to say – though I'll warrant they'll be speechless."

Her fighting talk made me think again of that medieval knight and it occurred to me that the corset and steel hoops constrained my movement as a suit of armour might. The comparison went further. Just as knightly garb gave access to great tournaments, so my own finery would allow me into the elevated circles where Lady Alice jousted with those Rebel-loving gentlefolk.

This was the moment when I knew I was ready for my battle.

*

Chilly October day. Liverpool drab-grey below an endless wash of overcast; Mersey, a gunmetal slab so flat it might have been solid. Through the thicket of masts and rigging in Canning Dock, I saw the great shipyards of Birkenhead on the far bank. One week gone since I arrived in Liverpool and this was the first time I'd come out on my own. Lady Alice was mighty anxious that I might get lost or waylaid, even though I pointed out that if I could escape from bondage and make my way across the Atlantic, a trip to the waterfront, not one mile from her house in Falkner Square, should not prove beyond me.

I turned away from the river, walking along Strand Street towards the colonnaded façade and pale blue dome of the Custom House, elegant echo of ancient Greece set amid a warren of grog shops, free-and-easies and laughing-gas parlours. Pungent dockside odours of tar and hemp and canvas mingled with town smells: horse dung and charcoal smoke, fish and fruit from shop fronts and hand barrows.

I paused at the corner of Canning Place where a small boy was dishing up licks of 'Hokey-Pokey' Italian ice-cream from a little cart hauled by a billy-goat. Never had ice-cream before and the prospect enticed me.

"That Hokey-Pokey's powerful tasty." Girl can travel to the world's end, but she's never going to mistake a South Carolina plantation accent. "You should try a lick, Missy Giddings."

Turning, I saw a young black man in a billycock hat, neat Belcher necktie and smart Chesterfield coat. He was young, perhaps my age, and appeared amused by my bafflement.

"How come you know my name?"

Boy's handsome face opened up in a grin that exposed big healthy teeth. "Read about you coming to Liverpool in the papers, Missy. And there ain't too many pretty young coloured women hereabouts – specially not coming into town by hansom cab all that way from the residence of Lord and Lady Featherfax."

"You followed me?" I'd be lying if I said I wasn't properly worried.

"This here's a serious business, Missy. Had to be certain you was the right lady."

"Who are you?"

Boy seemed to sense my concern and his cockiness receded. "Mighty sorry, Missy. My name is Blessing Dubois. Like you, I done ran away from the plantation, found my way here to Liverpool."

"You're from South Carolina, aren't you?"

He nodded eagerly and the luminous grin returned.

"Which plantation?"

"Rankin." His smile vanished and I could guess why.

My late brother Benjamin done been loaned out to the Rankin place where he was driven by the loathsome practices of Senator States Rights Rankin, the so-called 'big Massa', to walk into the Great Pee Dee River with his head filled with the devil and his pockets with rocks.

Blessing Dubois's tone obtained a note of urgency. "Like I say, Missy, I been studying on what they wrote in the newspapers, about you supporting President Lincoln and all. Figured I might help."

"Help how?"

"Can we go somewhere we can't be seen?"

"This is Great Britain, not South Carolina – we are free."

"This is Liverpool, Missy. Place where nothing moves but it gets wrote down and studied on by agents. Some work for the Yankees, others the Rebels. But either way I don't want this meeting knowed about by any side. I could lose my job – more."

Part of me cautioned against getting involved with this boy; another part urged me to find out more. "I'm really not sure – "

"Then I won't trouble you no further, Missy." He backed off, turned on his heel.

What to do? Every second I hesitated took him further away. Soon, he'd be gone, perhaps for good. And whatever opportunity he was offering would be lost.

"Mr Dubois – wait!"

Boy stopped, looked back.

Hastening along the street, I caught up with him. "If you wish, we can go somewhere quiet."

Walking quickly, he led me down the side of the Custom House towards a sail maker's workshop. It was shaped like a coffin stood on one end, with wooden doors, one above the next, rising all the way up to the fourth storey. Logical shape,

I supposed, to house those great fields of canvas they hung from the yards of tall ships such as the *Vigilant*. All the same, the casket-like aspect daunted me.

We entered through a small door off a side alley and I found myself in a towering store room with timber beams festooned with great lengths of sailcloth that grew fainter and fainter till they disappeared into grainy shadow, high above. Smells of musty textile and hemp and sawdust.

Blessing Dubois showed me to two seats fashioned from big barrels that had been sawed in half and bade me sit on one while he perched on the other. Alone with him in this strange building, I felt a twinge of apprehension grow and swell in my chest till I felt I couldn't breathe.

"When I got here, didn't have but two pennies," he said. "Old Mr Applegarth give me work in his shipyard 'cross the water in Seacombe, paid me well, made sure I had a place to live."

Despite these queer surroundings, I felt reassured by the familiar tones of his South Carolina lilt. Like a soft voice reached out from the hearth of some slave cabin, right across the grey Atlantic, and licked me with soothing tones.

"I ain't saying I'm not grateful for what Mr Applegarth done for me," he said. "But I tell you this, Missy, I ain't no traitor to my own kin."

I did like this boy, with his open face and trusting eyes. He wanted me to like him, I could tell that much. Not in a boy-girl way, more in a 'do what I want' way. At the time, I supposed this was only natural, given the risks he was taking simply by approaching me.

"Traitor in what way, Mr Dubois?"

Leaning forward across the work bench, boy lowered his voice. "They's building a warship for the Rebels. Mighty powerful one, like the Laird rams only bigger."

I gave him a baffled look. These 'rams' weren't male sheep, I knew that much. What, then?

Sensing my unspoken question, he leaned a little closer. "They's ironclad warships, Missy, built for the Rebels by Lairds, over at Birkenhead."

"Why are they called rams?"

Again, that open smile. "They got a sharp iron spike fitted to their bows that they ram into ships they attack, opening them up below the waterline."

Boy still wasn't making too much sense. I asked: "What with cannon and all, isn't that a little … old fashioned?"

"Not when it's a steel spike going into a wooden hull. But they also got big rotating gun turrets, like the one on the USS *Monitor*. Could be you seen pictures of it, Missy."

I nodded. Lieutenant Mill had shown me drawings of this USS *Monitor*, an ugly black Yankee craft that looked like a coal barge with a metal hatbox stuck on top and a big gun poking out. "Don't the Yankees have a whole fleet of these monitor boats?"

"They sure do. But monitors ain't sea-boats, they can only sail close inshore or up rivers. Yankees do have a deep water ironclad named *New Ironsides*, but she's slow and clumsy. Heard tell they even needs tug-boats to turn her in the right direction for firing her guns." His voice done sunk to a hissy whisper. "Those rams, they's fast and nippy. They could cross the Atlantic and break the Federal blockade. And that could mean the South winning the war."

"Where are these ram things now?"

He nodded over his shoulder in the direction of the river. "Moored on the Mersey after the British government seized them last week. The British done been arguing with the

Yankees nearly two years. Came down to the Yankees telling Lord Palmerston there'd be war between Britain and the Union if them rams was allowed to join the Rebel fleet."

I gave him a searching look. "But why build a third ram? Surely the British would seize that too."

"Not if they don't know 'bout it, Missy. Not if it's being built so it looks like a merchant ship."

"Are you certain it's *not* a merchant vessel?"

"Should be, Missy, I been working on that Satan-ship these twelve months gone, Lord forgive me." He put on a fearful face. "You gotta stop 'em."

Tried to collect myself, thoughts scurrying hither and thither. "Proof, Mr Dubois," I said. "We shall need proof."

"I got this."

Reaching deep into his coat pocket, he took out a buff coloured envelope, sealed with red wax. "It's what they calls an affidavit – statement I done sweared to all legal and proper in this lawyer's chambers. See, that's his stamp and signature right there."

I noted the official nature of the document. "Will the authorities act on it?"

"They have in the past, Missy," he said, "but …"

"But what, Mr Dubois?"

Boy gave me an uneasy look. "Before now, these affidavits been sweared to by whites. Lawyer reckons that don't make no difference. But you and me, Missy, we done been slaves. We knows the rule: don't never trust white folks – *any* white folks."

I took the envelope from him, tried to pump confidence into my voice. "We're not slaves anymore and South Carolina's halfway to hell. Here we have powerful allies – and they are committed to ending slavery wherever it may be."

Blessing Dubois attempted a half-smile but I could see he

remained somewhat unconvinced.

*

One of these powerful allies was the United States consul in Liverpool, Thomas Haines Dudley. Attorney by profession, looked it every inch. And though his job here in Britain was strictly diplomatic, lawyerliness reached into everything he did and said.

He was studying on Blessing Dubois' affidavit while a big old pendulum clock cut the passing time into thin, dry slices. Plenty to go round, since Lady Alice and I been sitting in his office in the Tower Buildings for all of eternity, and then some.

Lady Alice, sitting beside me, had brought me to the US Consulate after explaining that Mr Dudley had provided the evidence that forced Lord Palmerston's government to seize the Laird rams. This work meant he'd relied heavily upon many affidavits, such as the one furnished by Blessing Dubois.

At last he cleared his throat and looked up, peering directly at Lady Alice. Serious-looking fellow – were all Yankees this serious? – with a thick beard thatching his jaw and upper lip, and slick brown hair, parted on one side. Deep-set eyes peered from either side of a narrow nose. "There is sufficient here to warrant a further investigation, though we must tread cautiously."

There was a note of exasperation in Lady Alice's voice. "Am I to understand, Mr Dudley, that you're not going to press the authorities for an examination of the vessel?"

"Not at this point, Your Ladyship."

Lady Alice frowned icily. "I see."

"With respect, Your Ladyship, I suspect that you might not. Out there – " he gestured to the grand sweep of the Mersey, framed in the window at his back – "is a vast and complex world of high profit and low cunning. All too many business owners will instigate falsehoods about their competitors to gain a commercial advantage. Situations are seldom as they first appear."

Temper rising, I couldn't restrain myself. "Blessing Dubois has risked his livelihood to bring this news. I'm certain he's no schemer."

Lawyer turned his attention on me for the first time. "How long did you say you'd known your informant, Miss Giddings?"

I had to concede that I'd met Blessing for the first time just twenty-four hours ago.

"So you know nothing of this man's antecedents and have accepted everything he told you at face value?" Way that lawyer looked at me made me feel like some blunt-witted house-girl being addressed by a patient Massa.

Stood my ground all the same. "You can tell a great deal from a first acquaintance, Mr Dudley. Also, you can know someone all your life and yet be surprised by their trickery. I know Blessing is a truthful boy. I'm certain of it."

Lawyer rubbed the bridge of his nose with his forefinger and thumb. "I'm sorry, Miss Giddings, but I do not share your conviction – not on the evidence you have brought today."

"But, Mr Dudley ..." Words trailed away as I realised this was a lost battle.

He stood up, marking the end of the conversation. "I will, of course, look into the matter, but in the meantime I have much work to do. If you ladies would excuse me?"

As we were ushered from his office, I was powerful frustrated. What really raised hackles, though, was that this crusty old lawyer was right. Much as I wanted to trust Blessing Dubois, we needed solid proof that this Rebel 'Satan ship' was being built.

6

RECOLLECTIONS OF A CONFEDERATE GENERAL BY JUBAL DE BROOKE

East Lancashire and Liverpool, England,
October, 1863.

There was a satisfying click of wood on wood as my long-handled mallet struck the croquet ball and sent it bowling through the first steel hoop. I'd never played this game, but the rules were simple and the prospect of some uncomplicated activity before luncheon was appealing. So I'd left my room and come out to practise on the smooth lawn in front of the house.

The setting was quite magnificent and I paused awhile to gaze from the tame parkland to the Pennine scarps where bare fists of rock punched through the bleak fell-sides.

"Good afternoon, General."

Sarah McConville strode toward me wearing an emerald green promenade skirt with the hemline raised to display a pair of Bloomers – baggy silk trousers gathered at the ankles after the Turkish style.

She produced a croquet mallet. "May I join you for a game?"

"I can't promise you much competition."

"Nor I you." She made a faintly coquettish smile. "I hope you don't object to my Bloomers."

I told her I did not.

"My father disapproves – like much of the country. But it's so difficult to take part in any remotely active pursuit wearing full skirts."

Positioning herself over her ball, she placed the mallet between her ankles and took a couple of practice swings. "How are you feeling, General?"

"Better. Much better, thank you."

"I was worried."

"I'm touched, but you really shouldn't have been."

She whacked her ball and watched it roll unerringly through the first hoop, then gave me a bold look. "Shouldn't I?"

The forthright attitude that I had come to admire was now working against me. "I felt a little light-headed, nothing more."

Her determined aspect only intensified. "You were speaking to people who weren't there. A corporal, some others. You called them 'boys', but you weren't speaking to children. Other soldiers."

Standing over my ball, I swung too hard and the corner of the mallet sent it veering in the wrong direction. "I've been having occasional daydreams. My physician has suggested a period of rest, but it's of little consequence."

"I'm sure your doctor has only your welfare at heart." There was a muted thump and her ball went curving once more across the grass before passing through the next hoop. "You've seen so much suffering. It shouldn't be surprising that the strain should manifest itself in some particular way."

Moving to the far side of the court, I took my next stroke too hurriedly and my ball came to rest even further away from the first hoop than my starting position.

I desperately wanted to change the subject, but Sarah was too quick for me.

"I have a similar affliction," she said. "Recurring dreams – nightmares, really. You aren't alone, General: that's what I'm trying to say."

"Well, that's reassuring to know." I was unable to rinse my words of gentle sarcasm, but either she didn't notice or was too polite to say so. "What particular shapes do your dreams take, Miss McConville?"

Breaking off from lining up her next stroke, she gave me a fragile look that made me ashamed of my subtle derision. "My family has a humble background. Fifteen years ago, we lived in a grimy court off Scotland Road in Liverpool. We were Methodists and Chartists. A small share in the shipyard made my father a little better off. Then his partner died, the shipbuilding industry boomed and we became abruptly rich." She shrugged, as if helpless to determine her own destiny. "I am haunted by the fear of going back to where we came from. To be pitied, to be seen as worthless."

"Surely your father has laid up great wealth."

"Fortunes can be quickly lost as well as quickly made, General." Her mallet fairly clouted the ball. It hit one leg of the hoop and ricocheted against the other before spinning out on the other side. "Without pedigree and breeding – or title, such as, Arthur Harrowby's – you are scarcely more than one poor decision or unfortunate event away from ruin."

It suddenly came to me how much pressure had been placed on this young woman as a result of having to manage the affairs of a substantial business.

"You have nothing to reproach yourself for," I said.

When she spoke next, her voice had regained something of its flintiness. "I'll never go back there. I'd be better off dead."

The force of this utterance revealed such willpower as I had never before encountered in a woman. When I first met Sarah, in Charleston, I imagined her as a lady of leisure who had crossed the Atlantic to pursue a naïve notion of adventure. Now, I could readily picture her negotiating deals with tough-talking cotton merchants along the waterfront, examining their goods with a knowing eye, driving down their prices. Here was a woman succeeding in a man's world – one who would win, whatever this required.

I played my best shot but was soundly beaten.

*

"Stop, thief!"

I couldn't contain my mirth as Senator States Rights Rankin jerked his ankle up and down while Josie, his Jack Russell bitch, locked her jaws on the trouser leg as if attempting to apprehend a felon. The little dog rose and fell, growling and twisting with comical determination.

Everyone in the drawing room was laughing – and it pleased me greatly to see Sarah joining in.

Rankin, too, guffawed pleasantly. "Real show-stopper, ain't she?"

There was a loud ripping sound as the terrier's teeth got the better of the trouser cloth. I half-expected Rankin to cuff the dog in a fit of anger, but he responded with a kindly shrug and said, with startling tenderness: "Leave it, girl."

Obediently, the dog dropped from the shredded fabric,

sitting pertly on the parquet floor in readiness for the titbit that Rankin tossed.

Nap, the other Jack Russell – the pair were named for Napoleon and Josephine – came trotting from the library and sat by his sister.

"Can't give to one without the other." Rankin chuckled, dispensing another morsel for Nap.

We went through to the drawing room where sherry was served before dinner. The terriers padded gamely at Rankin's side, then sat by his torn trouser leg with their short back legs positioned in an amusingly side-saddle posture.

"I do admire your terriers, Senator," Harrowby said. "So well trained, so obedient. And yet so plucky, so devilish plucky."

"Might the same be said for your slaves, Senator?" Thomas McConville's words limped through his narrow lips, but they struck the room with the force of a shell-burst.

In the embarrassing hiatus, I remembered that we had been invited here as Sarah's guests, not her father's.

Rankin's voice remained amiable. "I take it that you disapprove of the particular institution, Mr McConville?"

"None of us here before you is a friend to slavery, Senator." McConville cast his pale, myopic gaze from one of us to the next. For me, there was the fleetest of smiles. "Including General de Brooke."

"And yet the general is prepared to fight for the Confederacy, while your own ships break the Federal blockade to sustain it." Rankin's tone remained ungrudging, even gracious. His bright white smile followed McConville's gaze around the room.

I didn't care for the way I was being discussed in the third person, and yet I was glad that I wasn't being drawn into what, for me, would be an invidious debate. My views opposing slavery were a matter of public record, but, by the same measure, I was here as an official representative of a government bound to support the institution. Whatever I said would very likely create trouble for me.

"We have no quarrel with the self-governing aspirations of the Confederacy." McConville's scooped-out features had a damp pallor that gleamed in the gaslight. "However, you would have many more friends in Britain if you rid yourself of slavery's taint."

As if at some invisible command, the two Jack Russells laid down on the floor, but kept their heads up and ears pricked. "Of course, we are all of us entitled to our views, Mr McConville." Rankin slowly whisked the air with his hand, as if to embrace everyone in the room. "Freedom of expression is, after all, one of the principal reasons we are fighting for our independence. And yet the opponents of slavery often fail to see it in the light of reality and of practicality."

"How so, Senator?" Sarah, slightly flushed, wafted her fan.

"Slaveholders take their responsibilities seriously, Miss McConville. The welfare of their charges is a moral obligation. And, aside from ethical considerations, a plantation simply couldn't function profitably without healthy and contented labourers."

"We hear of abuses," Sarah said.

I sensed her eyes alight on me, as if searching for support. Yet I could give her none without contradicting a member of the administration I was there to serve. Reluctantly, I said nothing and hoped I might later find an opportunity to explain my silence to her

"From whom?" Another imperceptible instruction from Rankin and the terriers placed their chins on the floor. White crescents in the corners of their eyes revealed how attentively they observed their master. "From the Yankee newspapers?

Abolitionist zealots prepared to peddle all manner of falsehoods in pursuit of their misguided ideals?"

"Abolitionism has deep roots in Britain, Senator." Harrowby affected a ruminative posture. "Whatever the merits of this paternalism you speak of, the vast majority of people here are vehemently, *vehemently* opposed to slavery."

"A fair point indeed, Lord Harrowby." Rankin's reedy voice enfolded the room with his air of accommodating geniality. "But … may I speak frankly?"

There was an edgy nodding of heads, a perceptible aversion to the creation of bad feeling. In a comparable well-to-do parlour in Massachusetts or Maine, Rankin would not have been heard. Here, his hosts were all too anxious that he should speak candidly.

"During my time here, I've visited Manchester and many of the Lancashire cotton towns. I've seen wage-slaves living in appalling, unsanitary quarters, while these same wretches – many of them children – are set to work in such dangerous conditions as would never be permitted even on the poorest plantation." He paused, surveying his uneasily tolerant audience. A barely discernible nod brought the terriers back to a sitting position and they tilted their heads towards him in an attitude of uncomplicated adoration. "Why, even my little friends here would turn up their noses at the notion of living in a Bolton slum."

Right on cue, Nap and Josie barked twice in perfect unison. Hear, hear! You didn't need to speak Jack Russell to understand their – or rather Rankin's – sentiment.

It was a damned clever trick, I had to give him that. And it restored the conviviality to the party like a hypnotist snapping his fingers to dispel a trance.

*

Liverpool had a confusing air of contradiction: familiarity and strangeness bound up in a single street scene. As Harrowby strode at my side along Lord Street, with its elegant stone-fronted shops, I reflected that this could easily have been a block on Broadway, New York. Yet there were also strident contrasts. In Liverpool, Negro sailors could be seen walking arm in arm with respectable British women. Even in America's free states, this would certainly have provoked a violent reaction among white folk.

"Jubal, there's a woman recently arrived in Liverpool," Harrowby said.

"And what is special about this person?"

"She's an escaped slave. Name of Trinity Giddings. I read an article about her this morning in the *Liverpool Daily Post*." He spoke with unusual urgency. "What the newspaper didn't report is that she is a handsome and resourceful young lady from South Carolina. This I learned from Mrs Marjoribanks whose intelligence is seldom, *seldom* erroneous."

Harrowby seemed to regard Mrs Marjoribanks – whom I hadn't met – as some omniscient sage, though from what I could gather she was nothing more than an indiscreet purveyor of gossip.

"Miss Giddings has been taken under the wing of Lady Alice Featherfax. Notable lady, formidable in her support of the North and zealous, *zealous* in her opposition to the Liverpool Southern Club. She is also my niece." By now, Harrowby's words were coming at me like bullets from a line of Yankee infantry. At the same time, his voice dropped to a panicky whisper so that I could barely understand what he was saying.

I gave him a worried frown. "Arthur, why are you speaking like this?"

He looked across the street with an incongruously gracious smile, then said between closed teeth: "Because Lady Alice and Miss Giddings are crossing the road, and heading directly towards us."

My eyes followed the line of his gaze to see an attractive, if slightly plump woman wearing an elaborate crinoline dress. At her side was a mulatto girl whose striking countenance forced me to admit that Mrs Marjoribanks had at least been correct on the subject of Trinity Giddings' good looks. Like Lady Alice, she was wearing a fashionable crinoline, though its more muted design allowed me to see the woman first and the garment second.

"Good afternoon, Uncle Arthur." Although Lady Alice addressed Harrowby, she was looking directly at me. "This must be Brigadier General de Brooke."

Harrowby had been bushwhacked for sure, yet he recruited himself remarkably well. With his assured thespian drawl, he presented me to his niece before inquiring if she proposed to introduce Miss Giddings.

When this had been done, Lady Alice returned her attention to me. "Well, General, I can warn you that any attempt on your part to return Miss Giddings to bondage will be met with *résistance considérable.*"

Harrowby retorted with silky alacrity. "Why should the General do that, Alice, when he has published newspaper articles entreating President Davis to abolish, *abolish* slavery?"

"Is this true, General?" Lady Alice's perforating gaze pinned me like a specimen of insect in a display case.

"Don't you read the newspapers, Alice?" Harrowby affected a dreary expression. "General de Brooke's letter to the

Richmond Examiner, setting out his moral objections to slavery, was republished in the *Times* only the other week."

Lady Alice's piercing expression did not waver. "Then why are you here, General?"

Harrowby was about to answer for me, but I was done with this antagonistic exchange between uncle and niece, and turned to Trinity Giddings. "Is Great Britain to your liking, Miss Giddings?"

I saw instinctive aggression in her eyes quickly tempered by a cooler, more mannerly expression. "This is a bountiful country, sir, where people may make the most of their talents and opportunities."

She had been well-schooled, so much was clear, but her almond-shaped eyes were so playful, I felt myself thrown off guard.

"That is good," I managed to say. "It pleases me that you are free."

Her lower lip dropped as she prepared to respond, but Lady Alice took her by the elbow. "Come, Trinity. We have tarried long enough."

Resisting her companion's shepherding, Trinity Giddings turned and faced me with a steely expression. "Why did you say that, General? Do you mock me, sir?"

Taken aback by the directness of the young woman's challenge, I almost lost my balance. "Quite the reverse. I wish you happiness in your new life."

Still she showed no sign of relenting. "Forgive me, General, but as one who has lately fled from bondage, I find it difficult to take the words of a Rebel commander at face value."

Despite her animosity, I detected a subtle impishness in her manner. "Your scepticism is understandable, ma'am, yet the Lord's truth is that I believe slavery to be a moral evil that cannot be ended too soon."

Her chestnut eyes locked on mine. "If you are so averse to slavery, sir, I'm perplexed as to why you fight with such vehemence in the interest of those who uphold it."

I braced myself for the tirade that was sure to follow.

7

EXPERIENCES IN THE LIFE OF A SLAVE GIRL BY TRINITY GIDDINGS

Liverpool, England, October, 1863.

Rebel general wasn't what I'd expected.

I'd felt a poke of apprehension and no little embarrassment as Lady Alice spotted him with her uncle and crossed the street to intercept them. Anxiety became astonishment when Jubal de Brooke ignored Lady Alice and spoke directly to me, apparently as an equal. Whether this was proper courtesy or sarcastic mockery, I couldn't yet decide.

Then he said he was pleased that I was free and I couldn't let that pass. So I collected my wits and gave him a flinty look, like I was fixing to scold him and asked him why he said that.

He flinched under my words. Yes he did! Perhaps it was wrong of me, but I did so relish the sweetness of that moment. A slave girl lording over a Rebel richcrat. That was something.

Confident now, this child continued with chilly politeness to inquire why he should fight for those who want to keep slavery alive.

This shook Jubal de Brooke once more. Those sky-blue eyes blinked real fast, smooth-boned features blanched. And the broad mouth, that could no doubt form a handsome smile, clamped tight shut. Problem was that I could tell from his reaction that he had indeed been addressing me as an equal and this made me feel a touch discourteous.

I was fixing to turn away and leave him in this defeated condition when he retaliated. "I'm fighting for the state of Virginia, Miss Giddings." His voice was so calm it stoked me right up. "My vehemence is in the cause of self-government and I'm not here in Liverpool to pursue you or any other former slave. I've come to get help for the families of boys held prisoner in the North. Destitute wives, hungry children. Is that so wicked?"

In a trice, he stole away my victory. Right then, I was powerful angry with Jubal de Brooke but for some reason I couldn't shake off the sound of his deep voice repeating the word 'wicked.'

*

Some half an hour later, Lady Alice and I were in the waiting room outside the office of the United States Consul, Thomas Haines Dudley, in the Tower Buildings on Water Street. We had gone there to find out what had become of the investigation into the Rebel warship, that Blessing Dubois told me was being built to break the Union blockade of Southern ports.

Lady Alice patted my forearm. "I'm sure Mr Dudley will have some news that will wipe the smile off the face of that hell-raising Rebel."

"He didn't seem like a hell-raiser," I said. "Quite

the opposite."

She studied on that a moment before deciding to agree with me, but only on her own terms. "Of course, the seemingly pleasant ones are often Lucifer's most assiduous agents. They ensnare you with their pretended civility and then, sensing that your defences are lowered, strike with viperish cunning. "But enough of General de Brooke. Let us sit, Trinity, my dear."

I was wearing a voluminous crinoline I would never have chosen, but which Lady Alice had given to me as a present. The great satin skirts were supported by the now familiar spring steel structure of hoops and stays, fastened at the waist. Although the cage was flexible enough for the wearer to sit down, doing so gave an unpleasant sensation, as if I was crushing the bones of some fragile creature.

When we were both seated on the leather armchairs, Lady Alice's alabaster face opened out in a beneficent smile. "I have some intelligence from Mrs Marjoribanks concerning the naval officer who showed you particular regard during your time at sea."

"Josiah Mill?"

She nodded

I'd be lying if I said my heart didn't skitter. Yet before I could inquire further, the consul's secretary came out and told us Mr Dudley would see us directly.

Lawyer looked much as he had last time round: grim. "I have ordered a thorough investigation of Blessing Dubois' allegations but there is no evidence that Applegarth's are building a warship for the Confederacy."

"How can you be so sure, Mr Dudley?" Lady Alice sounded suspicious.

Lawyer cleared his throat. "Gentlemen such as Mr

Applegarth are all too rare in Liverpool, for he is a staunch abolitionist who has donated considerable funds to the Union cause. I can only surmise the motives of your informant, Miss Giddings, but it seems you have been given false intelligence."

I opened my mouth to protest, but quickly closed it. As I'd been forced to admit last time I was in Mr Dudley's office, I could hardly vouch for a man I'd met but once.

Outside on the street, Lady Alice gave me a dejected look. "This is a terrible blow, Trinity, and an unexpected one. Mr Dudley is quite right, though – abolitionists are rare in Liverpool's commercial classes. Are you sure Mr Dubois is to be trusted? Could there have been some misunderstanding?"

I was as frustrated as my friend. "Something is awry, Alice, of that I'm sure."

Linking her arm through mine, she steered me along Water Street towards our carriage. "Until we can find out what, I'm afraid this investigation is at an end, at least as far as the United States Consulate is concerned."

Quite suddenly I saw a way to continue it.

As we sat in the carriage on the way back to Falkner Square, I turned urgently to Lady Alice. "Tell me more of this news regarding Lieutenant Mill coming to Liverpool."

My friend knew how much Josiah meant to me and gave me a warm smile. "According to Mrs Marjoribanks, the lieutenant is here to oversee the refitting of a steam sloop. When the work is complete, he will take charge of the vessel with the rank of commander."

Despite our disappointment at the consulate, I was thrilled to learn of Josiah's promotion, which I knew he wanted so much.

"Where is the ship moored?" I asked, excitedly.

Lady Alice made an apologetic expression. "I am sorry, Trinity, but Mrs Marjoribanks did not know."

"Did your friend know the name of the vessel?"

She laid a sympathetic hand on mine. "I am afraid not. All she knew of Lieutenant Mill's whereabouts was a rumour that he had taken temporary lodgings in Vernon Street. But it is a long and densely populated thoroughfare. It will not be easy to find him there – even if the rumour is true."

Late that afternoon, I strode with rising frustration along Vernon Street, a shabby, shadowy lane threading from Tithebarn Street to Dale Street. I was there, alone in the back alleys of this great city, trying to track down my friend.

Part of the street was flanked by tall warehouses similar to the one where Blessing Dubois told me his terrible secret. They turned the street into a sombre, sunless canyon. Air was heavy with stinks of animal parts from blood pudding makers, tripe dressers, purveyors of pigs' trotters, and manufacturers of neat's foot oil, produced from the shin bones and feet of cattle. Thin dogs, drawn by those rancid scents, nuzzled and snarled among piles of waste on the sidewalk.

The street was deserted but for an elderly fellow in raggedy clothes so frayed and tatty he looked blurred at the edges. Under one arm he carried a rectangular slab of a hard white substance that minded me of flaky marble.

He saw me and came hurrying. Thin voice scraped under the brim of his dusty hat, carrying with it a reek of onions and beer. "Look you here, Missy! Finest Cheshire salt." Old timer held out the hoary block. "Indispensable for all manner of domestic purposes. Fine ladies would gladly pay two shillings in St John's Market, yet it can be yours for only one."

I walked by without breaking my stride. "Thank you, sir, but I have no requirement for salt."

Yet he persisted, hobbling along at my elbow, swapping his shallow pretence at salesmanship for the instant mantle of a beggar. "Then spare a penny that this poor old soul might have a scrap of supper?"

"Sorry, mister, I haven't got but two cents." In my rising anxiety, I clean forgot I wasn't in America.

A deep voice spoke up behind me. "Here's a sixpence for you, Pete – but I want you on your way."

I glanced round to see Josiah Mill standing not five yards away, his hand extending a small silver coin. In his white naval officer's breeches and blue coat, trimmed with gold lace, he cut a commanding figure. Yet he seemed thinner, his face gaunter than when I last saw him, just two weeks gone.

Beggar accepted the sixpenny piece with a stooping nod, then scurried off along the cobbles.

"It's so good to see you." Unable to conceal my pleasure, I rushed forward and hugged him tight.

"I'm pleased to see you also." He held me back so he could look me in the face, "Why are you roaming the streets unchaperoned? Are you keeping well?"

"Yes, yes, I'm in powerful good health." At that point I done forgot my manners. "But you look a trifle sickly. And if I'm not mistaken, you've lost some weight."

He nodded and held his hand to his stomach, indicating he felt some pain.

"I read in the newspapers about your arrival in Liverpool with Lady Featherfax.

I glanced along the gloomy street. "Residing in this dingy alley can't do much good for your constitution. Won't the navy put you in a hotel?"

Wry smile, and he pointed to a sign above a shop window that read: JEDEDIAH DOBBY, MEDICAL BOTANIST

"My friend Jed is kindly allowing me to stay in his spare room. A fellow after my own heart and stockist of all the remedies I need." At that moment he appeared to sense that all might not be right with me.

"Step inside the shop so we can talk more freely," he said quickly glancing around.

Inside, I was enveloped by rich tangs of plants and earth that minded me of Josiah's cabin on board the *Vigilant*. The shop seemed to have been colonised by plants, its tall shelves and wide floor space smothered by an ever-encroaching jungle. Yet, amid this apparent chaos, I recognised familiar friends from childhood: henbane in bloom, a crop of mandrake apples, stringy seedpods of a milkweed and a handsome agrimony with its vivid spire of tiny clustered flowers. The brass cash register on the counter was engulfed by thick glass preserving jars containing seeds and berries, powders and salts.

Josiah led me through to a small parlour at the rear of the premises. I took a seat in one of the two armchairs by the hearth and he sat opposite. "Now, tell me how I might help?"

"There's a plan to build warships for the South," I began and gave forth at length about the whole scheme, barely pausing to take breath.

When I'd finished, he studied on my words a good while.

Then, with a polite cough, he went and struck me down. Not physically, you understand, but it surely felt that way. "You mustn't get involved in this. It's a murky business."

Jaw sagged. Not what I expected. No, sir. Not from Josiah Mill. What to say? I didn't know.

He leaned forward in his chair. "I'm sorry. I appreciate you came here expecting a different response. But this isn't your fight."

"You mean it's not *your* fight."

"That's not fair, Trinity."

I gave him an angry look, saw a look of trepidation similar to that I inflicted on Jubal de Brooke that same afternoon. Slave girl done come a long way from Society Hill. Yet my feeling of power was instantly snuffed by deep, cold hurt. "So we're on Christian name terms, are we? Very well, I'll call you by yours – *Judas*."

"Please try to be reasonable – "

My thoughts went skittering every which way, none of them reasonable. "Your skin's black sure enough, Josiah, but not one bit as black as your heart."

Long silence.

He spoke again and now his voice was awfully quiet. "You know, of course, that I'm the oldest lieutenant in the service?"

"You already told me that."

Still I heard no hint of provocation in those smooth vowels. "What I didn't tell you was that my promotion to commander was due last year, but something happened to prevent it."

Slowly, he came to his feet, poured himself a glass of brandy.

"You shouldn't be drinking hard liquor," I said. He swirled the amber spirit round the glass and swallowed some with a sour grimace. "Perhaps not. But then I shouldn't have embarrassed my own government over the Laird Brothers' construction of those two ironclad warships for the Confederacy. I shouldn't have helped the United States consul to obtain affidavits. Nor should I have spoken secretly to sympathetic newspaper editors, nor written a dozen reports to members of parliament, the Foreign Office, the Admiralty, everyone who cared to listen and everyone who didn't. So, in the measure of things, I dare say a glass of brandy will not weigh too heavily against me – "

His sentence snapped off and he set down the brandy glass, grabbing his stomach.

I hurried to his side, but he pushed me back. "I'll be all right in a few moments."

"Sit down." I urged him back to his armchair. "Why didn't you tell me these things?"

Shy shrug. "It would have seemed braggardly. Besides, I'd been led to understand that the promotion would still be mine when the *Vigilant* returned to Britain – provided I didn't cause any further trouble."

Ashamed, I looked down at my lap. "So here you are, waiting on your first ship to command. And here am I, scolding you bitterly for not risking it all for the second time round, on the say-so of some South Carolina boy I met but once."

Attempting to ease himself into a more comfortable position, he winced at a fresh stab of pain. When it relented, he admitted that perhaps he'd been too quick to dismiss Blessing Dubois' information – Josiah had also heard rumours that the Confederates were involved in a new warship scheme.

A private detective he'd hired during the Laird rams investigation had reported that a South Carolina trading enterprise, named Fraser Trenholm & Company, was expecting an important visitor that very next evening.

"This fellow is a Confederate senator," he said. "Apparently he goes by the curious, but quite proper name of States Right Rankin."

8

RECOLLECTIONS OF A CONFEDERATE GENERAL BY JUBAL DE BROOKE

Liverpool, England, October, 1863.

My host rose at nine-thirty o'clock that morning – moderately early by his custom – and bade me attend him as he dressed. I knew from experience that this was a procedure requiring only fractionally less planning than Lee's tactics for the battle of Chancellorsville, and prepared myself for a similarly lengthy encounter.

Arthur Harrowby was standing in breeches and shirt before a tall mirror, examining his fussily tousled hair. It created an aspect of heedless heroism that would doubtless have pleased Nelson or Byron, if they had attained Harrowby's vintage.

"Good morning, my dear Jubal!" He began brightly, but then his voice plunged into thespian melancholy. "But look at me! I am having the very devil of a time attiring myself in this shirt – too much damned starch. A vest of armoured steel would feel like gossamer, *gossamer* in comparison." He appeared amused by this simile and his abject frown transformed into cheery entreaty. "Be a capital fellow and assist me with my laces."

By this, he meant his corset laces, which drooped from the back of the buckram-stiffened garment around his midriff. Taking the cotton strings between my fingers, I pulled them tight, then tied a double-knotted bow.

"Fashionable garb is all very well, but I still hanker after the military life. You Confederate officers look so confoundedly splendid in your glorious, *glorious* grey." He regarded me with a covetous look, even though I had never worn a uniform outside America. "The very sight of all that gold lace twirling from cuff to elbow all but induces me to seek a commission from President Davis."

Struggling into a frock coat of burgundy challis, he examined his image yet again in the mirror and appeared content. "Pretty, though, ain't she? And clever with it."

We both knew he was referring to Sarah McConville. "Yes, Arthur, both of those, and more."

We travelled in an open landau from Dunstead Manor to Liverpool, where we were to have luncheon at the McConvilles' town house, and I was pleasantly invigorated by a redolent slipstream of equine odours and the tang of hoof-pulped autumn leaves.

As we passed through Speke, my host banged his fist on the upholstery and swivelled to face me. "Damn me for a forgetful dotard," he said. "I should have mentioned to you that I had the privilege yesterday afternoon of passing through the lobby of the House of Lords with one of your relatives."

I gave him an inquiring look.

"William Plantagenet de Brooke, twenty-eighth Earl of Puddlenorth. His grandfather and yours were brothers."

I couldn't believe that Harrowby had forgotten such a

memorable coincidence – if it was a coincidence – and suspected he'd been saving this disclosure for a suitably melodramatic moment.

"I took the liberty of informing him of your presence here in Lancashire and he was ineffably, *ineffably* enthralled by your story. So much so that he asked me to extend an invitation to visit him."

Despite Harrowby's undoubted good intentions, I felt somewhat piqued at his presumption.

Sensing this, he became a trifle sullen and put on a wounded tone. "As a son of the Old Dominion, Jubal, I'd imagined you would have been eager to attend the home of your ancestors. Since I seem to have behaved inappropriately, I must apply for your pardon."

My education at Harvard Yard and professional experience as a journalist had rid me of the romantic illusions, cherished by my father and grandfather, of Virginia's special position as Charles the Second's 'Old Dominion'. And yet there was a peculiar seductiveness in the image of a bloodline tracing its path through history's fog, from Fredericksburg to Hastings where my ancestors had fought alongside William the Conqueror. Of course, this was a fanciful conceit, but at that moment it presented itself with compelling allure.

"You cannot be pardoned, Arthur, because you have done nothing wrong," I said. "You thought only to act in my best interest."

My words ignited the beginning of a smile in Harrowby's solemn features. "Then you'll think on this invitation, Jubal?"

"Very well, Arthur, I'll think on it."

*

Luncheon at the McConvilles' house in Abercromby Square was enormously disappointing. This was not because of the quality of the cuisine, but the absence of Sarah. Apparently, she had been called to an urgent business matter at the shipyard in Birkenhead and asked her father to convey her apologies.

Waxen and wearied by consumption, Thomas McConville spoke feebly through mauve lips. The prospect of sitting round a dining table with him and Harrowby for two hours or more did not inspire me. Nonetheless, McConville was determined to entertain us and I had to admire his stubborn decency.

We ate an agreeable meal of mutton pie with vegetables, preceded by pheasant soup and followed by pineapple fritters. All the while, Harrowby gossiped entertainingly in a manner that contrived to be indiscreet without giving great offence to its various subjects.

Later, when Harrowby announced that he was going to visit his stockbroker in the Exchange Flags, McConville gave me a sly wink and bade me remain with him.

With Harrowby gone, McConville made a philosophical shrug. "Arthur is less likely to visit his stockbroker as his club, where I gather hands at faro are being dealt for considerable stakes. Then there is a certain young woman whose company he enjoys – not to mention that of a quite uncertain young man."

If the revelation of these vices was intended to disarm me, it failed.

Then I realised that McConville was not trying to shock, but help me to understand our mutual friend. "Whatever else he does, Arthur Harrowby does not judge or condemn. That he accommodates a vulgar chap like me is testament to the goodness of his nature. He regards you very highly, General. As does my daughter."

McConville's bluntness ambushed me completely.

"You shouldn't look so alarmed, General – nothing spurs a man to greater brevity than an unrefusable invitation to the grave." A dry chuckle clicked like a drowsy woodpecker in his throat. "I simply don't have the time for lengthy overtures so make no apology for plain talking."

"Some might say the world would be better if we all spoke more plainly."

"But it would be much less romantic." A suggestion of a smile shuffled the corners of his mouth and, for a moment, the opaque eyes sharpened. "If you regard my daughter as I believe you do, then you should come with me now."

At that juncture it occurred to me that Sarah hadn't been called away unexpectedly but had never been here at all. I'd been outwitted by a scheming invalid.

For one so ill, he moved with startling purpose into the lobby, where he gathered his pilot coat and hat, while calling for his carriage.

"Where are you proposing to go?" I asked.

He made another wink. "A short errand into the recent past."

*

His wink may have intimated humour, though our destination could not have been more cheerless. Scotland Road was not two miles from McConville's town house in Abercromby Square, yet it might have been on another star.

Through the carriage window, scenes of grand houses and elegant civic masonry were soon displaced by glimpses of meagre people and shabby shops with little to sell. These premises were tall and narrow, each distinguished from its neighbours by a facade of slightly different, but always grimy hue that called to mind a shelf of flaking book-spines. Outside a butcher's shop hung half a dozen carcasses, so scraggy that I couldn't identify the animals – though, for sure, they were better off dead. Nearby, a subterranean shoe repairer worked from a cellar, only his head visible at the level of the sidewalk, which served as his display counter.

Half a block along the road, a beggar whose legs had been severed above his knees played a fiddle from a wooden-wheeled chair. His sprightly tune briefly invaded the carriage.

"Very little astounds me these days, General." McConville turned awkwardly to watch the beggar until he vanished, like his music, in the turbulent street. "And yet, very rarely, the most improbable individuals insist on amazing you." He consulted his pocket watch, as if to assess whether time allowed for an explanation. "For example, this morning I received some extraordinary intelligence from Mrs Marjoribanks, who tells me that Senator Rankin, notwithstanding his reputation as an unconscionable slaveholder, has donated a large sum of cash for the establishment of a dispensary for Liverpool's destitute."

He looked at me questioningly. "What do you say to that?"

Reluctantly, I was impressed and was compelled to admit it. I surmised that Rankin had motives other than pure philanthropy, but could not air my suspicion without sounding churlish.

As we entered the residential district, my companion ordered the driver to stop and bade me follow him onto the street. We stood at the entrance to a tenuous alley, not more than four yards wide and hemmed on each side by four-storey tenements of sullied brick. Their upper floors leaned drunkenly together, shrinking the sky to a sallow strand.

At the end of the alley – or 'court' – stood a privy and

cesspool. Stenches of human waste and putrefying vegetable matter snarled with odours of unwashed bodies, gin and a pervasive rancidness that had no discernible source. As we walked further into the court I heard the muted mewling of babies, the hollers of angry mothers. A dog barked, a man cursed, a woman sang a jaunty music hall tune, all the more dispiriting for its imposture of jollity.

Despite these noises, no one was to be seen.

Leaning heavily on his walking stick, McConville nodded to each house in the court, as if renewing a broken acquaintance. "This is where the British keep their niggers. Rankin was right about that."

I didn't take kindly to his manner. "This quarter is certainly appalling. But the residents aren't forced to live here and can move away if they choose. Slaves can do neither."

My companion swivelled to face me on the axis of his walking stick and his crêpe-cloth face contrived a dour expression. "There are some eighty thousand Irish among Liverpool's population of one half million. Most live in squalor such as you see around you here. Their choice was to starve at home, or starve here. They can, of course, exercise the liberty of starving in some other resentful town. What sort of freedom is that?"

"I don't dispute the iniquity of their condition, sir. Nonetheless, they are not owned as chattels."

"Then they are but a whisker's width short of it. The policies of the English government ensure it."

This surprised me. "Are you not an Englishman, come into great wealth by your own enterprise?"

At this, he smiled at me fondly. "I say the English government, General, not the people. As to my Englishness, I came to Lancashire from County Sligo in 1828 and quickly learned that an Irish accent and Catholic faith were mighty handicaps to survival, still less improvement. To my shame, I eschewed both to acquire a local accent, a Wesleyan devotion and an English wife. Withal, we were terribly poor. My wife died in childbirth and this Scotland Road court was all Sarah and I knew for the following sixteen years, when providence smiled on us."

He turned away, moving yet further along the court. Still, no one appeared, although the distant crying of babes and that mockingly merry song continued to drift from one of the apartments.

At the end of the court he stopped, clearly exhausted by the thirty-yard walk from the carriage. At last he spoke, his voice a bronchial rasp: "I suspect you are asking yourself, General, why an Irishman who deplores English oppression in his homeland should tolerate the Confederacy, slaveholders and all?"

His question intrigued me and this, I conceded.

"The imperial designs of the Yankees disturbs me," he said. "In particular, the determination of the North to subjugate the South smacks of Ireland's treatment at the hands of the English. It is my strong conviction that the Confederate states have a right to self-government – a view that I understand is shared by a fellow Irish expatriate, General Cleburne. Are you acquainted?"

I nodded. "We met just once, during the engagement at Chickamauga Creek in September. He's an inspiring leader and correctly regarded as one of the finest commanders in the Confederacy."

A wistful chuckle rattled in McConville's throat. "Perhaps there is some aspect of the Anglo-Saxon character – common to New England and old England – that impels the conquest of neighbours, whether across the Irish Sea or across the

Potomac River."

I reminded myself, with some small satisfaction, that my ancestors were not Anglo-Saxon, but Norman. And yet who was William the First if not a conqueror?

These thoughts were banished by a sluggish breeze that stirred the sulphurous background smell and enabled me to trace its source to the cesspool. I was used to the reek of latrines, but there was an especially noxious intensity to this vapour.

Seeing my revulsion, McConville raised his walking stick to indicate a high wall at the end of the court, adjoining the privy and cesspool. "Yonder is a biscuit factory in which steam-engine boilers generate immense heat. Its proximity to the cesspool keeps the filth in a state of permanent fermentation, enabling those who live nearby to exchange cheap rent for poor health."

At this, I took his elbow and urged him back towards Scotland Road. "Then there's no better reason for us to quit this place at once."

His woodpecker chuckle drummed irrhythmically. "What can cholera do that consumption cannot?"

In vain, I tried to mask my exasperation. "Then spare a thought for my health."

"We shall leave soon enough, General, but not until we are done with our business here." His miry eyes wandered around the alley with a queer wistfulness. "If you wish to understand Sarah, you must understand the courts. They shape her mind and impel her actions. A young woman of thirty-two should not have to endure the burden of managing a substantial shipbuilding business. She does well, but I fear she is increasingly preoccupied by generating greater and greater profits driven by the prospect of sinking back into poverty."

Sarah had admitted these anxieties to me during our game of croquet on the lawn at the McConvilles' country seat. Now, as then, there was no relief in knowing that I wasn't alone in being plagued by the past.

"Come, General." McConville stepped across the threshold of the nearest house. Unlike the others, it had neither a door, nor window frames. Once inside the room, my shoes slithered on damp clay. Its earthy sourness conspired with the fusty tang of the sackcloth to increase my unease. I cast around the sepulchral murk but could see no evidence of previous habitation, save a few shards of crockery and broken liquor bottles.

McConville appeared to detect this and spoke reassuringly. "This apartment is unoccupied, General, so we are not about to be set upon as trespassers. You will, however, notice a complete absence of wood, which is because the previous tenants – now evicted and residing at the vagrant shed in Brownlow Hill – ripped up the floorboards, took the doors off their hinges and the windows from their frames to burn for heat."

Again, his filmy gaze swept this way and that, as if searching for something lost. "This tenement was once our home, General. You might not credit it, but Sarah and I enjoyed some happy times here. Of course, where I recall fond memories amid the hardship, she sees only wretchedness and despair."

The stench, the fetid air and the icy chill began to take their toll and I began to feel a little faint. I said gently: "It's very cold in this room. You could obtain a chill. We should leave."

At last he consented and I stepped into the relative brightness of the court. But my head felt no better, the music hall tune seemed to slow and distort then another song rose up, strangely familiar, strangely frenetic, and I gripped the wall lest I fell.

I'd last heard the song the evening before the battle of Gettysburg. It brought back a slew of memories, which I tried to banish from my mind.

Then, a young man stepped into the alley. He was gaunt and thin-shanked, with a countenance so faint that he appeared to quiver on the cusp of visibility.

Who was he? He looked familiar but his name escaped me … yet I knew he was not meant to be here, not here in Liverpool … Patterson, I remembered … It had been in my mind to make him up to sergeant after Gettysburg, only he hadn't survived.

The ground at me feet seemed to slant and I felt a sense of giddy detachment.

Turkey in the straw, turkey in the hay,
Roll 'em up and twist 'em up a high tuckahaw
And twist 'em up a tune called Turkey in the Straw

The song was being delivered far too fast – the singer struggling to keep pace with a banjo that had now struck up.

Where was that damned banjo player? I wanted to tell him to slow down, ask why the haste?

I realised why, but too late.

The Yankee infantry was coming – more than six hundred blue-bellies on the run.

Incredibly, Patterson had not seen them. He was standing by the door of an apartment, smoking a clay pipe, and singing along, unaware of the danger.

Went out to milk, and I didn't know how
I milked the goat instead of the cow
A monkey sittin' on a pile of straw
A-winkin' at his mother-in-law

I tried to warn him: "Patterson! Watch out, man!"

But the boy couldn't hear me. He began to dance a reel, skipping this way and that as the banjo player increased the tempo still higher.

Enfilade fire rippled along the line of Yankee rifles. I felt the air shiver, smelled the reek of scorched powder. Yet still the song rolled on, faster, faster, faster.

Bobbie Patterson, too, was moving faster. Possessed of supernatural speed, he danced so nimbly that his body smudged at the edges, those long legs shuttling back and forth like piston-rods in an overheated steam engine.

Somehow the boy was dodging six hundred-odd minié balls; somehow he was invulnerable.

Met Mr Catfish comin' downstream

Says Mr Catfish "What does you mean?"

Caught Mr Catfish by the snout

And turned Mr Catfish wrong side out

In that instant, Bobbie Patterson got turned wrong side out. He wasn't dodging the balls, but catching them. Every piece of him was laid open. Multiple spokes of sunlight passed through his body as if he was a tin colander. Lumps of butternut-clothed flesh flew outward, fell like sodden leaf mould on the ground. I gripped the wall as I slid to the ground myself.

The image faded away and the sounds and smells of the grimy streets returned once more. McConville was nowhere to be seen but scarcely fifteen yards from Scotland Road, the man in checked pants was handing one of his puppies to a young girl and potatoes baked in their jackets were finding purchasers at three farthings each.

I clung to this realisation, for it was the path to sanity.

9

EXPERIENCES IN THE LIFE OF A SLAVE GIRL BY TRINITY GIDDINGS

Liverpool, England, November, 1863.

Local folk called the offices of Fraser Trenholm & Company 'the Confederate Embassy', and I could see why. Big old building in Rumford Place was an elegant three storey affair with a large central gateway leading to a cobbled courtyard. Near to the waterfront as well as the commercial district, that place was comfortably as grand as the United States Consulate, some small piece up the road in Water Street.

Standing on the sidewalk in Rumford Place in the early evening, I turned up the collar of my reefer coat as a fresh gust swept off the Mersey and came hunting through the streets. If nothing else, this exercise allowed me to discard my dress and its cumbersome cage of spring-steel hoops. I'd replaced this fashionable attire with common mariner's garb, purchased from a store in Albert Dock, which more resembled a walled city than a wharf.

Short time later, this child was spying for President Lincoln. Yes I was!

On the surface, Fraser Trenholm & Company was the British division of a successful Charleston trading enterprise. In truth, I saw before me the headquarters and treasury for all Confederate activity in Europe. This notion caused my stomach to agitate. Dipping a hand into my coat pocket, I felt somewhat reassured by the cold hardness of the knife that I'd also purchased in Albert Dock.

Quick glance round showed the street was empty, save for a beggar-woman on the corner. Sun seeped pale and weary through grey sky like a bar of soap left in laundry water. Dusk already creeping across the city – something I hadn't reckoned on.

This troubled me some since I'd paid no mind to Josiah's stern advice and come here unaccompanied.

Beggar-woman extended her tin cup as some passer-by approached unseen from the direction of Chapel Street. Abruptly, the air got torn open by throaty snarling and I looked up to see that poor crone go scurrying across the street as two Jack Russell terriers appeared from around the street corner, yapping and snapping and straining like the devil on their leashes.

Holding onto those leashes was States Rights Rankin.

No risk of my mistaking that man: shoulders so powerful his legs seemed to bow outward under the weight; whiskers sprouting like hedgerows from that shovel-shaped jaw; pink hands, big and dangerous as clubs.

I also recalled my late brother Benjamin telling me that those two terriers got better fed and more fairly treated than any slave.

This I could readily understand. Any proper gentleman

would chastise his dogs for attacking an unfortunate beggar-woman, but States Rights Rankin was manifestly amused.

I'd be lying if I said the sight of the big Massa striding down that sidewalk didn't scare me some. Even in my mariner's garb, I felt exposed. Caught my breath and held it till he passed through the tall courtyard gates of Fraser Trenholm & Company.

*

Night fell all too soon on Liverpool. Gas lights didn't cast out the darkness, but fashioned lemony islets in the soupy gloom. Lamp flame flared and faded, tossing slow-shifting shadows across street cobbles.

States Rights Rankin had been in the offices of Fraser Trenholm & Company the greater part of an hour and there'd been no other arrivals or departures. Yet what did I expect? President Jefferson Davis handing over a cartload of gold bars to the shareholders of Applegarth & Company, right there in the street?

Some spy I'd turned out to be. Loitering on the sidewalk under a street lamp, the disguise I thought was so clever a few hours past now felt a little absurd.

"Gas is singing – you hear it?"

Unexpected voice set my thoughts scurrying. Cramming my tarred mariner's hat tighter on my head, I looked round to see a coloured boy whose appearance was downright startling. See, I'd never seen an overweight Negro. Under a velvet stovepipe hat, his quilted cheeks and plump lips created a cherubic aspect that made it difficult to guess his age. Wore an emerald green frock-coat and jacquard-patterned waistcoat that constrained a mighty bulge of belly. Thighs like Virginia hams swelled his britches.

I gave him an irritated look. "I don't see how a gas lamp can possess the capacity of song."

"You've got to listen!" Fat-boy cocked one ear at the lamp overhead.

Against the distant clatter of horse hooves and muted scrape of carriage wheels, I heard a whistling exhalation of gas rushing from the pipe and the faint crackle of the flame in the burner.

"You hear it?" he said.

"I hear," I said. "But that's no song I can understand."

He gave me a knowing look. "That's because it sings in a secret tongue."

I decided to indulge this curious stranger. "What does the gas tell you?"

Fat-boy chuckled. "Now that, I don't know. Sounds like it's singing, though, don't it?"

His accent was local to Lancashire, and this colloquial pronunciation sounded still more peculiar in the throat of a Negro than Josiah's gentlemanly elocution.

He asked if I was a mariner, and since this was precisely the impression my disguise was designed to convey, I nodded.

"What ship you from?"

At first I thought his question was plain cheeky, but his guileless smile suggested he was simple rather than rude.

"The SS *Pembroke*." I'd noticed a large merchant ship of that name lying in Albert Dock only that afternoon, so my deception was sound enough.

Fresh gust snatched the lapel of my reefer coat, tugging it open. Underneath I was wearing a saggy sailor's smock that only partly concealed the swell of my bosom. Fat-boy's eyes seemed to settle there before I could fasten up my coat. For an instant I minded how that unfortunate southern boy Nate saw through my disguise – and suffered for his alertness.

But this slow-witted Fat-boy was quickly distracted by an almighty sneeze. Unfurling a voluminous crimson handkerchief, he set about cleaning his nose with elaborate industry.

He muttered some concern about catching a cold, but I was no longer paying attention. My gaze was distracted by a flurry of movement in the gateway of Fraser Trenholm & Company. Bulky frame of States Rights Rankin appeared from the courtyard with his two white terriers and set off along Rumford Place in the direction of Chapel Street.

"You must forgive me," I said, without taking my eyes off the senator. "I have to go now."

Walking briskly along Chapel Street and across the Exchange Flags, I trailed my quarry into Dale Street.

There, I stumbled into a giddy daze.

Scores of shops and stalls, each mantled in gaudy lantern-light. Felt like I'd gotten drunk and was peering into some distorted kaleidoscope. Jewellery stores sparkled in gaslight from ground-glass globes; tea dealers' shops reposed in softer gleams of octahedral lamps. Further down the street, a butcher done unscrewed the burner mechanisms from his gas pipes so naked flames grasped and flapped above roasting spits laden with joints of yellow veal and carroty hogs, complete with sorrowful heads.

Moving into the thoroughfare I found myself quickly engulfed in a chaotic tide: folk bustling this way and that; hawkers hollering their wares; mish-mashed tangs of spattering fat and stale horse-sweat, roasted coffee and fish, fresh that morning, now on the turn.

And in all that confusion, States Rights Rankin done vanished.

Staving off a poke of hysteria, this child cast around in a frantic attempt to pick him out among that concealing hubbub. Big fellow like him couldn't have moved but ten yards from where I last saw him. Yet the harder I searched, the less I saw. One person blurred into the next and the next till all I could see was a swim of featureless faces.

Never thought I'd admit this, but I was mighty indebted to those two Jack Russell terriers. There they were, right before me, barking at some poor stallholder of oriental descent; and there was the senator, grinning as he indulged their aggression. Though I felt sorry for the Chinese boy, I was powerful glad to see those dogs.

After that, I stayed much closer.

Soon, he turned into Crosshall Street and made his way toward Bell's English & American Hippodrome and Circus, a hump-backed monster of a building constructed of wood and canvas, with a red, white and blue façade. A large crowd of working men thronged the street outside, barging and shoving as they funnelled towards the main entrance. I caught sight of a billboard advertising 'A Scientific, Rational and Manly Display of Fistic Talent' and deduced that this was a fancy way of describing pugilism.

Despite the air of aggression in the throng, a path seemed to open up before the big Massa, minding me of the Red Sea parting for Moses. I followed in his wake to the junction of Crosshall Street and Whitechapel.

At this point he hesitated, glancing across his shoulder this way and that in a manner at odds with his customary boldness. Quickly now, he moved along Whitechapel, not with those long deliberate strides I'd followed all the way from Rumford Place, but rather a swift, scurrying gait.

He was fixing to do something secretive, I could tell

that much.

In that moment, this entire subterfuge revealed itself to me: directly before States Rights Rankin stood a grand stone building with fluted columns and a polished brass plate that bore the name Henry Applegarth & Company.

With a furtive pause on the doorstep, States Rights Rankin entered the offices of the very shipbuilding concern that Blessing Dubois done risked so much to tell me about.

Now I had solid evidence that even that dry-boned lawyer of a United States consul couldn't ignore.

*

Aware of the lateness of the hour, I hurried in the direction of Lady Alice's house in Falkner Square.

Walking fast was easy – felt like I had springs in my heels now that I had that wicked richcrat all but locked up in prison. Turning into a partly derelict locality known as Sir Thomas's Buildings, I noticed a dapper gentleman strolling by the big soap-boiling factory. Flickering gas lamp on the wall opposite illuminated an advertising bill for *Orpheus and Eurydice* at the Amphitheatre.

As the man stepped into the miry yellow light, I recognised him.

Jubal de Brooke – swear to God!

Now this was an intriguing encounter and my mind went scrambling among the possibilities it tossed up. My disguise meant I could walk right up to Soldier-boy, perhaps inquiring after the time of day, or for directions to this place or that, and he wouldn't know who the devil I was.

My amusing reflections quickly turned to concern when four ragged figures emerged from the shadows. They moved towards Soldier-boy with swift, stealthy strides.

Caught by surprise, he wasn't aware of their presence until one raised hefty a wooden club and thumped him hard across his back. Soldier-boy dropped to the ground where another attacker kicked him hard in the kidneys. Two more hung back, ready to join in. Prospects looked powerful ugly for that Soldier-boy.

Just what was in my mind, I didn't correctly know; but the sharp knife was in my hand and a piercing holler in my throat.

Robbers looked round, plainly shocked.

"You boys better get gone." I let the knife glimmer in the wavering gaslight. "'Less you want to get laid open with this here blade."

"Yankee nigger, huh?" Leader made a throaty laugh and glanced at his companions. "You reckon you can do the four of us with that little knife?"

"Maybe not four. One for sure. Maybe two." My words came slow and steady. To this day, I don't know how I managed to stay so collected. "Depends how much value you place on obtaining this gentleman's property."

Long pause. Almost heard those boys' brains ticking and turning. From Dale Street, the sweet aroma of roasted chestnuts mingled with the rank stink of beef fat from the soap boiling factory and a sour odour from the muddy ground at my feet. Hadn't occurred till then that I may well end up bleeding to death in that mud.

Robbers' leader found some voice. "We could rush you easy."

I shrugged. "Opened up a white boy down South Carolina way only last month." How true that was. Poor Nate. Never knew whether he done intended me harm, but of these boys I had no doubt. This knowledge steeled me. "Might do the same here in Liverpool just as quick."

Someplace vague at the back of my head, I heard myself asking what folly done led me to risk my life in a reckless attempt to save my enemy. The simple act of walking on by could have rid President Lincoln of a formidable foe at a stroke. Mule-headed girl hadn't thought things through.

Those robbers would come at me any instant. Fingers tensed round the knife handle.

Yet their victim was not as helpless as we all thought. Rolling sideways, Soldier-boy came nimbly to his feet. With one blow to the jaw, he knocked down the robber with the club then snatched up the weapon for himself.

"That makes the odds a shade more even," he said. "Now, if you boys still want the shirt off my back, I'd be obliged if you'd make the attempt."

With no stomach for a balanced contest, those robbers took one look at their leader and fled, each in a different direction. Seemed like a well-rehearsed move to outwit the constables, though neither me nor my new 'ally' were in any fit condition to chase them.

"I'm indebted to you," he said. "That was an exceedingly brave and Christian act. Let me get you something strong and hot. Then we can talk. I can't let your kindness go unrewarded."

Soldier-boy took me to the George Hotel, nearby.

Once inside, he tossed a shilling for two glasses of hot whiskey and asked my name.

"Pete Johnson." I gave the first two names that came to mind.

He'd taken off his stovepipe hat and placed it on the table between us. Etiquette required that I should do the same, yet if I removed my hat, my hair would spill out and my disguise fall away.

"My name is Jubal de Brooke, and I'm pleased to make your

acquaintance, Pete." He extended his hand, which I gripped firmly, as men did.

Taking a good draught of his whiskey, he gave me a handsome smile. "You mentioned South Carolina previously. Is that where you're from?"

I took a big old swallow of liquor and nodded.

All around, patrons of the George Hotel jostled and hollered in a fog of pipe smoke as I pondered on the irony of this happenstance. Here I was, chattel slave lately held in bondage, having saved a Rebel general from an ugly beating or worse. One part of me counselled caution; the other bade me let this high-minded Soldier-boy know just who it was stuck her neck out to save his.

He leaned forward and gave me a solicitous look. "Would I be correct in surmising that you're a former slave?"

When I didn't reply, he added: "It's not my intention to embarrass you, Pete. I'm a Southerner certainly, but no friend to slavery. In fact, I've expressed my views in a letter to the *Richmond Examiner* that was republished here in England by –"

"The *Times*. Yes, General, you already told me that." Words rose up from my throat like they had minds of their own, rushing out through my lips before I could even think about stopping them.

Soldier-boy's face made a wonderful sight: baffled blue eyes skittering this way and that across my own countenance.

Swept along by my impetuous outburst, I removed my tarred hat with a flourish, determined to enjoy the theatre of revelation before the mist cleared behind that educated brow of his.

Tilting his head to one side, he regarded me from a slightly different angle. "I'll be damned if it isn't Miss Giddings."

10

RECOLLECTIONS OF A CONFEDERATE GENERAL BY JUBAL DE BROOKE

Liverpool, England, November, 1863.

"You'll be damned all right, General, for all those dead on your account fighting for the wrong cause." Trinity Giddings spoke with an odd mix of anger and satisfaction.

"That's as may be, but my immediate concern is that you've been tracking me, disguised as a seaman."

She made a disapproving expression. "It would be a vanity to imagine I'd been tracking you. I encountered you entirely by accident. But perhaps you should be grateful for my mariner's garb. I doubt those ruffians would have taken me quite so seriously had I been decked out in petticoats."

The merest smile tickled the corners of her mouth and I felt compelled to return it.

"This city is full of danger, Miss Giddings. You shouldn't be wandering its streets unattended, still less at night."

"Advice that you would do well to heed, General."

"Your impudence does you little credit, Miss Giddings."

"My impudence? Remind me, who saved who back there in the street?"

The sharpness of her wit made her all the more intriguing. "Of course, I'm grateful for your assistance," I said. "The Good Samaritan himself could hardly fail to applaud you. It's your recklessness that worries me."

"You shouldn't concern yourself with my welfare."

"I believe I have a duty to, Miss Giddings, since you concerned yourself with mine." I saw my small success register in her features. "Why *did* you come to my aid?"

She blinked quickly. "I don't rightly know. I acted without thinking."

Her manner had become flustered and I pressed home my advantage. "Equally interesting is why you chose to remove your disguise? If you have been busy in some clandestine purpose, surely I am the very last person who should know about it?"

"I fear your imagination runs away with you, sir," she stammered.

"Well, I am forever in your debt, Miss Giddings, whatever your motive."

She looked at me thunderously. "You can't be a Rebel and an abolitionist, General. You can't ride those two horses over any proper distance."

Finishing my whiskey, I gave her a quizzical look. "I do believe you would rather I upheld slavery. Perhaps that would make matters conveniently straightforward so that disliking me would be so much simpler for you."

"That, General, already comes quite easily."

She snatched up that tarred mariner's hat and headed for

the exit.

I thought to follow, but desisted. She would resent any further intrusion on my part. Besides, I had no doubt she could take care of herself – and I was still feeling the worse for my experience of being set upon. What I needed was to rest – rest and recovery before facing another day.

*

The next morning Sarah McConville and I took a carriage to St George's Hall where the Grand Liberty Bazaar would be held, some four weeks hence. The brougham clattered along the uneven road surface of Mount Pleasant, intensifying the ache in my shoulders, lividly bruised by the clout of that club the previous evening.

The incident had exercised my thoughts on Trinity Giddings and her curious subterfuge, which was certainly contrary to the interests of the Confederacy. Yet I was in a quandary. I could, of course, report the matter to States Rights Rankin, or perhaps inform James Dunwoody Bulloch, the Confederate purchasing agent in Liverpool. But what could they surmise that I could not? There was also the matter of my pride. A Rebel General rescued from a band of guttersnipes by a former slave girl? It didn't sound too edifying.

"Here we are, Jubal – St George's Hall!" Sarah's excited voice was a welcome intrusion.

As our carriage halted in Lime Street, I caught my first sight of the colossal structure. Its pale ochre masonry was a graceful alignment of classical columns and porticoes, sculptured pediments and ornate entablatures. Stone-flagged plateaux surrounding the great edifice were strangely clear of hawkers and beggars, imparting an aspect of fresh-scrubbed repose that seemed incongruous in this noisy, unstill city.

At the north front we approached a semi-circular apse and made our way towards one of three doorways attended by lamp-bearing statues of nereids and tritons. We were there to reconnoitre the Great Hall, where our bazaar stalls would be set up – thirteen in all, representing each of the eleven seceded states, as well as Kentucky and Missouri. As the president of the organising committee, Sarah had made herself responsible for managing the Virginia stall.

Her voice effervesced with enthusiasm. "Lord Northycroft has already donated a race horse for our raffle, while the Duchess of Athlone has pledged a pair of Constables which will undoubtedly fetch a very fair price at auction."

Sarah was dressed in a sumptuous crinoline of Wedgwood blue, with a starched plastron of intricately embroidered bows covering her breast. She cut a resplendent figure, yet there was something a little overstated in her appearance as she led me across the flagstones to the central door.

"Why, look who this is!"

A sharp-featured woman was heading from the hall to the stone steps in the direction of Wellington's Column. Instantly, Sarah put on a turn of speed and altered course to intercept.

For a moment I entertained a faint hope that I was about to be presented to Mrs Marjoribanks, the most prolific broker of gossip in Liverpool.

I was quickly disappointed when Sarah introduced me to the Marchioness of Chalcross.

"This event of yours has a ring of vulgarity, Miss McConville." Her voice was dour. From the side of her head, one diffident eye scanned me, parrot-like, as if I might be a carrier of some infectious disease.

"We are asking patrons to suspend matters of taste in the

greater interest of Confederate success, Lady Chalcross." Sarah spoke with a deference that was at odds with her usually direct manner.

Now the marchioness turned both eyes on me. "And you, sir, I trust you are more rebel than rabble?"

Irritatingly, Sarah replied for me: "General de Brooke is a relative of the Earl of Puddlenorth."

"I see." She regarded me with just a fraction less hostility. "Then I do hope all those years in our former colonies have not too greatly diluted your breeding."

"Quite the reverse, ma'am. In America we recognise that nobility cannot be inherited by the privileges of birth, but is acquired instead through individual endeavour."

If the Marchioness of Chalcross had been chewing lime-rind, her expression could not have been sourer.

When she had gone, Sarah made a coy smile. "Lady Chalcross is invigoratingly candid, is she not?"

I was in no humour to indulge silly euphemisms for plain rudeness, but said nothing as we entered the immense building.

"I'm afraid she's never been quite as congenial after the fiasco of my Bloomer Ball." Sarah affected an unconvincing chuckle. "I aimed to promote the new style for women, but succeeded only in embarrassing my friends and bringing a crowd of protesters onto the street."

I grinned at that. "In America we march to war over secession, while the British, well – you rise up on the momentous question of … Bloomerism."

My derision was intended to be gentle, but provoked an expression of asperity.

"It's not funny, Jubal. There was violence – the constables had to be called."

As we approached the Great Hall's enormous doors of

wrought bronze, she indicated the monogram 'SPQL'.

"It stands for 'The Senate and the People of Liverpool' – a rather pretentious association with the SPQR motif of ancient Rome. If I were a Roman ruler, Celia Chalcross would be fed to the lions in no time."

I shrugged. "Then damn Lady Chalcross; damn them all."

She gave me a shocked look, then a small smile. "That's what my father said."

"Your father is a man of profound insight."

"Yet he rarely leaves the confines of our house." A hint of rancour now stole into her tone. "He doesn't have to live among these people, attend their functions, do business with them."

So why, I pondered, had she provoked them by organising an event such as her Bloomer Ball? It seemed that Sarah wanted to shock and appease Liverpool's socialites in equal measure. Perhaps she was trying to do what Trinity Giddings had accused me of attempting – riding two incompatible horses.

Stepping inside the Great Hall, I was overwhelmed by a graceful confluence of art and science; of light and space jubilantly joined.

The roof was a vaulted tunnel of heraldic designs, no less than eighty feet high, and shouldered by columns of vermilion granite. High in the walls, wide-winged seraphs gazed down from the spandrels between classical arches, illuminated now by natural daylight; after dark by ranks of glittering gasoliers. The floor comprised thousands of tiles laid out in vivid symmetry as if describing the orbits of planets and moons. Everywhere I looked, there were images of the red rose of Lancashire, St George and the dragon, and that most curious of creatures, the heron-like Liver bird.

"Will it do?" Sarah's tone was a little nervous.

I heard my laughter resonate in high-flung recesses. "It might just pass muster."

She walked to the far end of the hall where an arched window loomed above a set of doors adorned with bronze scroll-work. "This is where our stall will be. Virginia will be represented here, if only for a few days."

"It will be Virginia's honour."

When she turned to me I was glad to see a return of the familiar frankness I admired so much. "Yet, in truth, you would sooner be in Virginia with your soldiers than here with me."

"I'd prefer to be with my brigade than taking part in this war of opinions in Great Britain. But being here with you makes it an entirely different question."

She looked at me so hard I had the impression she could see deeper into me than I ever could.

"Nonetheless, this war of opinions is important. My accountant estimates that the function in this very hall will raise at least twenty thousand pounds, which is to say more than one hundred thousand dollars."

"You could do a great deal with that much money."

"You could win a war." She was close to me now, though I wasn't aware of either of us having moving toward the other. My nostrils flared as the muskiness of her perfume braided with the lavender-scent of her hair.

"It takes more than money to win wars," I said.

"What then? Courage? Valour?"

Our closeness might have appeared unseemly in such a public place and I wondered what Lady Chalcross might have made of it. Then I found myself not caring if the whole of Britain was watching – the whole of America too.

"Those, yes. But also luck and audacity."

With surprising firmness, she took my hand then led me from the Great Hall, across the corridor outside, and into a small wood-panelled room.

"Welcome to the headquarters of the Grand Liberty Bazaar."

It wasn't much of a headquarters: a scuffed table, four chairs of mismatched styles, and half a dozen wooden shelves bedecked with envelopes and letters.

With her back to the door, she turned the brass key in the lock and crossed the room to stand before me.

"Would it please you if I was to be audacious, Jubal?" Despite the boldness of her question, her voice trembled.

So did mine. "I can't imagine that it wouldn't, Sarah."

There was more fumbling behind her back. I sensed deft manipulation of ties before the hooped crinoline fell away in one piece. Underneath she wore no corset, nor petticoats, nor undergarments of any description. The movement was so quick that, for the merest instant, it distracted me from the fact of her nakedness.

After that, the situation in my trousers vanquished all intellectual function. For here was an entirely lovely woman for whom I had the greatest affection. And if three damnable years of soldiering had taught me nothing else, it was that those who deferred the pleasures of this short life were often dead before opportunity next tapped their shoulder.

11

EXPERIENCES IN THE LIFE OF A SLAVE GIRL BY TRINITY GIDDINGS

Liverpool, England, November, 1863.

Lady Alice Featherfax elevated her chin, projecting her voice heavenward and I imagined the Almighty shielding His ears against her booming tones: " 'Then the Lord rained upon Sodom and upon Gomorrah brimstone and fire … And he overthrew those cities, and all the plain, and all the inhabitants of the cities, and that which grew upon the ground.' " She looked up from the King James Bible on her lap and the fierce gleam in her eyes told me she wasn't so much thinking of Sodom and Gomorrah as Richmond and Charleston.

"The Good Book shows us, does it not, Trinity, that those panderers to the devil's doings are most certainly bound to tumble into his blazing abode? By which, of course, I refer to that *rebelle diabolique*, States Rights Rankin."

It was late on Sunday morning and I'd waited, until we got

back from church, before telling Lady Alice how I followed Rankin to the head office of Applegarth's. Risky business for sure, she reckoned, although she soon accepted that my mission had been justified by the value of the intelligence I'd obtained. Indeed, my story got Lady Alice so stoked up that she immediately took out her Bible and went straight to the Sodom and Gomorrah verses, which I suspected she quoted often.

"I also encountered General de Brooke."

Snapping shut the heavy Bible, Lady Alice fixed me with a penetrating stare. "I thought that double-talking dandy would be involved in this subterfuge."

"If he is, it wasn't apparent from what happened last night," I said. "This was a separate incident that occurred as I made my way back to Falkner Square. I spotted the general near Sir Thomas's Buildings and followed him into the George Hotel."

"You are so very daring, Trinity." Lady Alice's eyes moistened in excitement. "What did the rakehell get up to?"

I shrugged. "Nothing more incriminating than taking a drink." Saw Lady Alice's deflated expression and added with a wry grin: "However, I did stand right beside him at the bar – as close as you are to me."

She smiled back. "And he was oblivious to your presence?"

I nodded, unhappy at withholding information from my friend, yet reluctant to tell her the whole tale. If I'd done so, all Liverpool would have known double-quick and that Soldier-boy would have been mightily embarrassed. So why did I pass up such an opportunity? That I had no satisfactory answer was a source of agitation.

"But this is icing on our cake, my dear – and I know precisely how to exploit it." Lady Alice gripped my forearms and looked at me directly. "Mrs Marjoribanks is holding a reception this afternoon at her address in Abercromby Square, to which you and I are invited. I had decided against attending since certain unpalatable members of Liverpool Southern Club will be there – and very probably my uncle and General de Brooke. But in view of your disclosure, I feel we must go. We cannot spurn the prospect of tweaking the general's nose yet again."

I said nothing, my mind grappling with the implications of another meeting with Jubal de Brooke. If Lady Alice got her dander up – which was entirely possible – and attempted to embarrass the general by revealing the half-true yarn I'd just spun, I'd be exposed to both as a two-faced tattler.

"I'm not so sure I feel up to another exchange with those people ..." My words trailed into silence as I realised how unconvincing I sounded.

My friend gave me a disappointed look.

I struggled for a more satisfactory explanation but could find none.

Awkward quiet was broken when one of the maids entered the room to announce the attendance of a young man at the door, a young black man, asking to see me. Name of Blessing Dubois.

*

Last time this child saw Blessing Dubois had been in that coffin-shaped sail-maker's warehouse on the waterfront.

As he was shown into Lady Alice's drawing room, he had that same billycock hat, with a smart Belcher necktie and dandy Chesterfield overcoat. Yet his cockiness done vanished, I could tell that much. Boy calls at the house of a wealthy abolitionist, he's bound to get noticed. For a slave lately escaped from the Rankin plantation, coming here must have taken powerful courage.

"Blessing – what a truly Christian name." Lady Alice made a pleasant smile. "But please sit down, Mr Dubois, and tell us how may we assist you?"

Blessing looked up from the chair to which Lady Alice had shepherded him. "Ain't no disrespect intended, Your Ladyship, but my business here's with Missy Trinity."

Lady Alice whisked away his protest in a flutter of laughter. "You must believe me when I assure you, Mr Dubois, that there is nothing you can tell Trinity to which she would not want me to be party."

"Go ahead, Blessing," I said. "You can trust Lady Alice."

Boy hesitated. Loss of nerve, maybe; good reasons, for sure. "It's about Applegarth's and that Satan-ship they's building," he said. "I got more proof. Better proof. But you got to come with me to Mr Longinch's house."

"Who is this Longinch?" Lady Alice narrowed her eyes, thrilling to the air of conspiracy.

"Mr Longinch is the chief clerk at Applegarth's, Your Ladyship," Blessing said. "He has the proper plans and papers for this ship they's building for the Rebel navy."

Taking me by the arm, Lady Alice steered me across the room to the large bay window, where we could speak out of Blessing's earshot.

"Can we afford to trust this fellow?" she said.

"Can we afford not to?"

She bit hard on one corner of her lower lip, as if the pain might summon up insight. "He was right about Applegarth's in the first instance. As you discovered for yourself only yesterday evening."

"I should go with him."

"Yes, we should." Lady Alice nodded vigorously. "It might

prove quite enlightening. To the devil with Mrs Marjoribanks' reception – I suspect we will have bigger fish to fry."

To say that I felt some relief at this unexpected turn would be an understatement.

12

RECOLLECTIONS OF A CONFEDERATE GENERAL BY JUBAL DE BROOKE

Liverpool, England, November, 1863.

The journey from Liverpool to the country seat of my ancestors at Astrop Castle in Warwickshire illustrated the flux of time in a way that would not have been possible in America. After travelling by steam locomotive through miry canyons of mills and kilns and coal mines, I was presented, at last, with this scene of timeless repose.

Until then, I'd felt a shade resentful that Arthur Harrowby had arranged this visit without my knowledge. He was peculiarly determined to re-establish the bonds linking the American and British lines of the de Brooke family. I'd agreed to come out of regard for my friend's efforts, but having arrived, I felt a rising sense of gratitude for his perseverance.

It was only as I approached the castle's walls that I noticed evidence of change: windows in the grey stonework filled in with red brick, presumably to avoid paying window tax;

medieval chimney stacks topped with modern terracotta pots; tarpaulin sheets covering the roofs of shabby outbuildings. A steam traction engine grinding noisily across a flaxen field completed the destruction of my illusion of timelessness. The Nineteenth Century was as present here as it had been in Manchester or Stoke-on-Trent or Birmingham.

All the same, Astrop Castle was an imposing sight. The original structure had been built in the fifteenth century and its ramparts had endured Yorkist siege engines in the Wars of the Roses, as well as Cromwell's artillery in the English Civil War.

Clattering over the drawbridge that spanned a mirror-faced moat, my driver stopped the pony and trap outside the great hall. This was an elegant building with mullioned panes and gargoyled walls.

A footman bade me follow him into the building, where its master, Charles Plantagenet de Brooke, Earl of Puddlenorth, greeted me with a firm handclasp.

He was a slender man, perhaps in his early to mid-forties. Wispy side-whiskers flowed onto his chest, imparting the look of an underfed lion.

As he escorted me into his drawing room, my eyes scanned his face for signs of physical resemblance, but saw nothing familiar. I reminded myself that we were, after all, only second cousins; that similarities were not always evident between first cousins, even siblings.

"Our mutual friend, Arthur Harrowby, tells me you have become acquainted with Thomas and Sarah McConville." My cousin offered me a glass of brandy, which I accepted. "How is Thomas' health these days?"

"He insists he won't see another summer," I said. "Although Sarah is equally adamant that he will see several."

My cousin smiled faintly. "Thomas has suffered long and

painfully with consumption. Baden Baden, Marienburg – there are few watering places to which his search for a cure has not taken him. Yet it would appear to no avail. When we last spoke, I sensed an unremitting weariness about him."

I sipped the fine brandy and felt its welcome scorch in my chest. "And yet he has a formidable force of will."

My host peered at me over the curve of his brandy glass. "So, too, does Sarah."

This, I couldn't dispute. At the time of our adventure in St George's Hall I'd considered the excitement to be peerless. That was until the next time, and the one after that, and the half dozen that followed.

"I suspect that Thomas' refusal to depart this mortal coil is deeply rooted in the welfare of his daughter."

"How so?"

"If it is possible to die happy, seeing Sarah betrothed would settle it for Thomas." My cousin's glance was no doubt innocuous, although in that panicky instant I imagined he knew precisely what had gone on and struggled to stop myself coughing back the liquor I'd just swallowed.

My cousin looked at me anxiously and asked if I was well.

Thanking him for his concern, I assured him that I was fine.

Yet my thoughts remained with Sarah. For all our voluptuous activity, she'd never suggested that it should signify anything beyond immediate pleasure. Coupled with her determination to run the shipyard single-handedly, I suspected she regarded any prospect of marriage as an obstacle to her commercial ambitions.

*

The tap of my shoes on dark floorboards brought hollow echoes from the ancient recesses of Astrop Castle's east wing. Apart from the tall stained window at the far end, the only light was generated by wall-mounted candelabras. The air was burdened with the tang of scorched wax and old timber.

On the walls, portraits of armour-plated ancestors gave the unsettling impression that I was being judged as I passed under their gaze.

This started with the first Earl of Puddlenorth, ennobled by Henry Tudor for his part in defeating Richard III at the battle of Bosworth Field, almost four hundred years ago. Since then these forbears had fought hard and often in the cause of the English and later the British crown. Yet my reaction was not what I'd anticipated. I found no sense of heritage or kinship.

I walked by paintings of forbears who had fought at Naseby and Blenheim, Quebec and Waterloo and it meant nothing. Reminding myself that my presence in Britain was chiefly the result of having fought too many battles, I put this lack of excitement down to my weariness of war.

My cousin had brought me to this gallery and left me to explore, explaining that the portrait of our mutual grandfather, the Honourable Robert Plantagenet de Brooke, could be found at the furthest extent of the corridor, near the coloured glass window.

Strangely anxious to find the one face I would recognise amid all this history, I bypassed a century of family portraiture in a few seconds.

The painting I was looking for depicted Robert Plantagenet de Brooke in the scarlet coat of a British infantry officer, on a chestnut stallion.

I blinked, took a step forward; looked again, but couldn't sustain my focus.

Instead I examined the battle scene in the background – grey and indistinct: I made out horsemen galloping through garlands of cannon-smoke; a field, a river; somewhere distant, a fortress. Its walls had been damaged by artillery fire. Smoke coiled around a tower. I looked at the gilt frame – an object of art in itself, elaborate scroll-work with florid motifs and a pair of cherubs linking hands across the top.

My eyes scanned every aspect of that portrait, save its subject. After those first, fleeting glimpses I did not want to look again.

With a rising sense of hysteria, I looked around the gallery for an explanation.

There must have been a mistake.

I had to be looking at the wrong portrait.

Yet my host had been very explicit. I'd come exactly as he directed, to the last painting on the wall, the one nearest the stained glass windows.

My fears were confirmed by the title of the portrait, set in a small plaque on the frame: The Honourable Robert Plantagenet de Brooke, 1774.

I lifted my eyes to the man on that chestnut horse.

The thin countenance of the fellow in the portrait bore not the smallest resemblance to the bold features of the man I'd known as my grandfather.

Yet it was the other discrepancy that shook me with such violence: the subject of this portrait had lost his right arm. Where the limb should have been, an empty sleeve was pinned across his chest.

I shut my eyes, praying that I might have tumbled into one of my episodes.

But this sober, solid truth was far more disturbing than any delusion my mind could conjure. Unless the man pictured before me had obtained a new face and re-grown a severed arm, he was not my grandfather.

13

EXPERIENCES IN THE LIFE OF A SLAVE GIRL BY TRINITY GIDDINGS

Liverpool, England, November, 1863.

Blessing Dubois did not please Lady Alice by insisting that we leave the elegant carriage a small piece up Vauxhall Road and walk the remaining hundred yards along Naylor Street.

Yet she soon appreciated the need for an inconspicuous approach. The area was respectable enough: rows of good-sized houses with fancy bay windows and small grass plots in front of them. Blessing explained that these were the homes of draftsmen, foremen and clerks who were by no means poor, but at the same time rarely saw a liveried carriage draw up on their doorsteps.

At last we arrived at a house with plaster-cast horses decorating the fanlight above the door. As we approached, I saw the venetian blinds of the front window stir a fraction. Seconds later the door opened and we were ushered by

Blessing into a gas-lit lobby.

Our host introduced himself as Cuthbert Longinch, chief clerk at Applegarth's shipyard. He was a chubby fellow in his early-middle years with a small O-shaped mouth and fleshy folds puckering up around it, minding me of a draw-string purse. This combined with wide-spaced bulbous eyes and a wispy-whiskered moustache to give him the aspect of a catfish decked out in waistcoat and necktie.

Showing us through into his parlour, he bade us take seats around a japanned dining table. Glass display cabinet by the window contained ornamental mineral spar, trinket boxes and porcelain figurines. Sharp odours of brass polish and turpentine and linseed oil gave the impression it had been meticulously prepared for this very visit.

Mr Longinch's bug-eyes flicked uncertainly between Lady Alice and me. "Young Blessing has no doubt explained the nature of my predicament? For some half-score weeks I have been tormented on the rack of my Christian conscience. I was a torn soul, ladies, utterly torn."

He paused, as if recalling a moment of epiphany, and resumed in a more uplifted tone. "In such a fix, there is but one hope of obtaining salvation: to beseech the Lord."

Lady Alice nodded her approval. "Entirely the correct resort, Mr Longinch."

He made a modest smile. "The Good Book left me in no doubt that I could not keep my peace on the matter of this wicked undertaking. Thus girded in the armour of righteousness, I secreted these plans and brought them home for the purpose of disclosure to Miss Giddings – and, of course, Your Ladyship."

Reaching behind his chair, he produce a rolled-up sheet of waxy paper and unfurled it on the dining table. I saw intricate designs depicting various plans and elevations of a sleek-looking ship. She was powered by a steam engine with masts and yards to carry supplementary sails. A formidable vessel for sure, yet I saw no cannon. Clerk made a knowing expression when I mentioned this.

"The Foreign Enlistment Act prohibits the supply of warships built in Britain to any belligerent power, Miss Giddings," he said. "However, this is circumvented by sailing unarmed vessels under a British flag to a neutral country where the flag is changed and guns installed."

Lady Alice laid a bejewelled finger on the drawing, tracing a line of rectangular openings that ran along the side of the hull. "I am certain Mr Longinch will correct me if I'm wrong, but I believe these are gun-ports – each with an ammunition rack nearby to accommodate shot and shell."

Clerk nodded eagerly. "Your Ladyship is entirely correct. You will also see that the vessel is equipped with a fire-proof ammunition magazine, steel-lined throughout and situated substantially below the waterline. What purpose the fire-proofing, other than to store gunpowder? And why else so deep below the waterline, save to give protection from enemy fire?"

Nodding, Lady Alice leaned over one of the plans to indicate what seemed to be a rectangular box incorporated into the hull. "What is this arrangement?"

Mr Longinch made a broad a smile. "Your Ladyship's eye for detail is exceedingly sharp. For this is a citadel of armoured steel, designed to shield heavy guns and vital machinery during battle."

Lady Alice cleared her throat, as a judge might before pronouncing sentence. "I have no doubt, Mr Longinch, that these designs are those of a most diabolical ironclad that the

Rebels intend to use to sweep President Lincoln's warships from the ocean."

This to me: "Come, Trinity, the Lord's work brooks no delay."

*

The Lord's work may well have demanded urgency, but before taking these matters back to the US consul, this child was determined to show the designs to Josiah Mill, whose knowledge of such matters was second to none.

Initially exasperated by my insistence, Lady Alice eventually concurred when I explained Josiah's role in the thwarting of Confederate plans to obtain those two ram-bowed warships from the Laird Brothers' yards.

I found Josiah's lodgings at the botanical shop in Vernon Street much more easily on this, my second visit.

I was thankful to see Josiah come to the door, but concerned at his much depleted appearance. He'd lost a great deal of weight, giving his countenance a whittled-out appearance, while his previously stout frame seemed round-shouldered and diminished. Nevertheless, his solemn expression brightened when he saw me standing there on the doorstep.

"Come inside, Trinity. What a very pleasant surprise it is to see you." His voice, too, sounded thinner, huskier.

In the botanical shop, I was again immured by towering shelves of vegetation; immersed in earthy aromas of plants and peat. There was the lily-like bloom and ochre-knuckled root of Solomon's seal; spiny flourishes of horsetail and werewolf root with its pink bell-shaped flowers and long stringy seedpods growing in pairs, like pincers. This being the Sabbath, the shop was closed and Josiah explained that his landlord had gone to visit relatives in St Helens.

Following Josiah into the parlour, I declined his offer of a seat and instead asked for his opinion on the warship designs which I laid out on the surface of a walnut bureau.

Placing a pair of silver-rimmed spectacles near the end of his nose, he peered down at the plans. I watched his eyes shifting every which way as he sought to determine the nature of the draughtsman's drawings.

At last, he looked up at me with a worried frown and asked how I'd come by the plans.

I told him, holding back nothing.

Removing his spectacles, he tapped them on the waxy-textured drawing paper. "This is the design of a formidable ironclad warship, similar in many ways to the Laird rams, but much larger."

"Then we have those fiends!" My voice was laden with vindictive fervour, but at that moment I didn't rightly care. Girl lives in thraldom her whole life, she's going to relish any opportunity to strike back against her oppressors.

"What do you propose to do?" Josiah looked at me squarely.

"Why, to take these plans to Mr Dudley at the United States Consulate."

I was half expecting him to counsel caution. Instead, he nodded soberly. "Then that is what you must do, Trinity."

"Will you come?"

"If you wish."

His features clenched in pain and he pressed one hand against his stomach, placing the other on the bureau to steady his balance.

I took him firmly by the upper arm, guiding him to the sofa, and sat close by, hoping the pang would subside.

"I believe it is an ulcer which brings on this wretched

condition."

"You must rest, Josiah." Still I held onto him. "You mustn't become entangled in this business with Applegarth's."

Slowly, he loosened my grip on his arm and placed it around my shoulder, tugging me close with surprising strength. "I am already entangled, my dear Trinity. We must both of us see this through."

We sat quietly in the dim light while he recruited his energy some. I'd have waited there with him for ever. But at last he came to his feet and announced that he would hail a cab to take me home.

At the door, he gave me a stern look. "I have no doubt that this powerful evidence will enable the United States authorities to take firm action. However, Mr Dudley is correctly suspicious of all allegations brought before him, so we must be entirely prepared."

As the sweaty, steaming horses drew up in Vernon Street, I leaned forwards and touched my lips to his cheek. His skin felt soft and clammy, like damp silk. "You have a fever, Josiah. You should take some of your friend Mr Dobby's calendula flower tincture."

He laughed. "You are rather a youthful grandmother, Trinity, to be instructing me in the sucking of eggs."

I chuckled too, for that instant it was enough that we could both find the capacity for mirth.

14

RECOLLECTIONS OF A CONFEDERATE GENERAL BY JUBAL DE BROOKE

Liverpool, England, November, 1863.

The liberal dimensions of the parsonage dwarfed the squat Saxon church I'd passed, some fifty yards down the lane.

The parson, George Micklewycke, showed me into his drawing room whose lofty walls were adorned with watercolours of rustic idylls. There was nothing about this well-appointed country house, some one half mile from the gates of Astrop Castle, that spoke of ascetic devotion.

"Lord Puddlenorth sent word of your requirements, General," he said. "Of course, I will do whatever is within my gift to aid you." His pillowed cheeks and ample belly suggested a life of plenty. So, too, did his attire: a fine velveteen frock coat over a black satin waistcoat and back-to-front dog collar that I understood to be a distinguishing feature of the Anglican high church.

He offered me refreshment – a glass of port wine, or

perhaps some buttermilk – but I politely declined, explaining that I had only recently taken luncheon.

At supper the previous evening, I'd mentioned to my cousin Charles that I would like to gather more information about our grandfather's life in England before his departure for Virginia in 1775. Charles had immediately identified Micklewycke as the ideal person to assist: the parson was not only the keeper of the parish records, but also an antiquarian of some repute.

Micklewycke led me through a door at the opposite side of his drawing room and into a capacious chamber that more resembled a museum than a clergyman's office.

All manner of artefacts had been laid up in display cases and on shelves. There were marble figurines; silver vases; clay pottery; sections of mosaic; gilded icons; one tray containing flint arrowheads; another, intricately worked copper jewellery. In one corner, papyrus scrolls were stacked like tusks of ivory.

A leather-bound book lay open on his desk and I saw bold, forward-sloping handwriting on the sallow pages. This was grandfather's diary for the year 1775, which had been donated to Micklewycke's collection by my family – or at least, what I had believed to be my family until yesterday. That portrait of a one-armed Robert de Brooke had undermined the foundations of my life. Every assumption and belief was now open to doubt. For if my two-armed grandfather was not Robert de Brooke, who was he?

Who was I?

*

The diary of Robert de Brooke spoke of many aspects of his life in the period preceding his departure for Virginia in the spring of 1775. There was a description of the appalling riding accident that left his arm so badly damaged that amputation was the physician's only recourse. He wrote at some length about the painful months that followed and his despair at the premature end of his career in the army. Casting about for alternative ambitions, he had decided – as had so many others – to leave the old world behind and start afresh in the new. The prospect of owning a tobacco plantation in Virginia represented a means to this end. The people he spoke of included his parents, elder brothers James and Edward, and younger sister, Melissa, for whom he appeared to have a particular regard. He was also evidently fond of a baffling fellow named Lazarus, who sometimes appeared to be a servant and at others, a companion.

Lazarus was an unusual Christian name and stirred a brief flutter of association in the dimmer cloisters of my memory.

I mentioned my puzzlement over the identity of this individual to Micklewycke.

"Poor Lazarus was an indentured servant to your grandfather, and a companion also," the parson said. "The diary suggests they were born in the same year, which I confirmed by reference to the parish register. It seems they knew one another as children – your grandfather taught young Lazarus his letters – and the pair would have become friends had not their social stations precluded it."

Micklewycke had applied the adjective 'poor' to Lazarus in a way that indicated misfortune rather than simple penury. Still more mystified, I asked him to explain.

"The lad contracted a fatal disease during the voyage to Virginia and died not two weeks after arriving. This was explained in a letter to his mother in Astrop."

"From my grandfather?"

"In a manner of speaking. Your grandfather was temporarily

unable to write as a result of an accidental injury and so dictated the letter to a clerk at the tobacco plantation."

I made a humourless grin. "It seems my grandfather was uncommonly prone to accidents."

"Quite. He says as much in the letter."

This made me look up from the diary, my heartbeat quickening. "You've seen it?"

The parson nodded. "Lazarus' mother could not read, so the letter was sent to my predecessor at this parsonage, petitioning him to communicate tidings of the tragedy. The letter has remained on the parish files."

Rising from the desk, I followed his bulky frame across the room to a great wall of shelves containing large, leather-bound ledgers. The one seemed much the same as the next, although as I glanced down the long ranks of books I saw that their spines grew more and more flaky as they receded through the nuances of antiquity. My host went to a section of relatively recent registers and he pulled out one marked 1775. Laying this flat on a sturdy table, he turned to the back page, to which a stiff card wallet had been attached.

From this Micklewycke pulled out a letter written on a sheet of stained and crinkled paper.

I took it from him, struggling to prevent my fingers from trembling.

My eyes darted along the lines of awkward, crammed script without comprehending any of it, as a shell is deflected by armour plate. Placing the letter flat on the table, I held down its edges with my palms, as if attempting to subdue an assailant. Employing all my will, I tried once more to concentrate, reading with slow deliberation.

The message was from Robert de Brooke and requested Micklewycke's predecessor to convey to Mrs Elizabeth

Hotchkiss, a widow of his parish, the dreadful tiding that her son had lately died of smallpox in Smithfield, Virginia. Lazarus had passed away, said the letter, wishing to be lovingly remembered by his dear mother.

Incongruous reminiscences sprang out at me from the page: conflicts of logic and sanity that cast me into a vertiginous plunge. Pressing still harder on the letter, I compelled my mind to interpret the information before me. The letter was certainly from my grandfather. I knew as much because I recognised the handwriting as his own. Yet this was very different to the elegantly sloping calligraphy in the diary of Robert de Brooke. Still more disturbing was the question of why my grandfather should have pretended the letter had been set down by a clerk at the plantation? What reason could he have for practising this deception?

One explanation that struck an unsettling agreement with the other contradictions was that my grandfather was aware that the handwriting of the real Robert de Brooke would have been recognised by anyone who knew him.

Another memory blundered into my chaotic thoughts. This was not the first time I had come across the name of Lazarus Hotchkiss.

*

Hurrying back to Astrop castle, I went directly to my bedroom and took out my grandfather's ancient black Bible – the token of my heritage that I had carried at every engagement from First Manassas to Chickamauga Creek.

Turning to the fly-cover, I examined the dedication with fresh interest: To Robert de Brooke, from his good and loyal friend Lazarus Hotchkiss. The wrinkles on my brow deepened.

The name of Lazarus Hotchkiss had been written in a lighter shade of ink than the rest of the inscription.

Of course there could be many explanations for what was nothing more than a trifling inconsistency. But the one that returned most insistently was this: the Bible's true owner was Lazarus Hotchkiss, who cherished the book and had written his name in it to mark it as his property. Some time later, Lazarus Hotchkiss had added the extra words, using different ink, to give the impression that the Bible had been a gift from him to Robert de Brooke. Why else would he have done this if he had not assumed the identity of Robert de Brooke?

Consumed by sudden rage, I hurled the Bible across the room. Brittle pages tore from the spine, floating to the floor like the feathers of a shot bird.

"Damn you, grandfather!" I shouted at the disintegrating Bible.

What odds that the body at St Luke's Church in Smithfield, Virginia contained the bones of a one-armed man? What odds that Lazarus Hotchkiss had stolen Robert de Brooke's name – not to mention his money – and written that counterfeit letter to the local parson by way of bidding farewell to his mother?

What odds that I was no progeny of a Norman knight, but the grandson of a shameless thief?

Of course there could be no odds. Not when the outcome was certain.

*

Early that evening, unable to settle, I took a turn around the grounds of Astrop castle. Despite an excellent dinner, I felt compelled to walk awhile in hopes of resolving the myriad questions infesting my mind.

I strolled by a forge and threshing barn, a stone-built granary and cow house, into the small wood.

Powerful sunshine transformed the trees' scant remaining leaves into gilded pennons, picking out exuberant variegations of copper and lemon and carmine among fallen leaves, shunted by the wind into crescent-shaped shoals. Animated by erratic gusts, they stirred and settled, over and over. The air, too, carried a promise of decay in its astringent mouldy tang. The tumbled leaves shifted again and the world seemed to tilt.

I was not certain precisely when those fallen leaves became fallen boys. Their bodies blanketed David Miller's cornfield under Nicodemus Hill, sporadically groping and grunting, giving the impression that the land was attempting to shirk its unwanted mantle of brokenness. Dusk could not come swiftly enough, though even in the crepuscular light I glimpsed those boys' hopeless gestures; heard their feeble whimpers. With each passing minute, the movements diminished, sounds softened.

It was all I could do to lie still amid the cover of the trees with my shoulder still bleeding from a canister blast, and pray for midnight to bring silence and stillness.

Yet for all the exaggerated sharpness of my perceptions, I knew this was not really happening.

For the first time since my mind succumbed to this illness, I was aware that what I could see had no substance. This was not Antietam Creek, but Astrop Castle. There were no dying boys, only piles of leaves.

And although I could mark this as a triumph over my malady, I sensed more tangible perils that had yet to reveal themselves.

15

EXPERIENCES IN THE LIFE OF A SLAVE GIRL BY TRINITY GIDDINGS

Liverpool, England, November, 1863.

We stepped down from the hansom cab in Canning Place and I followed Lady Alice along the sidewalk towards the colonnaded portico of Custom House. Salt tang carried from Canning Dock, stirring in with scents of fresh manure and spiky whiffs of grog shop gin and pickled whelks.

Organ grinder in a dented derby hat cranked the handle on his music barrel while a little monkey, decked out in a scarlet pageboy cap, capered on the cobbles. Tune was so out of key that I pondered whether the seagulls up above were mewling in accompaniment or protest. Folk watched, grinning, on occasion tossing pennies, and I stole a moment to study on the plight of that monkey, so removed from his place of natural habitation. So lonesome, I thought.

Monkey done raised his red cap to Lady Alice who turned a powdered cheek and lifted her formidable voice above the cacophony. "Come, Trinity, we should not tarry."

She was right enough in that regard.

Inside the great building we were directed to an office given over to the temporary accommodation of Sir Eustace Baggott, principal minister to the foreign secretary, Lord John Russell. On the way over, Lady Alice explained that Sir Eustace had been given responsibility for investigating the activities at Applegarth's shipyard.

He looked up from a large table on which the warship designs had been laid out, and hurried to greet us.

Neatest little fellow I ever done seen: every smallest detail of his attire perfectly aligned, precisely symmetrical. Sparkly brown eyes regarded me through gleaming brass-framed spectacles that ornamented a pleasant countenance. I guessed he'd be in his early thirties.

"Miss Giddings, what an incomparable delight. I trust you are well?" Garbed in a light grey frock coat and striped trousers, he was a fraction shorter than me, yet seemed possessed of titanic industry. If Sir Eustace had been raised in a tribe of red Indians, they would surely have named him Little Big Man.

Behind him, Josiah was resplendent in his navy uniform and I noticed the extra gilt ring on his coat cuffs, denoting his promotion. Despite the momentous nature of the occasion, my heart swelled at the sight of my dear friend: no longer the Royal Navy's oldest lieutenant; now its newest commander.

We were invited to take seats round the table and my eyes alighted on the draughtsman's technical designs for the ironclad.

"We have confirmed that the drawing is authentic enough," said Sir Eustace.

"Of course it's authentic." Lady Alice gave Little Big Man a powerful frosty look, as if he'd caused her some personal slight. "I could see as much the first time I laid eyes upon it. As the wife of one of this country's foremost *ingénieurs éminents,* I have come, over the years, to recognise – "

"No one in this room would doubt your expertise in these matters, Lady Alice." Little Big Man cut across my patron with silky diplomacy. "However, we must also consider the credibility of certain parties and sensitivities in relation to others. We must take into account also what is at stake: we cannot afford to be too circumspect, yet nor can we act on presumptions without first substantiating them."

I blinked. He had a way with words, I could tell that much. What I couldn't tell was what they meant.

Josiah appeared to sense my confusion. "What Sir Eustace is saying, Trinity, is that our agents have confirmed that Mr Longinch is who he claims to be."

"Quite so, Commander." Sir Eustace gave Josiah a look of mild irritation.

He paced towards the tall window overlooking Canning Dock and remained there with his back to the room, as if arguing with himself.

Earlier, Josiah had told me the recent Yankee victories at Gettysburg and Vicksburg done shifted the stance of the Queen Victoria's government. Upshot was the prime minister, Lord Palmerston, was much less willing to turn a blind eye to the purchase by the Confederacy of British-built 'merchantmen' that everyone knew were really warships. For all that, the secessionists could yet count on powerful supporters in Lord Palmerston's cabinet. I was sure the mind of Little Big Man was filled to brimming with these and other concerns.

At last he turned back into the room – an actor swivelling to face his audience.

"The moment for action is upon us. Commander Mill

will receive immediate orders to accompany the collector of customs for Liverpool to Applegarth's yard, there to carry out an inspection of the vessel currently under construction."

"That is exceedingly good to hear, sir." Lady Alice's voice was shrill with enthusiasm.

"Lord be praised," I said, trying not to cry out in jubilation. It was like this: you treat black folk – any folk – like brutes, they'll surely rejoice at biting the hand that kept them down. I'd be lying if I didn't admit to a sense of revenge – which, I know, properly belongs to the Lord – yet it was true also that this was a mighty blow struck in the name of President Lincoln's crusade to set my people free.

*

Josiah's ship, HMS *Shearwater,* was fitting out in Bramley Moore Dock off Regent Road, a piece north of Liverpool's commercial quarter.

Work on the *Shearwater* was all but done and I believed Josiah wanted to deliver the tidings regarding Applegarth's while, on the same occasion, showing me his new command.

The inspection of the yard done taken place that morning. Having received a terse note in Josiah's hand, asking me to attend the *Shearwater* directly, I'd wasted not a moment in taking a cab from Lady Alice's house to the dock.

With my heart askitter, I approached the *Shearwater's* companionway where a young officer asked me to wait while he informed Josiah of my arrival.

The dockside was a busy place, a miniature city built of casks and barrels, boxes and bulging hemp sacks that were being swayed on board by pulley hoists, or carried across the companionway on the shoulders of sailors. Musky scents of warm tar and fresh-sawed wood, overlaid by sour wafts of coal dust and engine oil. In a timber yard on Regent Road opposite, enormous beams and masts poked heavenward like whale-ribs. For one idle moment I imagined Jonah standing amid them, yet in the belly of the great sea-beast, somehow overlooked by the Lord, still waiting for redemption.

Scolding myself for a fanciful child, I directed my attention to the fine appearance of Josiah's *Shearwater* – truly a command he could be proud of. Somewhat knowledgeable on maritime matters after my time crossing the Atlantic Ocean, I recognised her as a wooden steam sloop, smaller than the *Vigilant*, yet leaner and sleeker. Displacing some eight hundred tons, with a company of one hundred and thirty souls, she carried eleven big guns and could steam at nine and one half knots. These facts about the *Shearwater* I'd learned so that I could converse with Josiah knowledgeably on the characteristics of his ship.

"Commander Mill's compliment, ma'am."

I turned to see the young officer had come back from his errand and was gesturing that I should accompany him on board. Despite my voluminous crinoline, I managed to negotiate the cable-strewn quarterdeck and descended the stairs that led to the captain's cabin.

I was surprised he wasn't present, yet there could be no mistaking the identity of the occupant. Every horizontal surface supported potted plants, jars of dried herbs, flasks of infused flowers and vials of viscous tincture. Even the goose-necked alembic still was on board, stealing pride of place on a table intended for Admiralty charts. Blanketed tight in that soft, peaty redolence, I obtained a powerful sense of homecoming.

Yet this notion of wellbeing was soon burst by a sharp prick of anxiety. For if Josiah's little apothecary shop had been brought on board, the departure of this ship – and therefore

Josiah – must be close by.

"Trinity."

Swinging round, I saw Josiah enter the cabin.

Something not right in the way he spoke my name. No word of welcome, no inflection of pleasure.

Forcing a laugh, I waved my hand at the scene around me. "You have a fine ship, Josiah, and I see that you have lost no time making a home of it."

Close to me now, Josiah was not smiling. Took my hands in his, squeezed tight.

"My dear Trinity, I must tell you candidly that the ship in the Applegarth yard is not a ram or any other type of ironclad warship. She is a legitimate merchant vessel. The plans were clever forgeries, our informants even cleverer scoundrels. We have been duped."

Laughed at that.

Thought he done said the Applegarth ship was legitimate; somehow imagined he told me Blessing Dubois and Mr Longinch were tricksters; that they fooled us. Girl believes in a cause so long, so hard, there's the devil to pay when all that hope – no, all that vanity, that damned vanity – spills down on her stupid stupid head.

Josiah repeated his words slowly, deliberately. This time hysteria gave me no refuge.

Crying now.

Hands, firm on my shoulders, guiding me across the cabin, pressing me down into a chair. "Please, sit, my dear Trinity."

*

This child's tears dried soon enough. I'd learned early in life that they served no purpose, save to expose weakness to those who might exploit it.

Took a glass of brandy tincture from Josiah and harnessed its fiery shock to tug myself back out of that tub of self-pity.

Then I looked at him, hard and even. "Please, Josiah, tell me what happened."

"The moment I stepped into that shipyard, it was clear that the ship under construction bore no resemblance to the plans and contract purveyed by Longinch. The proprietor, Mr Applegarth, was understandably incensed. A longstanding abolitionist and Christian supporter of President Lincoln, his reputation has been badly damaged by this conspiracy."

Sipped more brandy tincture. "Fellow's bound to be mad."

Rare occasion when Josiah gave me a downright despairing look. "Anger isn't the half of it, Trinity. He's instructing his lawyers to draw up writs for defamation, for consequential loss of profits, for the breaching of laws I've never heard of. There'll be one for each of us – you, me, the US consul, Baggott, Lady Alice."

"Alice knows?"

"She was informed by that inveterate gossip, Mrs Marjoribanks."

I paused, not wanting an answer, yet needing to know. "How did Lady Alice react?"

"Inscrutably." Josiah made the merest of smiles. "It was the briefest of meetings at the US Consulate." Dreaded to imagine what that Yankee lawyer would be thinking of me. Anticipating my question, Josiah told me this: "Mr Dudley was entirely collected. Like the rest of us, he was too keen to believe what he wanted to believe."

Josiah poured himself a tot of brandy. We both knew he shouldn't drink, what with his ulcer, but neither could call up the energy to debate the question. "Sir Eustace Baggott is distraught. He considers himself to be a statesman of substance and this fiasco will mean considerable loss of credibility in the parlours of Whitehall and Westminster."

Poor Little Big Man, I thought.

"What of Mr Longinch? Of Blessing Dubois?"

Thus far Josiah had kept his tone level, no doubt for my sake. Now I detected an uncommon note of anger of in his voice. "Bloody rogues, both. Blessing Dubois is a slave owned by Senator States Rights Rankin, who is clearly the architect of this entire miry subterfuge."

Rankin? That name lashed me.

Hadn't suspected this, not for one trice. Yet it prompted reluctant stirrings in my head; recent events began to rearrange themselves like camouflaged lizards exposing themselves by the merest of movements.

Striding across the cabin, as if to moderate his temper, Josiah hesitated by the bulkhead door, then turned to face me with stoical dignity. "It now seems clear that Rankin's first ploy was to have Blessing Dubois approach you with his counterfeit affidavit. That ruse was frustrated when the US consul decided there was insufficient evidence to act. Yet this didn't deter Rankin. His people made inquiries that led them to Cuthbert Longinch, formerly chief clerk at Applegarth's, who had been dismissed this June gone for accepting bribes from suppliers. Apparently, the matter had not been brought to a court of law because Mr Applegarth believed the scandal of a criminal trial would have damaged his business."

Josiah paced slowly back towards me. "Longinch would have been a ready recruit to Rankin's conspiracy. Already resenting Mr Applegarth for the loss of his employment, he must have savoured the prospect of payment *and* revenge. With both Dubois and Longinch at his disposal, Rankin's second attempt to trick us was as simple as it was effective."

Yet those lizards went on revealing themselves in the thicket of my memory, obtaining bloated proportions that made my belly wriggle. So obvious now, but not two minutes ago I'd never have picked them out. Rankin done made fools of us all, but no one more than me.

Minded that Fat-boy with the velvet stovepipe hat and plumped-up cheeks who I'd put down as a simpleton, but was, in truth, the very opposite. Another of Rankin's people. They must have spotted me loitering out on the street outside the offices of Fraser Trenholm & Company and sent Fat-boy to investigate. He'd have seen right through my silly disguise. Recalled the wind blowing open my mariner's coat and his eyes alighting on the swell of my breast. If any doubts done lingered in Fat-boy's mind, that would have shifted them because very soon afterwards, he sneezed and flourished that big red handkerchief – signal to Rankin, no doubt watching from a window, that I was, indeed, spying on the premises.

No coincidence, then, that Rankin done left Fraser Trenholm & Company moments later. That rakehell had no doubt delighted in leading me like a bullock with a ring in his nose though the streets of Liverpool to the premises of Applegarth's. All he needed to do to spring the trap was walk inside, perhaps to pretend an inquiry about business or ask directions to some location or other.

The very next morning, who should arrive on Lady Alice's doorstep but Blessing Dubois, powerful eager to invite me into the parlour of Cuthbert Longinch? And all this while I'd not once thought to question the strangely convenient happenstance of these events.

How foolish I'd been to imagine I could outwit such a man as Rankin.

Minded that monkey back on the sidewalk with its scarlet page-boy cap, same colour as Fat-boy's handkerchief. Asked myself who was the monkey now?

Still worse was the trouble I'd made for my friends and allies. Yankee consul Mr Dudley, stern-faced but well-meaning; Little Big Man with his powerful but unavailing energies; and Lady Alice, bossy and brassy yet withal a true friend.

And what of my dear friend Josiah? What ruinous effects would my folly have on him? This distressed me more mightily than all else.

"I'm so sorry." Without looking at him, I took his hand, pressed it against my cheek.

Taking my hand in his, he urged me up from the chair and looked at me directly. "I cannot accept an apology when none is due."

"But I've put at hazard all that you so rightly deserve."

Slight smile, fractional tilt of the head. I never done seen such gentlemanly self-possession, not among the grand houses of South Carolina nor the stately palaces of Great Britain. "I did nothing without accepting the risk," he said. "Moreover, Trinity, you are overlooking an important consideration."

"What would that be, Josiah?"

Tilting my chin upwards with the tip of his finger, he allowed his smile to lengthen just a smidgeon. "We are not yet defeated."

16

RECOLLECTIONS OF A CONFEDERATE GENERAL BY JUBAL DE BROOKE

Liverpool, England, November, 1863.

The footman who opened the front door of the McConville's house did not invite me inside, but instead bade me wait on the doorstep.

For an instant I feared I was not welcome – that Thomas and Sarah had somehow become aware of my counterfeit ancestry. Yet I quickly collected myself: they could not possibly know since I had not told a soul of my revelations at Astrop.

At last, Thomas McConville appeared in the doorframe, attired in a pilot coat and derby hat.

I had come to Abercromby Square at Sarah's request so that we could go as a couple to a reception at the home of the Marchioness of Chalcross, the sourly-disposed matron Sarah and I had encountered as we entered St George's Hall. Lady Chalcross' remark to me – that she hoped I was 'more rebel than rabble' – had not endeared her and the discovery that my forebears were rabble of the worst kind had done nothing to diminish this aversion.

"Sarah will not be ready for one half-hour at the very least," McConville said. "In the meantime, my dear Jubal, I would be grateful if you would accompany me for my daily turn about the shrubbery."

I followed him down the steps and across the sidewalk towards the 'shrubbery', a tree-flanked rectangle of planted lawn around which the great town houses and church of St Catherine had been constructed.

The temperature was unseasonably mild as we walked slowly along a gravelled pathway to a white circular garden house at the centre of the shrubbery, where McConville took a seat.

Sitting beside my friend, I followed his gaze across the carefully tended verdure to see a red squirrel picking among shawls of fallen leaves, not ten yards distant.

McConville spoke softly, so as not to disturb the foraging creature. "Quite beautiful, isn't she? And yet somehow frantic. Ceaselessly searching for something that is not to be found."

"So much more colourful than the grey critters we get in America."

There was a moment of hesitation. When my friend spoke his words came quickly. "I need your advice. It's a matter of enormous concern and sensitivity."

I detected a hint of alarm that seemed to make his breathing even more difficult. "Take your time, Thomas."

I continued to watch the squirrel until my companion was able to resume. "I was visited today by Donald Gunby, the chief draughtsman at the shipyard. Gunby is a trusted manager who has been with me since the very early days, though we have seen little of one another since the deterioration in my health. That he should have come to see me at the house when

Sarah was at the shipyard was not a good potent."

My gaze followed to the squirrel as it moved some yards across the grass and started to scrutinise the rind of a horse-chestnut.

Somewhere in the half-focused background over my friend's shoulder, I became aware of quiet movement amid the bed of hydrangeas.

McConville pressed on. "When I was running the business, Gunby had always been aware of the company's financial situation, but Sarah had ceased to involve him in money matters two years ago. I didn't approve of this decision, but was too ill to take issue with her."

A cat's face emerged from the vegetation; the squirrel laid down the horse chestnut rind, turning now to pick up a cluster of berries.

"Nevertheless, business went on much as it had always. Profits accumulated, doubts diminished and very soon the whole matter had been forgotten."

The cat – a sturdy tabby – was moving purposefully across the grass towards the squirrel.

McConville also remained unaware of the stalking predator. "Gunby's ignorance of the company's finances ended yesterday when he entered Sarah's office to find the sales ledger lying open on her desk. The poor fellow was clearly embarrassed at having to admit this to me, yet I sensed that he was driven by a deeper anxiety."

Moving with unerring stealth amid the wreckage of leaves and twigs, the cat continued to close with its quarry.

Another harsh intake of breath from my friend seemed to halt the cat, but the squirrel paid no heed to any activity save its own. "Gunby could not help but notice a very considerable level of credit extended to one particular customer, the Pasham &

Edgeport Steam Navigation Company, which placed an order for a large merchant vessel two years back – soon after he'd been excluded from financial management. This ship is to be called the *Himalaya* and her name reflects both her enormous size and the value of the contract – some £180,000, to be paid in six equal instalments. Although the ship is now fitting out in the Great Float at Birkenhead, the final instalment fell due some six months ago."

The cat moved nearer ... nearer still.

One half of me wanted to alert the squirrel; the other was locked fast by the anxiety of my friend for his daughter.

"Gunby then noticed a letter from the bank, stating that the shipyard was struggling to service a loan for almost exactly the same amount as this final instalment. The letter was written with great courtesy, but Gunby knows bankers well enough to recognise the warning signs of a foreclosure. Put bluntly, Jubal, the bank wants its money within the month or they will call in the debt and shut us down."

The cat punched into the air.

All but a fraction too late, the squirrel squirmed to one side, throwing up a welter of leaf litter. I couldn't tell what was happening as both critters went skittering behind the trunk of a horse chestnut. There was a dreadful scream. All movement ceased. Clenched by unrelenting tension, I was unable to remove my eyes from the tree trunk.

Then, after a few seconds, a small auburn head appeared atop a bough, perhaps six feet from the ground, and I felt a somewhat ridiculous sense of relief.

"Thank God."

I wasn't aware of having spoken aloud until McConville turned to me.

"It was a small miracle that your man discovered the situation when he did, while there is still time to find a remedy."

Ignorant of the drama that had enfolded behind him, McConville came unsteadily to his feet and started back towards the gate.

Quickly catching up with him, I noted the cat circling the tree trunk. The squirrel, though, was already gone from view.

"Sarah has always been too headstrong, too willing to gamble." My companion lifted one quavering hand, as if to fend off an anticipated argument. "I accept that some hazard is always necessary in business, yet there is a clear distinction between calculated risk and recklessness. I fear Sarah has tilted our company towards the latter and I blame myself for failing to correct her."

He paused, as if fatigued by so much talking, but continued in a sterner tone. "The question I must put to you, Jubal, is this: do I confront Sarah directly? Or do I go to the bank's principal, Erasmus Pickering – who is the son of an old acquaintance – and plead for more time, all the while hoping the final instalment on the *Himalaya* will come through?"

I struggled to disentangle this unexpected collision of my own loyalties. I felt myself being pulled in two directions: I was preciously fond of Sarah; yet I had obtained this knowledge in the confidence of her father, who was also intensely concerned for her welfare.

Turning to face him, I saw in those worn-down eyes a peculiar alloy of defeat and defiance. Placing one hand on his slender shoulder, I ordered myself to offer up a smile. "I don't know what you should do, Thomas, at least not immediately. But what I do know is that a solution will be found."

*

The short journey from the centre of Liverpool to the country residence of Lady Chalcross at Grassendale was tedious. Sarah sat opposite me in the brougham; she seemed distracted and responded without enthusiasm to my efforts to kindle conversation. After a while I gave up the struggle.

As we'd clambered into the carriage she complained that she'd not had enough time to prepare herself as a result of being detained on a pressing matter at the shipyard. This haste was reflected in her appearance: the normally immaculate arrangement of her hair had an unfinished aspect, loose straggles falling randomly across her brow and around her ears.

I suspected the cause of her delay at the shipyard was related to the financial problems surrounding this large merchant ship, the *Himalaya*. Yet there was nothing I could say or do without betraying her father's confidence. So I sat back and listened to the dissonant squeaks of the stiff leather upholstery and the iron leaf-springs supporting the carriage.

I was relieved to step down onto the gravelled apron in front of Lady Chalcross's residence – a flamboyant brick mansion of the late Eighteenth Century, set amid formal gardens and parkland where red deer grazed among Andean alpacas, as if nothing could have been better fitted to nature's design.

Arthur Harrowby rushed to meet us, his handsome features arranged in an expression of practised elation.

"What a to-do! We are about to engage the Yankee sympathisers in a duel of considerable, *considerable* significance. Many of the *haut ton* are present – on both sides."

Harrowby was a leading figure among the *haut ton* – the 'high-tone' of fashionable European society. Yet I was at a loss to understand how such refined individuals could have become involved in any activity more bellicose than card games.

"Garden parties!" Harrowby took Sarah and me by our

elbows and urged us towards the rear of the house. "Garden parties at twenty paces …"

"I'm in no humour for your silliness, Arthur." Sarah sounded irritated, though I was pleased that Harrowby had at least transported her from her mood of sombre introspection.

Raising an eyebrow at her forthrightness, Harrowby began to speak in plainer terms. "Intelligence from Mrs Marjoribanks lately revealed that a picnic ball aiming to raise charitable monies for the Federal cause was to be held on the lawns of Lady Chalcross's neighbour, the Countess of Frocester."

According to Harrowby, the countess was an ardent supporter of President Lincoln and an implacable enemy of Lady Chalcross.

"But we are in the month of November." Sarah's tone had lost none of its frostiness.

Harrowby made an accommodating chuckle. "Uncommonly pleasant weather, though, ain't it?"

This was true. With the sun shining warmly from an unblemished sky, the air was still and I estimated the temperature to be in the region of sixty degrees on the Fahrenheit scale.

"It appears that Lady Frocester aimed to exploit the exciting novelty of hosting an autumnal picnic ball." Harrowby continued to steer the pair of us towards the distant sound of music emanating from behind the great house. Clearly, he had not enjoyed himself so much in a very long while. "However, Mrs Marjoribanks obtained knowledge of these plans through her association with my niece, Lady Alice Featherfax. Therefore it was decided by the Organising Committee of the Ladies' Forum that a counter-offensive should be mounted in the Confederate interest."

"Why was I not consulted?" Sarah's voice had taken on a note of indignation. "I am, after all, a founder member of the

Organising Committee."

Making a diplomatic cough, Harrowby explained that this was something she would have to take up with Lady Chalcross, though he understood Sarah had been asked to attend the emergency meeting, but could not be contacted.

By now, we had passed through a gate at the side of the mansion and the elaborate dispositions of the two opposing camps lay before us.

On the 'Confederate' side, aromatic dishes were being prepared under a large canvas marquee, while some distance to the left a light orchestra was playing an aria from Rossini. Between the fiddlers and the food, a crowd of Harrowby's beloved *haut ton* mingled in a chattering melange, the women fashionably vivid, the men more soberly attired. An area for dancing had been marked out in white lime on the smooth lawn.

Perhaps one hundred yards distant, across the stream that formed the boundary of the two estates, an identically lavish event was being staged. Indeed, the two parties were so close that occasionally one gentleman would recognise another and both would uncover with a decorous flurry of hats and bowing of heads.

I noticed Trinity Giddings standing quite still, surrounded by the *haut ton,* yet in no sense one of them.

News of the fiasco at Applegarth's shipyard had quickly spread across the city and, indeed, the country. Yet I could no more derive pleasure from this situation than from the destruction of the Yankee brigade I'd defeated at Chickamauga Creek.

Without thinking, I raised my hat to her and was pleasantly surprised when she returned my courtesy with a wave of her hand.

"Jubal, come and join us." The slap of Harrowby's hand on

my shoulder broke off the momentary connection and I was manhandled across the lawn to a small circle of people that included our hostess, the Marchioness of Chalcross and States Rights Rankin, together with his Jack Russell terriers.

Sir Eustace Baggott, a minister of state at the Foreign Office, was also among the group. Like Trinity Giddings, his reputation had been badly damaged by the embarrassing *faux pas* at Applegarth's and I figured he was there alongside Rankin in an attempt to mend the British government's fences with the Confederacy. Baggott was a diminutive and talkative fellow who I thought was trying too hard to please the indifferent senator.

Casting around for Sarah, I saw her locked in earnest conversation with a florid young man who, I recalled, was Erasmus Pickering, director of the bank that was owed so much money by the shipyard.

To my right, I heard Baggott speaking to Rankin about the Applegarth affair. According to the minister, it had been an unfortunate episode precipitated by Trinity Giddings, a naïve and credulous young woman, who was all too typical of the Negro race.

Perhaps I was being unduly harsh on Baggott – when all was said and done, he was a servant of his political masters. Yet there was something unpleasant in his calculated duplicity. Trinity Giddings might have been made to look foolish, but she had not ordered the inspection of Applegarth's yard.

Rankin made a modest smile. Events could not have played more obligingly into his hands if he had planned them from the outset, which was probably not so distant from the truth.

All this while, Harrowby had been scanning the event opposite through miniature binoculars of the kind used at horse races. Without lowering them, he said to me: "Don't we look the very devil of a sight, Jubal, ourselves and Catherine Frocester's people across the stream, there?"

I smiled weakly. "Yes, Arthur, the very devil."

"Tell me, do not the two marquees resemble general headquarters, and we gay picnickers – are we not infantry battalions? The dancers, cavalry troops? And what are the orchestras, if not representations of each side's batteries of artillery?"

A broad impression of a civil war engagement was no doubt the effect desired by the Ladies' Forum.

"How would you assess our mutual dispositions, General?" Rankin waved a cigar at the far bank.

I lifted a glass of champagne from the tray of a passing waiter. "Compared to what is happening in America, Senator, I would say the situation here today is a fanciful confection."

Rankin chuckled. "Well, quite. After all, this is hardly our great triumph at Chancellorsville."

"Nor our great defeat at Gettysburg." I swallowed more champagne and quickly looked around in hopes of finding Sarah.

Eventually I saw her in the marquee, speaking to a man whom I didn't know, but guessed was another financier. It was all too plain that Sarah was using the event as a means of raising business finance, yet she was looking less a director of commerce and more an importuner of favours.

I lost sight of her as Rankin moved in front of me. "Then what strategy would you advise for today's encounter, General?"

This was the moment when the conceit of the occasion overwhelmed me, though I kept my tone light as I indicated the 'Federal' camp with a sweep of my arm. "An infantry charge is often the only way to victory, Senator. Let me demonstrate."

Setting my champagne glass on a waiter's tray, I turned smartly and began to march down the grassy bank.

It was later suggested that I didn't know what I was doing, that my actions that day were a product of the problems that had brought me to Britain in the first place. This was not true. I knew exactly what I meant to accomplish.

As I moved closer to the stream, the Rossini aria of the 'Confederate' musicians clashed with strains of the 'Federal' orchestra's rendition of Bellini's *La Somnambular* and I found myself caught in a crossfire of discord that added an extra dimension of parody to that already absurd situation.

Splashing into the stream, I winced as its water flooded into my shoes and around my ankles. After a few steps I was up to my knees. The sudden chill stole my breath. Surprisingly strong currents coiled around my calves as if a great eel was attempting to draw me downstream where the water became dark and deep. My stomach lurched in anticipation of an icy plunge.

Moving more cautiously, I was uncomfortably aware that one half of European society was watching me from behind, and the other from the bank ahead. I was already a spectacle – one slip and I'd be a laughing stock. Did I care? I didn't rightly know.

Half way across, my right foot jammed between two rocks. I almost howled as the current spun me round, wrenching my ankle. Raising my arms, I tried to steady myself in the manner of a tightrope walker. For a few moments I wobbled, this way and that, as dignity locked horns with gravity. The former prevailed: my balance returned.

Turning once again to face my objective, I set off toward a mass of curious faces.

17

EXPERIENCES IN THE LIFE OF A SLAVE GIRL BY TRINITY GIDDINGS

Liverpool, England, November, 1863.

Caught my breath as Soldier-boy started wading across that stream.

Minded me of my journey down the Great Pee Dee River. Very different situation, but it was like this: folk place themselves at hazard crossing water, so they need a powerful strong purpose. The nature of Soldier-boy's purpose was another matter, though revelation would come all too soon.

Though the stream was not more than ten yards wide, it churned white through rocky shallows, turning glassy-still where the riverbed shelved into steep trenches.

Deeper he went, until the water was up to his knees. Must have been powerful cold. Slippery too. One part of me hoped he'd take an embarrassing tumble, another prayed he wouldn't. Tension and bafflement burdened the air all around me. Same question on everybody's lips: what was this boy doing?

The Liverpool Southern Club had already created a stir by staging a picnic ball right opposite the event arranged by the Countess of Frocester. After the fiasco at Applegarth's shipyard, I'd not wanted to show my face, but Lady Alice insisted we attend this function to show people we'd not admitted defeat. Nothing like adversity to reveal folk's true measure. Lady Alice emerged with great credit. Not so, Sir Eustace Baggott. Even now I spied him ingratiating himself among the richcrats of the Liverpool Southern Club. Josiah told me to expect as much, given that Little Big Man was an ambitious politician. All the same, I felt betrayed.

A great gasp went up from the folk around me. Soldier-boy done stopped, right in the middle of the stream. Thought I saw his face twist in pain. He teetered on the brink of a fall, arms outstretched as he fought for balance. My belly agitated. Said a quick prayer. Perhaps I shouldn't have, but the Lord answered it quickly enough because Soldier-boy appeared to recover. Following a moment's pause, he continued, but more slowly now. Seemed to take him an age to wade those last few yards, but at last he came splashing through the shallows and stepped onto this side of the shore.

Peculiar anxiety quivered through the people round me – as if they'd been confronted by some great army, not one solitary soldier, not in arms, not even in uniform.

I do confess to sharing this apprehension.

Soldier-boy came striding up that bank; what he wanted I couldn't tell – until he changed direction and headed straight towards me.

Pausing, he raised his hat as he'd done earlier, and made a curious smile. "I wonder, Miss Giddings, would you do me the honour to dance with me?"

Struggled to keep the astonishment from my face. Soldier-boy done splashed through that chilly stream, decked out in richcrat finery, all so he could ask me to dance? Now, that was something!

Kept my tone flinty, though: "You're somewhat wet for dancing, General."

"As you can see."

"Should I be flattered?"

"This isn't something I would do in the normal course of events."

"Then why today?" Lord, this boy was a puzzle.

"Weariness and optimism, Miss Giddings: weariness of playing the Dixieland grandee for the delectation of the Liverpool Southern Club, and optimism that you will enliven this occasion."

"You think to shock your hosts?"

"Rather to educate them. They consider these two picnic balls to be a representation of an American Civil War battle and I was asked to explain how I would engage the enemy. So I took the opportunity to present them with a practical illustration of the infantry charge."

"Am I the enemy, General?"

"Only inasmuch as the silliness today is an actual battle between the Union and the Confederacy."

"And if I decline your request?"

"You have the perfect opportunity to make a complete fool of me."

"You presume I will not?"

"I gamble you will not."

Boy risks so much for so little, he's got to be crazy. "Why so?"

"If you wanted to humiliate me you could have done so after our last outing." Small pause, then a mischievous grin invaded those pretty features. "Besides, would it not be amusing to turn all these gossiping heads? Furnish them with something truly novel to chatter about?"

Hare-brained, maybe; appealing, for sure.

Before I could move, Lady Alice appeared at my side. Didn't take my eyes off Soldier-boy's, though I could discern the attitude of my friend by her formidable register.

"Trinity, come away from that hell-hearted heathen. *Rapidamente, s'il vous plaît!*"

My failure to respond lifted Lady Alice's voice half of one octave. "I implore you – why, he may have a weapon."

"I'm sure General de Brooke means me no harm," I assured her. This to Soldier-boy: "Yes, I would like to dance."

He made a courteous bow and asked the orchestra's conductor to play a tune suited for the *varsovienne*.

The musicians struck up and I joined with my enemy in that simple but elegant dance. Its three-four time rhythm carried us in slow, graceful curves across the lawn.

All around, richcrats stood still and silent, minding me of the painted lead figures Missy Honoria done arranged in her fancy doll's house when we were children. I sensed an odd weave of fascination and embarrassment, though none of it distracted me.

After a while, Soldier-boy spoke. "I was very sorry to learn of the situation at Applegarth's."

"Forgive my scepticism, General, but why should that be?"

"An axiom among soldiers is that your enemies are sometimes least where you expect them. So, too, are your allies."

"Are you suggesting we should be friends, General?"

"Is that so outrageous? Are we not both Americans? Does any sane person expect this dreadful war never to end?"

Couldn't answer that one directly, so I deflected it, though not untruthfully. "It was a gallant thing you just did."

We said nothing after that. If we were not friends, I doubted we could be enemies.

Queer place to be; yet in that moment, no place else I cared to go. Whisking gentle arcs in windless air under the gaze of the powerful and the privileged. Yet not in their orbit, and shone upon by a different sun.

*

Later that week, as I followed Josiah into the crystal structure at the rear of the medical botany shop in Vernon Street, I was abruptly shawled in damp, clinging heat. Air was a whiffy stew of warm manure and musky tree-bark, piquant shrubs and sour bitumen. Although no longer than fifteen yards, the glasshouse seemed more extensive, perhaps because of the variety of vegetation that sprouted forth on every side, including most of the floor and vine-bound roof. There were trees bearing limes, tangerines and pineapples, exotic plants with flamboyant leaf-patterns. One section done been given over to orchids, their flowers a tumult of garish colour and strange configuration, sometimes minding me of fairytale critters rather than botanical specimens.

At the end of the building one half-dozen long timber boxes, each with a sloping roof of glass supported by stout wooden frames.

Josiah, clad in shirt and breeches, stood among them, scratching the back of his head as if contemplating which task to perform next. "These are Wardian cases," he said. "My friend Jed Dobby uses them to transport botanic specimens and has given me half a dozen."

I made a dubious expression. "They look like coffins with

pitched roofs."

My friend smiled. "Quite the opposite, Trinity: they are containers of life rather than death."

He explained that these boxes would allow him to keep plants on board his ship, regardless of the climes of her station.

I didn't wish to dwell on the departure of the *Shearwater*, so I altered the topic, telling him instead of the peculiar developments at Grassendale.

Josiah found this amusing. "To rival the Wars of the Roses, we now have the Wars of the Rose Gardens, with your friend Jubal de Brooke making a bold offensive. Ha–ha."

"That Soldier-boy is no friend of mine." This I said with a little too much vehemence.

Of course Josiah discerned this and raised one eyebrow. "Why, then, did you agree to dance?"

"A refusal would have been discourteous."

My friend chuckled at this. "To think that you Americans mock us British for our obsession with the strictures of etiquette. Yet I believe it's entirely acceptable to enter into friendships with certain supporters of the Confederacy. By all accounts, Jubal de Brooke is an honourable chap."

"This isn't about honour, Josiah. It's about liberty and justice – and the fact that we black folk don't get either. Not from the Confederate States, nor it seems, from Queen Victoria's ministers of state. That turncoat Baggott showed his true colours."

Josiah's expression of subtle enjoyment persisted. "Perhaps you have been expecting too much of the British government, Trinity. Not one member of Lord Palmerston's cabinet would countenance slavery, yet Great Britain must accept the possibility that the South may yet win her independence. If that was so, Palmerston would have to re-establish trading links with the Confederates – a far more difficult task if he had made enemies in Richmond."

Once more my friend's even-handedness done riled me. "So Palmerston is betting on both horses. I call that double dealing."

He shrugged. "It's the way of the world, Trinity."

"Rankin was also at this 'War of the Rose Gardens', as you refer to it. Would you stay seated on that pretty fence of yours in the matter of that damned rakehell?"

Josiah frowned at my outburst and I knew I'd gone a piece too far.

He took my hands in his, holding them with tender firmness. "I've suspected for some time that you have a special cause to loath this man. Would you like to tell me why?"

I looked away, tearful-angry. 'Massa Zebulon loaned my big brother to Rankin. On those rare occasions when I spoke with him about his life at the Rankin plantation, he never once complained, but nor did he say much else. For a firecracker of a boy such as my brother Benjamin, that told me everything."

Josiah waited patiently, not moving. Good like that, was my friend. When I was sufficiently collected, I continued, but still couldn't look at him directly. "See, there'd always been rumours that Rankin and his overseers took their pleasure – if you can call it that – with boys. Word was they'd pick out one boy and abuse him over and over, never letting up, no not ever, not those men."

"How did you find out?" I turned back to Josiah now, placing my head on his shoulder. "Boy goes swimming in the Great Pee Dee River, pockets jammed with rocks, that tells you more than you need to know."

"I'm so sorry, Trinity."

"How many other boys has Rankin destroyed?"

"May he rot in hell for it."

"Lord knows I'd kill Rankin this instant and happily follow him." Standing as close as I was to Josiah, I felt the sudden spasm in his belly, heard a whisper of pain as he staggered back, clutching his abdomen.

"Come, you should rest."

Tried to usher him from the hothouse, but he resisted. "I shall be well in a few moments."

"You must lie down, Josiah, and I won't brook any argument." Sharpness in my tone surprised us both, yet achieved its aim and he allowed me to guide him back into the shop and slowly up the stairs, each step followed by a pause, into his bed chamber. There I laid him on his bed and tugged off his boots.

His face appeared more relaxed as he looked up at me. "The worst is over, Trinity."

"I'll administer some medication," I said. "Where do you keep it?"

My friend managed a bleak smile. "My need of medication is passed."

Casting all notion of propriety aside, I climbed onto the hard bed and lay beside him, putting my arm across his chest, clinging to him as I never done clung to anybody. Strange churn of anger and sorrow brewed up deep inside.

I must have sounded like the most selfish child, yet I could do nothing to stop my gush of sentiment. "The Lord isn't content to take away my loving mama and papa and my sweet brother, but now also my dear, dear friend. What a bitter world this is."

A catch in his throat caused me to fear a return of his pain, but then I realised he was laughing. "The Lord isn't about to take me, Trinity," he said. "Of more immediate concern are

175

their Lordships of the Admiralty."

Pitching myself up on one elbow, I gazed at him with intense puzzlement.

His grin seeped away and he fixed me with a most earnest expression. "My need of medication is passed because my illness is all but cured. What you witnessed in the greenhouse was nothing more than a cramp of the stomach."

"You're not about to die?"

Seeing the consternation in my face, Josiah took my head between his hands and pressed a kiss on my brow. "Please be calm, Trinity. My physician told me this very morning that I have been suffering from a peptic ulcer, not a cancer. Equally encouraging is that the ulcer has responded favourably to his treatment."

"Why, that's the most wonderful news, Josiah!" Despite my eruption of joy, some other thing gnawed at my thoughts, bent on wrecking the moment. "But what did you mean when you mentioned the Admiralty?"

The furrows on his brow deepened. "I have received orders. When the *Shearwater* is ready for sea, I am to take her to the China station."

18

RECOLLECTIONS OF A CONFEDERATE GENERAL BY JUBAL DE BROOKE

Liverpool, England, November, 1863.

The opening day of the Grand Liberty Bazaar was distinguished by skies as blue as the bloodstock flowing into St George's Hall. The event, orchestrated to raise funds for the Southern Prisoners' Relief Fund, was expected to occupy three days and its list of 'Lady Patronesses' read in the fashion of a roll call of Europe's *haut ton*.

Of course they all considered my lineage to be among the noblest, little suspecting that I was the grandson of a low-born impostor, fraudster and thief. Whether this was a cause for hilarity or despair I couldn't correctly discern.

"They're all here!" Sarah leaned from the window of our carriage as it drew into Lime Street. "I can see the Duchess de Beaupierre and the Countess Giavoglio – and there – there's Lady Veronica Fane. Can you see her, Jubal? Just by Wellington's column. All the great families of Europe are present!"

What to do about my family was another matter. My grandfather had died more than twenty-five years ago and the truth of his deception would utterly destroy my father, now approaching his seventieth year. So, short of adding patricide to my family's lengthening list of crimes, I would have to maintain the name of de Brooke at least as long as he lived.

After that, I couldn't say.

I stepped down from the carriage opposite the Royal Amphitheatre and Sarah followed, entirely engrossed by the panoply of privilege laid out before us.

As we entered St George's Hall, Sarah turned to me with an anxious look. "Before we go in, Jubal, I want your word of honour that there will be no repetition of your antics at Grassendale."

"Unless there is now a stream flowing through the building, that is hardly possible." I grinned in an attempt to soothe her, but provoked the opposite effect.

"How can you be so flippant, knowing how concerned I am that this event succeeds?"

I apologised, assuring her my behaviour would be impeccable. I might have reminded her that she had not even seen my so-called antics at Grassendale. When I returned to the 'Confederate' picnic-ball, Sarah was not to be found and I learned from Arthur Harrowby that she'd gone back to Liverpool with her banker friend, Erasmus Pickering, presumably to arrange a further bank loan.

Sarah's attitude to money was an additional worry. Despite the ruinous finances of the shipyard, she was attired in a cerulean crinoline of luscious *poult de soie* which, she'd told me, cost twenty guineas – more than five times the monthly pay of a private soldier in the Army of Northern Virginia.

"Come, Jubal." Sarah said. "Mrs Marjoribanks is currently

in charge of the Virginia stall and we owe it to her not to be tardy."

She hastened through the doors as if she was leading an army to the relief of Vicksburg.

The transformation of the Great Hall came as a shock to the senses. Its cathedral elegance had acquired the gimcrack aspect of a circus. The majestic pipe organ was concealed behind a billowing skirt of red, white and blue canvas. Similarly garish awnings were fixed to the balcony balustrades to mark out the stalls below, representing the ten seceded states as well as Kentucky and Missouri. Each was festooned in Southern Cross and Union Jack bunting that did nothing to promote the dignity of either the Confederacy or Great Britain.

An aviary of piping bullfinches and an operetta company's rendition of Offenbach's *Les Deux Aveugles* might have raised the tone, but both birdsong and music sounded incongruous amid the hubbub and billboards declaiming opportunities to gaze upon 'A Southern Mermaid' and 'The Two Headed Marvel'.

This unreal mood was intensified by an equine theme that included the raffle of a racehorse and pony rides around the circumference of the Great Hall. Initially aghast at the effect of shod hooves on the tiled floor, I saw on closer inspection that protective raffia matting had been laid down. The racehorse standing nearby seemed in curiously poor condition and I later learned that the animal being raffled was too excitable to be brought into the hall, so was represented by an elderly stable-mate whose erratic bowel movements were being carefully monitored by a groom with a dainty silver pan and trowel.

I reminded myself of the laudable objective of this event – to relieve families left destitute by war. There was also an enlightening aspect to the circus-like feel of the bazaar:

for all their cut and poise, Arthur Harrowby's *haut ton* were little different to common folk in their enjoyment of tawdry spectacle.

"Come along, Jubal." Sarah tugged my arm. "Mrs Marjoribanks will be holding the fort of Virginia alone."

The Virginia stall, I was pleased to discover, was less ostentatiously furnished than the others. Beside a portrait of Stonewall Jackson, looking much as I remembered him, lay a Bible and sword that were to be presented to Robert Lee.

Fancy goods were displayed for sale, but the stall was deserted.

This left me unable to resist a jibe. "If President Lincoln could be persuaded to let Mrs Marjoribanks hold *his* forts, a Confederate victory would be guaranteed."

"Such silliness does you no credit, Jubal." Sarah hurried behind the counter, flinging me a reproachful glare. "Mrs Marjoribanks suffers from recurring lassitude and her energies are quickly depleted. We are fortunate that she was able to attend at all."

The bulky frame of States Right Rankin emerged from the crowd, thankfully preventing further debate on the subject of Mrs Marjoribanks.

Rankin tipped his hat and made a lavish smile. "Good morning to you, Miss McConville; General de Brooke."

Sarah's reply was brief and prickly – and I was reassured in the knowledge that I was not alone in attracting her disdain. After a minimum of polite conversation, she excused herself and headed in the direction of the Lady Chalcross.

We were approached by a small boy of perhaps five years who wanted to pet Rankin's Jack Russell terriers. Wearing neither leashes nor collars, they were sitting motionlessly at his heel like porcelain ornaments.

The senator made an avuncular smile. "Of course you may stroke them, son."

The boy extended a hand, then hesitated. "They don't bite, do they, sir?"

Rankin laughed. "Only when I tell 'em to."

This had been meant as a joke, but the humour evaded the little lad and he quickly retreated behind a wall of skirts and trousers.

"He'll come back later," Rankin said. "I'm sure he'd also like to see a small monkey I've acquired. You may have seen him when you arrived."

I recalled just such a creature dancing to the tune of a barrel organ at the entrance. The little monkey had extended a scarlet pageboy cap into which people tossed coins for the benefit of the Liverpool Christian Mission for the Deserving Poor. This, I now remembered, was the charitable organisation founded by Rankin in an impressive act of philanthropy.

"Your efforts on the part of destitute folk are to be applauded, Senator," I said.

Rankin inclined his shoulders. "It is merely an expression of gratitude to the Liverpool Southern Club. Their ladies' work in the Confederate interest has been nothing short of Herculean."

"All the same, you chose an especially praiseworthy means of expressing your appreciation."

As he turned towards me, I detected a mystifying aspect of relish in his eyes. "Do you want to know why I chose to establish the mission, General?"

I had no choice but to invite an explanation.

"The British are an admirable people – they are, after all, our brethren. However, there are certain elements of British society that exceed even the worst excesses of the Yankees.

I had my mission built to assist in the removal of a particularly egregious condition, namely the sight of Anglo-Saxon men begging in the streets of Liverpool while American-born niggers are openly walking out with British ladies – and I use the latter term most loosely, sir, most loosely."

No small wonder he'd savoured this disclosure, knowing as he did my publicly expressed opinions on emancipation. Wrapping such virulent bile in a parcel of apparent altruism was an astonishing feat, even by Rankin's measure. Yet I felt compelled to keep my counsel. As at the dinner party at the McConvilles' house, it wouldn't do to take issue with a member of the government I was here to represent.

Rankin, on the other hand, was enjoying this moment too much to restrain himself. "The nigger, you see, General, is but a child. If Mr Darwin's theory of natural selection is to obtain universal acceptance, then he must identify the Negro as a separate and inferior species to the Anglo-Saxon."

"Senator, I believe you know my views on this matter."

"We are free men, are we not, General? From a land that is free?"

"This is not an appropriate venue for debate." I moved closer to him, speaking in an angry whisper. "If you have any regard for our mutual cause, you will desist."

Ignoring my appeal, he continued in tones that sounded entirely affable, despite the repugnant content. "You have to understand, General, that the nigger could no more elect or run a government than – than why, Nap and Josie here."

Smiling affectionately, he looked down to the small white dogs, still sitting obediently to heel, avidly watching their master for the merest suggestion of an instruction.

I wanted to suggest that even a government of Jack Russell terriers could make a better fist of governing the South than the present administration, hamstrung as Jefferson Davis was by the narrow perspectives of individual states and self-interested politicians such as Rankin.

Instead, I made an unfelt chuckle and attempted to divert the course of our discourse by reaching down to fuss his beloved dogs. Instantly realising my mistake, I pulled back my fingers from their snapping jaws with not half of one inch to spare.

I gave him a stern look. "You would do well to keep your dogs better disciplined, Senator."

"And you, General, would do well to keep *yourself* better disciplined."

"I'm not altogether sure I care for your tone."

"I'm not altogether sure I give a damn."

"Explain yourself, Senator."

Placing his thumbs beneath the lapels of his frock coat, he thrust out his chest in the manner of a belligerent walrus. "Your fondness of the Negro race has always been vexatious, General. However, it became downright embarrassing following your … dalliance with that Giddings girl at Grassendale."

My smile surprised him. If common sense was proving ineffective, perhaps hogwash would do the trick. "I fear my dalliance may have been a trifle too subtle, Senator, since my aim was to obtain a diplomatic advantage for the Confederacy."

His walrus chest sagged a fraction as I continued. "By extending the hand of friendship to Trinity Giddings, I demonstrated to the most influential people in Britain that some in the South are capable of liberal attitudes. It may have escaped your notice, but even our most ardent supporters in Britain will not brook slavery." I extended my smile. "This is the political reality here, Senator. No matter how distasteful you may find it."

Rankin regarded me dubiously. "Pity, then, that she didn't

slap your face – insolence in the face of kindness. Now that would have been useful."

A stir in the centre of the Great Hall provided a welcome diversion.

As the hubbub increased in volume, I located its source: Trinity Giddings and Lady Alice Featherfax were walking directly towards Rankin and myself. As they approached, the thong of *haut ton* shifted discreetly aside.

There was a boldness about the arrival of Trinity Giddings that was both admirable and daunting. If my behaviour at Grassendale had been audacious, hers here today was doubly effective, stealing at a stroke the accumulated thunder of the Ladies' Forum. For tomorrow's newspapers would be dominated not by the attendance of Europe's most fashionable socialites, but the appearance of an escaped slave girl.

Half of me savoured the prospect of another encounter; the other half shrank from it. Was this a riposte to my crossing of the stream, or was I flattering myself even to imagine that I was a factor in her presence?

Recruiting my wits, I kept my eyes on the attractive figure of this bold young woman while addressing my voice to Rankin: "Why Senator, I do believe this is a first-rate opportunity to induce Miss Giddings to slap *your* face."

19

EXPERIENCES IN THE LIFE OF A SLAVE GIRL BY TRINITY GIDDINGS

Liverpool, England, November, 1863.

St George's Hall was the most splendid building this child ever done seen. As I approached with Lady Alice from Lime Street, its fawn flanks and aspect of sedate grandness minded me of a big old lion resting on his haunches.

Once inside, though, these refinements were scorned by activities more suited to the free-and-easies and laughing-gas parlours of Tithebarn Street. Hectic dealing across gaudy stalls called to mind the money-changers' tables in the temple of the Lord before Jesus overturned them.

Sight of that red-clad monkey scampering around to the barrel organ's tune did nothing to bolster my spirits. Little critter done portended calamity once already when I arrived at that first meeting with Little Big Man, and this second appearance didn't bode so well.

As we entered the Great Hall, the babble of that multitude

fell to a ripple of whispers.

A sea of richcrats receded as we moved into their midst – we'd gone and bushwhacked every last one. Now that might sound a touch mean-spirited, but it was this way: girl comes up in bondage, she gets a firm appreciation of the social order and her place in it – right at the very bottom. Just then, I was top of the pile and that was something – yes it was!

Then I saw Soldier-boy standing next to States Rights Rankin and this stole the wind from my sails some. Hadn't reckoned on an encounter with the both of them together. Yet I'd already entered the lion's den and wasn't fixing to spin on my heel – especially since we were attending the Liberty Bazaar at my insistence. So I pressed ahead with my friend Alice at my side.

Jubal de Brooke had a fidgety look, as if he wasn't entirely sure whether he was predator or prey. And yet his confusion was strangely comforting, perhaps because it reflected my own state of mind.

As for States Rights Rankin, murderer of my dear brother Benjamin, I would have gladly shot him down right there if I'd had a gun in my hand. Swear to God.

Nonetheless, I had brought a weapon of sorts and noted, with quiet satisfaction, the small white dogs at his heel.

Soldier-boy made the formal introductions, for which I was genuinely grateful. All this while, Rankin's discomfiture was plain. That a big Massa should have to endure social intercourse on equal terms with a runaway nigger clearly scandalised him.

Determined to grasp my opportunity, I addressed Rankin direct. "You may consider, Senator, that your present advantage means you have us beat."

Big Massa looked flustered. "I'm at a loss to understand."

I was amused by his stifled outrage, his inability to address me as 'Miss Giddings' as Soldier-boy did. Didn't relent: "You have never been at a loss, Senator. But I'll tell you this: I shall repay your consideration in full and in kind."

Big Massa could no longer bear to speak to me directly, addressing his comments through Soldier-boy. "Did you hear that, de Brooke? Why, I do believe she's making menaces."

I laughed to scorn him. "She surely is, Senator. I suspect you'd like it better if I called you Massa, though you have no power here. Allow me to me demonstrate."

Anxious murmuring among the richcrats gathered nearby. They sensed an embarrassing episode – and this child was oh-too-happy to provide one.

Taking two small slices of liver from waxed paper in my purse, I tossed them a few yards across the floor. Never known a dog to turn up his nose at a piece of liver and those two little devils were no different. For all Rankin's schooling, they went skidding across the mosaic tiles, nails scratching, teeth gnashing.

Big Massa's dignity went skidding with them. Angry commands – all the louder for the embarrassed hush – eventually brought the two dogs back to heel, tails tucked, ears flat.

Tawny rubble of his countenance shovelled itself into a furious snarl. By rights I should have been scared. Yet amid all Rankin's fury, I knew I done snapped his power, if only for an instant.

Small victory though it was, I did so cherish it.

Dapper old boy I recognised as Lady Alice's uncle, Lord Arthur Harrowby, seemed to emerge from nowhere and placed himself between Rankin and myself – though I noted he was careful not to present his back to either of us.

Soldier-boy also seemed to appreciate the need to avoid a

'scene' and I felt his hand at my elbow, steering me ever so gently in the direction of the Virginia stall.

Kept my voice sparky: "I must inform you, General, that I need no protection from Senator Rankin."

Soldier-boy put on an ironic grimace which was so very endearing. "My concern, Miss Giddings, is that *he* needs protection from *you*."

Didn't drop my guard – not right then. "I do wish you were a general in the Union army."

"Why should you wish that?"

Now I allowed myself a smidgeon of a grin. "So that I might admire your wit and kindness without the burden of guilt."

Looked at me earnestly. "Yet I feel not in the least conflicted in my admiration for you."

Our eyes engaged for one moment longer than was proper. Interesting that Soldier-boy turned his gaze first.

It was to be a morning of victories.

*

An afternoon of equal reward was in store, also.

After leaving the Liberty Bazaar, Lady Alice displayed an almost vulgar delight in the way I'd dealt with the big Massa's dogs. By way of reward, she announced that we were to visit Hengler's *Grand Cirque Variété* in Newington, a large wigwam-shaped structure with a classical portico that was fashioned after the *Cirque Napoleon* in Paris. Looked impressive till you came up close and realised the crumbling plaster façade was but a poor imitation of marble. Yet the entertainments were truly memorable. We saw a man and woman dancing on a tightrope and feats of equestrianism that involved a boy riding two horses at once (this minding me, with some discomfort now, of what I accused Soldier-boy of attempting). Best of all was a selection of scenes from Hamlet, performed by a small group that included Charles Hengler himself. How I loved that play, recalling as it did my memories of Missy Antonia and those evenings by the hearth in the Big House when we'd read Shakespeare and Milton and Wordsworth and even, on occasion, some verse by Walt Whitman.

Emerging from the *Cirque Variété* towards the end of the afternoon, there was still a good hour's sunlight, though the lamplighters were beginning to appear on the sidewalks.

Approach of dusk did nothing to slow the street traders: fiery sparks fizzed from a knife sharpener's grindstone, its big treadle wheel giving the appearance of a stationary bicycle; a crone hawked a basket of oranges so large that Lady Alice remarked that they had probably been boiled to make them bloat; faint-faced boy vended matches from a dinky tray hung from his neck; a still fainter urchin swept horse dung and all manner of filth from a road crossing so ladies like us needn't bemire our skirts.

Hard to say when I noticed Lady Alice was no longer at my side. Quick glance round the bustling street failed to reveal her. Retraced my steps to the circus portico, but no sign of her there, either. No matter. I could find my way back to Falkner Square easily enough.

Made my way briskly along Renshaw Street to its junction with Leece Street, where a newspaper vendor was selling copies of the *Liverpool Daily Post* from a tarpaulin satchel. Not till I reached the end of Leece Street that I realised the newspaper vendor was but two paces behind. Happenstance, maybe, yet I'd had my fill of unwelcome attention and wanted to be sure this man wasn't pursuing me. So I headed for a milliner's shop window and pretended to look at a display of hats and bonnets. After perhaps one half minute, I looked round and, with some relief, noted that he'd vanished.

Reproaching myself for a high-strung fool, I turned to resume my journey.

"Miss Giddings, isn't it?"

Newspaper man was standing directly behind me. Been there all that while. Though this spooked me some, I was reassured by the busy scene around: he could hardly attempt any untoward action in the midst of all those folk.

All the same, whatever he wanted was an annoying intrusion. "I'd say that was my business and no other's, Mister."

"Leatherbarrow, ma'am, William Leatherbarrow. I apologise for my direct approach. I saw you leave Hengler's circus with a lady I knew to be Lady Featherfax and deduced your identity."

Told him I did not wish to converse; he paid no heed. "I read of your unfortunate involvement in the investigation at Applegarth's yard," he said. "Miss Giddings, I believe the entire episode was a ploy to discredit you so that no one would listen when the true conspiracy was revealed."

I'd had quite sufficient of this. Girl gets bit a first time, she'll make sure there won't be a second. Maintained a temperate voice, though. "Mr Leatherborough, I don't care to listen to any more talk of conspiracies."

As I started to move away, he placed himself before me. "Leather*barrow*. My name is Leather*barrow*."

"Mister, I don't give a hoot if your name's Abraham Lincoln, I have no interest in what you have to say."

"Then I was mistaken to consider you a crusader in the cause of righteousness and liberty."

Now that stoked me right up. Rounded on him, tigerish-angry. "Listen, Mr Leatherbarrow, and listen well. My friends have sacrificed much more than you can possibly know seeking justice for black folk held in bondage. But we'll not get taken for dupes again."

Still he refused to shift aside. "That is my point, Miss Giddings. What possible reason could your enemies have for wanting to discredit you *twice*?"

This was a fair question, I had to give him that much.

Shouldn't trust anyone after what happened over Applegarth's. Yet all he was asking was a hearing. And if there was substance to his tale, here was an opportunity to take the fight right back to States Rights Rankin.

Looking at that newspaperman straight on for the first time, I saw a face that had once been handsome, but was disfigured by a broad scar that ran vertically each side of an eye that seemed milky and unfocused. Garments were beggarly: dusty coat torn along almost every seam; patched up trousers that were more patch than trouser; these mimicked by shoes with balled-up newsprint bulging from numerous rips. Impression I got was not of an entire man, but a creature of haphazard manufacture – a jigsaw man made up of old scraps and shabby shards that didn't fit but done been jammed together anyhow.

Not a newspaperman, then, but a jigsaw man.

His good eye – clear blue like Soldier-boy's – regarded me as if to say: 'I haven't always been this way.' Yet he wasn't seeking pity, I could tell that much.

"I have nothing to gain from telling you this except my own belief in doing what is right, whatever it may cost."

"Very well," this child said at length. "I'll listen."

"What I have to say is best said in private." He indicated a small public house called The Ring O' Bells, opposite St Luke's Church.

With some apprehension, I followed him into the dim-lit establishment. Odours of ale-hops and rancid tobacco; damp sawdust and old sweat. Men stood by the bar tossing coins for beer and spirits. Grimy faces looked round at me with shiftless interest.

"Do they look because I am black?"

Half smile – best Jigsaw-man could manage with only half a face. "They look because you are a lady."

Strange way he had with him of putting folk at ease. Again, this minded me of Jubal de Brooke. Yet, unlike Jubal, this Jigsaw-man proved that a fellow had no need of blue blood to deport himself as a gentleman.

Pulling back a chair, he waited until I was seated before sitting down opposite.

"May I offer you a drink, Miss Giddings?" he asked. "This is a poor district, though the beer is good."

I glanced through the miry window at the folks walking by – mostly pale and tattily dressed. "Beer would be welcome, thank you."

He called for a pint bottle of ale and two glasses.

Sipping the warm, hoppy beer, I gave him a forthright look. "I would be grateful, Mr Leatherbarrow, if you would come directly to the point."

Slowly, he poured himself a drink, occasionally missing the rim of the glass so the ale splashed onto the table top, perhaps, I thought, due to his partial blindness. When he was done, he addressed me briskly but in low tones so that I had to listen hard to catch his words above the babble of voices. "Very well, Miss Giddings, my point is this: I believe the entire Applegarth's investigation was a decoy to divert attention from a much more menacing Confederate manoeuvre to acquire a warship similar to HMS *Warrior*."

Swallowed more ale, gave him a stern look. After the fiasco at Applegarth's, I'd made it my business to study on these vessels and wasn't about to be gulled again. "Secretly building another ship as powerful as the *Warrior* is hard to believe ..."

"This one will be superior to every Union warship in every respect. It will have twice the firepower, twice the armoured protection and a much greater turn of speed than the two ironclad warships known as the Laird rams, lately seized on the Mersey by the British government. In short, a warship that could break the Federal blockade of southern ports."

"Twice the firepower and even faster, you say?" I felt a rising sense of panic. Could this tale be true?

Jigsaw-man swilled some beer and took out a long-stemmed clay pipe. "Are you familiar with the British government's stance on international law relating to blockades?"

Told him I was not.

Producing an oilcloth pouch, he used his forefinger to shove tobacco into the bowl of his pipe. "I'm no legal expert either, but my understanding of Lord Palmerston's position is that for the Union's blockade to be legitimate, it must be enforced by enough warships to create 'evident danger' to any merchant ships entering and leaving Southern ports. If the Confederates could show that there was no danger by sweeping away any Union ships in their path, Britain – and France also – may be persuaded that the blockade does not meet the requirements of international law. That being the case, they could resume normal maritime commerce with the South – protected by the Royal Navy as well as the French Navy."

"And you believe this could happen if the Rebels obtained a *Warrior*-standard ship?"

Jigsaw-man placed the pipe in his mouth. "If they start trading with the South again it will likely mean that Britain and France would recognise its independence."

"Then the South would keep its backward government and

the whole damned war will have been for nothing."

"Barring a miracle, President Lincoln would lose the election next year. With a Peace Democrat in the White House, an armistice would be signed and the Confederate States would have successfully left the Union."

Jigsaw-man's opinion was a hotchpotch of guesswork, imagination and supposition, I could tell that much. Yet it all made a worrying sort of sense. How I wished Josiah was here. He would know immediately what to do.

"How do you know about this *Warrior*-standard ship?"

Jigsaw-man puffed on his clay pipe and the redolence of the Virginia baccy brought to mind my father sitting by the fireside in our cabin. "Until February I was a foreman at a well-known shipyard on the Mersey. The announcement of an order for a large merchantman for the China run was great cause for celebration as it meant work for two, even three years. The owners placed great demands on the workers, but we were paid handsomely and there were few complaints."

Jigsaw-man explained that things turned sour when he came to suspect this great vessel wasn't a merchantman at all, but a powerful warship, funded by Confederate gold.

I tried to think as Josiah might; ask questions he would ask. "What exactly made you think this ship was intended for war?"

Leaning back a fraction, Jigsaw-man stroked the cheek below his sightless eye, "Why should the builders of a merchant ship construct her hull with iron plates, five inches thick and weighing four tons apiece?"

This did set my heart a-skitter. He'd described what Josiah called *Warrior*-standard armour. The gun that could pierce it had yet to be invented.

Disguised my concern well, though. "Do you have any proof, Mr Leatherbarrow?"

Jigsaw-man fingered his buckled jaw. "The very day after I made my protests to the owners, an iron bar fell down from a scaffold and struck me, causing the injuries you see before you. I was attended by a physician who pronounced me unfit to continue any manner of work at the yard."

Another bellyful of ale appeared to douse the smouldering bile in his voice. "However, I realise you seek harder evidence than the anger of a crippled man."

Dipping one arm into his crookedly stitched jacket, he pulled out a two-foot long, circular iron bar with a trumpet-shaped end.

"This is a countersunk bolt of the kind used to secure armour plates to the hull of a *Warrior*-type ironclad. I'd smuggled it out of the McConville yard before the so-called accident befell me. Look you here." He tilted the bolt in the guttering gaslight to show me some letters stamped along the shank. I read the name of a business, 'Haslam & Oglethorpe, Sheffield', followed by a long row of numbers. "Haslam & Oglethorpe are the manufacturers and these numbers correspond to the order, placed by McConville's, for thousands of these bolts."

Jigsaw-man handed me the iron bar. Felt heavy and cold in my hand and its sour chemical odour rose to my nostrils. "But how can this small piece of metal represent evidence that the McConvilles are building a Rebel ironclad?"

One-sided smile. "You will have to make your own inquiries, Miss Giddings. For my part, I can do no more. The fact that I have given you a puzzle rather than a complete story should tell you that I am not another trickster."

Coming to his feet, Jigsaw-man pressed a thin scrap of paper into my hand.

"If you pursue this matter, you'll need to speak to me further. This is where I'm to be found."

Opening the folded paper, I read in a scrawled hand the name of the Jamaica Vaults public house on Strand Street and the name of its landlord.

When I looked up, Jigsaw-man done gone.

20

RECOLLECTIONS OF A CONFEDERATE GENERAL BY JUBAL DE BROOKE

Liverpool, England, December, 1863.

The drawing room at Dunstead Manor was a peep-hole into the soul of its owner: a carefully arranged chaos. Harrowby vacillated on where to position the various statuettes, vases and sundry *objets d'art* lying haphazardly on the floor. Strewn among these were books of poetry, illustrated volumes of flora and fauna, scientific tomes and philosophical treatises, each left open at the page where the reader's itinerant mind lost interest and wandered to the next all-consuming but short-lived distraction.

Sitting opposite each other, we exchanged polite smiles and pleasantries about the continuing mild weather as we commenced our forenoon ritual of tea and cakes.

Perhaps I should have inferred something peculiar was afoot when Harrowby set about the pouring of the tea without involving a domestic servant.

"The Grand Liberty Bazaar was an unqualified, *unqualified* success, was it not?"

This was true: in its three days at St George's Hall, the bazaar had attracted prosperous individuals from Britain, France, Germany, Italy and beyond. The *haut ton* had not only attended in large numbers, but spent lavishly.

"Would it be indiscreet to enquire how much cash has been laid up as a result of this great enterprise?"

"I deposited more than £28,000 at the bank earlier in the week," I said.

Leaning over to dispense a stream of amber tea from the silver pot, Harrowby made an arch smile. "Then Mrs Marjoribanks' intelligence was correct, as it invariably, *invariably* is."

I felt a powerful urge to tell my friend just what I thought of Mrs Marjoribanks, but desisted. Harrowby was convinced that she pretended friendship with his niece, Lady Alice, for the purpose of extracting information for the Southern Club. I had no doubt that Lady Alice thought along similar lines, but with the roles reversed.

I was still musing on the apparent obviousness of Mrs Marjoribanks' duplicity when Harrowby sprung his ambush. Sometimes, I could sense a surprise attack. Not this one; not in a hundred lifetimes.

"I'm afraid, my dear Jubal, that I must ask you to hand over the entire sum."

Noting my expression of surprise and bafflement, he nodded slowly, as if to confirm that I'd heard him correctly. "It's one lump you take, isn't it?"

"Yes, one lump, thank you, Arthur." As he used delicate silver tongs to drop the single sugar lump into my cup, I considered whether this was actually happening; whether my hallucinatory episodes were returning in an altered guise.

"I'm terribly, *terribly* sorry to have to tell you this, Jubal, but I'm in a position to blackmail you most ruinously."

"You'd better explain yourself, Arthur."

He made a dreary sigh, as if this was all very taxing and unpleasant but had to be gone through. "I know your grandfather's secret; that his true identity was Lazarus Hotchkiss."

The mention of that name struck me hard. Harrowby must have noticed it register on my face but remained silent, allowing the implications to do their work. Someplace at the back of my mind, unsettling awareness shuffled forward. My friend's peculiar determination that I should visit Astrop Castle began to explain itself.

"And you mean to use this information against me?"

"Not necessarily against you, Jubal, but rather as a means of persuading you."

"To part with the monies from the Liberty Bazaar?"

"Well, yes."

"But you must know the cash is not mine to give."

"That is merely a matter of interpretation, as will become clear." Indicating two little jugs on the tea tray, he glanced at me, apologetically. "You must forgive me for a forgetful dotard, but I can't remember if it's milk you take, or cream?"

"Just a small amount of milk, Arthur, if you please."

When the ceremony of the tea-serving was accomplished, I gave him an uncomprehending frown. "I thought you were my friend."

"I *am*, my dear Jubal." His guileless smile made the conversation appear all the more unreal. "And I very much hope our friendship will continue. You see, when you arrived from America it was my most earnest hope that I should thoroughly dislike you. Yet the moment we met, I knew this would not be possible. You are a far better man than that nitwit Charles Puddlenorth. Yet this makes what must be done so much more disagreeable."

"Please enlighten me, Arthur."

Leaning back in his seat, Harrowby allowed his gaze to meander from his teacup to the window, as if he was about to recount a cherished memory.

"I first met your grandfather in Virginia in the spring of 1823. He must have been over seventy and I would have been twenty-three. And here's the queer thing, Jubal: I knew instantly, *instantly* that the man before me was an impostor. You see, I'd learned two years earlier from the real Robert de Brooke's younger sister, Melissa, that he'd lost an arm in consequence of a riding accident shortly after his twenty-first birthday. Melissa had explained that he'd set forth for a new life in Virginia in 1775, but contact had been lost during the Revolution."

I recalled the name of Melissa from Robert de Brooke's diary, shown to me in the study of Parson Micklewycke.

"May I have another lump?" I'd heard sugar was good for shock.

With meticulous attentiveness, Harrowby set down his own cup and busied himself with the silver tongs.

He resumed his account with the same air of fond reminiscence. "I was a young hot-headed fool in those days – as distinct from the old hot-headed fool who presently sits before you – and my attempts to blackmail your grandfather were crushed, *crushed.* He had me thrown out of his house with a kick up the backside and a stern warning that any defamation of his character on my part would be met with the full force of a libel action."

My friend – it was impossible, even then, to regard Harrowby as anything else – permitted himself a resigned sigh. "Since I couldn't prove my allegation without bringing Melissa de Brooke, by then aged sixty and in poor health, into an American courtroom, I had to accept that your grandfather had me beat."

Abruptly, his mood became chipper. "I hadn't returned to America for nigh on forty years, but had substantial, *substantial* interests in the supply of cotton and travelled to Charleston after the outbreak of the civil war. Can you imagine my delight when I learned that your late grandfather had a dashing young grandson named Jubal? It was then that I realised my fortunes had at last changed for the better."

He looked at me across the paraphernalia of tea and cake with a sparkling expression, as if I should share his elation.

"Hear me out, Jubal," he said quickly, "then perhaps you'll not look so po-faced."

With mounting enthusiasm, Harrowby recounted that he'd returned to Britain in 1861, determined to investigate the possibilities of his new intelligence. He'd been at school with the current Lord Puddlenorth and a little research at Astrop Castle led him to Parson Micklewycke, who revealed to Harrowby, as he did to me, that Robert de Brooke had travelled to Virginia in 1775 with his servant Lazarus Hotchkiss, also aged twenty-three.

"When Micklewycke showed me that letter, ostensibly from Robert de Brooke, in which he announced that poor Lazarus had died of smallpox, I quickly worked out the likely sequence of events. No one in America could tell Robert de Brooke from Lazarus Hotchkiss and no one on that vast continent was better equipped to assume the identity of de Brooke than Hotchkiss, his intimate since childhood. Your grandfather,

Lazarus Hotchkiss, grasped his opportunity to obtain de Brooke's money and purchased the plantation, using the family name to forge relationships and build a reputation among the southern gentry. I don't criticise your grandfather, Jubal: quite the opposite – I applaud, *applaud* his enterprise."

"You must forgive me if I don't, Arthur." I sipped my tea.

"Would you care for a spot of jelly roll, Jubal?" He nodded at the plate of sliced sponge cake with its pleasing spiral of raspberry preserve. "Fresh from Mrs Trudgeon's oven this very morning and devilish, *devilish* tasty."

"My appetite is lacking."

"I understand," he said. "Yet it's my firm conviction that it will soon return."

"You've been damned clever, Arthur. Did you pay Puddlenorth and Micklewycke to take part in your scheme, or were they also blackmail victims?"

Ignoring my jibe, he severed a slice of jelly roll and began to nibble at its edges. "In truth, I didn't need to be particularly clever, nor implicate Puddlenorth or Micklewycke. All I had to do was persuade you to visit Astrop Castle and I was confident the revelations would follow, as they had for me."

Setting my cup and saucer on the table, I gave him a hard stare. "Your blackmail won't work, Arthur. No matter what you threaten, I can't deliver the proceeds of the Liberty Bazaar to settle, what? A private gambling debt?"

There was a look of genuine shamefacedness about him. "I cannot deny that my fondness for the faro tables has played an unwelcome role in the present financial entanglement."

He took a moment to trace the coil of raspberry preserve in the jelly roll between his fingers. The twisting confection appeared to gratify him and he turned to me with a look of instant ebullience. "I'm certain, *certain* you'll experience a change of heart when I tell you what these monies are needed for."

I had a terrible sinking feeling which set off a thirst for a more robust stimulant than the orange pekoe on offer, now stewing in the silver teapot before me.

21

EXPERIENCES IN THE LIFE OF A SLAVE GIRL BY TRINITY GIDDINGS

Liverpool, England, December, 1863.

The Jamaica Vaults were located in a row of red brick buildings on Strand Street, opposite Canning Dock. As our brougham carriage pulled up on the cobbled road, I noticed a pair of constables, with their stovepipe hats and smart blue tailcoats, standing beside a tarpaulin sheet thrown over some object on the ground.

"You shouldn't look, Trinity," Josiah said. "It's a body they're attending to. No doubt hauled from the Mersey after some appalling assault."

Josiah had reluctantly agreed to meet Jigsaw-man after he'd examined the long iron bolt and conceded that it was manufactured for the purpose of fixing armour plate to an ironclad warship. Yet he remained deeply sceptical about Jigsaw-man's story. After all, there was nothing but a sequence of numbers stamped on the side of the bolt to link it to the

McConville shipyard.

I'd countered Josiah's doubts with Jigsaw-man's argument that if this was another Confederate plot, why honey the trap with such shoddy evidence? Just as important, why should Rankin want to discredit me twice? Surely once was enough, even for a scheming devil such as the big Massa? Logic of my argument – that there *was* no logic – done pleased me as much as it irritated Josiah.

Jamaica Inn was much the same as the Ring O' Bells, where I'd originally met Jigsaw-man: gloomy, miry and filled with listless men who supped liquor and spat tarry wads of baccy on the mucky straw-strewed floor.

Josiah tossed a copper coin to the barmaid and asked to see the landlord.

He appeared from a room at the rear of the premises, wearing a cantankerous look. Averse to black folk, maybe; suspicious of strangers for sure.

I showed him the note from Jigsaw-man.

"Billy Leatherbarrow ain't here." The landlord didn't appear to be in cooperative humour.

"Then where?" Josiah sounded impatient.

This provoked a hostile frown. "I was given to understand only that an African lady might inquire. Who might you be, sir?"

Piped up quickly, before Josiah could inflame matters still further. "This is Mr Mill, my friend. Surely Billy wouldn't begrudge me a chaperone?"

Landlord's voice softened just a fraction. "Billy don't want to take no risks, ma'am. You already seen what they done to him." He nodded toward the open door and the two constables with their tarpaulin-covered charge on the street. "That poor wretch was found in Canning Dock this very forenoon. Body with no head. Earlier, in Canada Dock, someone found a head with no body. They don't match, so that makes two murders discovered in the span of three hours. Now, I'd lay handsome odds that both are the work of soulless devils who'll stop at nought to obtain intelligence for the Rebels about the Yankees or the Yankees about the Rebels. That's why Billy is right to be cautious."

Josiah spoke again, but this time more temperately. "We understand that Billy has put himself at hazard. But we must speak to him if we're to pursue the matter he's brought to our attention."

Landlord looked from Josiah to me and back again. "Go to the quarry at St Domingo Road in Everton. I'll send word to Billy that he's to meet you by the watchman's shack at a half past two o'clock."

*

Quarry was a queer place. Sandstone cliff fell sheer some two hundred feet, with big squared-off slabs protruding from the salmony rock-face. As we approached, we saw winches and lifting tackle on ledges high above but not a soul working them.

Leaving our carriage on the main road from Everton to Kirkdale, we walked down a mucky track towards the watchman's shack. Nothing but timber laths with a crumbling brick chimney that minded me of the cabin I'd grown up in.

The sound of a gun being cocked close behind us snapped me from my reverie.

"That you, Miss Giddings?"

I recognised Jigsaw-man's voice. "Yes, Mr Leatherbarrow. I've come with my friend Commander Mill, of the Royal Navy."

Turning, I saw Jigsaw-man standing in the shadows below the eaves of his shack. He'd lowered his revolver and beckoned us to follow him into his cabin. Inside, a low-banked fire glowed in the grate and two grease lamps smouldered on a splintery wooden table.

Jigsaw-man bade us take a seat and offered us tea or liquor, which we politely declined.

Josiah opened up in his usual forthright manner. "Mr Leatherbarrow, the countersunk bolt you gave to Miss Giddings is certainly the type used to build powerful ironclad warships, though we have yet to verify the serial number."

He paused to clear his throat as pungent fumes from the grease lamps choked the air. "Before taking matters further, I need to find out what you know about the construction of this ship at McConville's."

"Ask what you will, Commander." Jigsaw-man took out his baccy pouch and began filling his pipe-bowl.

Josiah took out a small pocketbook and pencil. "I know already about the armour plate used in the construction of the hull, but were there any other aspects of this ship – no detail is too small – that made you suspect she was an ironclad?"

The disfigured side of Jigsaw-man's face was hidden behind a cloud of pipe-smoke, giving him a momentary appearance of wholeness. "One day, a solid teak stem with a tapered end was delivered to the yard; next day, we received a consignment of rounded iron plate of matching diameter. I believed these were the components for a ramming beak to be fixed to the ship's bow. When I made inquiries I was informed the stem was to support the mainmast and the rounded iron was to protect the propeller shaft. I'm no engineer, but I sensed immediately that this was not true."

Josiah took up his pencil and wrote a few lines in his

pocketbook. "You were quite right – those materials are precisely what is need to assemble a ram beak."

Looking up from his pocketbook, Josiah made a small smile. "Did anything else strike you as unusual about the ship's construction?"

Jigsaw-man sucked on his pipe. "This might be quite unconnected," he said after a while, "but her coal bunkers could be flooded with sea water when empty. I only mention this because I can't think why the skipper of a merchant ship would want to slow himself down in such a way."

More scrawling in Josiah's pocketbook. "A merchant skipper wouldn't, but a warship commander might. For example, if he wanted to take on ballast to make his ship more stable when firing his heavy guns, or to add to her momentum when planning to ram another vessel."

My heart punched in excitement. "Does this mean we got 'em?"

Josiah closed his pocket book. "It means we have a fighting chance. Yes."

This child's spirits lifted some. Tough path ahead for sure, though I sensed deep down it was leading in the right direction.

22

RECOLLECTIONS OF A CONFEDERATE GENERAL BY JUBAL DE BROOKE

Liverpool, England, December, 1863.

As if to emphasise the importance of what he was about to tell me, Arthur Harrowby placed his slice of jelly roll back on his plate. "The monies raised by the Liberty Bazaar are needed to obtain a ship, Jubal. A ship that could scarcely be more vital, *vital* to the Confederate cause."

Returning his straightforward look, I replied with equal vehemence. "I cannot imagine any vessel more important than the relief of destitution among the wives and children of those boys held in Union prison camps."

Harrowby's voice deepened as he affected an air of melodrama. "This ship I speak of will achieve the release of your soldiers and the relief of their kin. It is a remedy for all issues. It will win the war for the South."

"That, I doubt." How many rogues had I heard espousing those very words in hopes of selling idiotic inventions and crackpot notions to the credulous or the desperate?

"You must trust me, Jubal." In other circumstances, the suggestion by a self-proclaimed blackmailer that he was worthy of his victim's trust would be downright comical.

I swallowed some tea to ease the prickly dryness in my throat. "If I refuse?"

Harrowby, who had again picked up his jelly roll, hesitated in mid-bite. "You will leave me no alternative but to use my intelligence to your detriment, and that of your family."

"Surely it would damage your own reputation Arthur, were it known that you had deliberately passed me off as a relative in a scheme to pay off your creditors?

Harrowby raised one eyebrow. "Whose word would be believed on that score, Jubal? I'm related to everyone who *is* anyone in this county. And they'd never support a person descended from a fraudster and a thief."

"You must realise, Arthur, that my hands are tied. I'd be ruined anyway if I handed over those funds."

"Not so, Jubal!" Already perched on the edge of his seat, he banged a fist on his knee with such violence that he almost knocked himself from the chair. "This is the beauty of my proposal. Powerful, *powerful* interests in the Confederate government will ensure your family name is preserved."

As my mind began to explore the various threads of Harrowby's blackmail scheme, it became clear that there was another, equally ominous weave to his subterfuge.

"I'm intrigued, Arthur, by these interested parties. If they're powerful enough to conceal such massive deception, they must also possess sufficient influence to manipulate my posting to Britain, as the chief agent of this fraud."

In the uneasy pause Harrowby's ancient pendulum clock marked time with slow, hollow beats.

This was drowned by a deep-bellied holler: "Give the general a prize!"

The inevitable Jack Russell terriers came trotting into the room ahead of their master.

He stood on the threshold a moment, as a showman might await applause after pulling off an audacious sleight-of-hand illusion. In a sense this is exactly what he had done, though sleight-of-mind better described it.

As I watched him approach, I recalled Harrowby informing me, soon after my arrival in Liverpool, that Rankin was investing in one of his companies. This was an engineering firm that had once manufactured steam engines for textile mills but had been forced by the cotton famine to make engines for blockade runners, which were Rankin's line of business. And the number of blockade runners was growing larger as each month passed, due to the huge profits being made by those fast enough to outrun the Union fleet and deliver much needed supplies and munitions to the Confederate Army.

I remembered, too, that conversation with my commanding officer, James Longstreet, who informed me of the War Department's decree that my next battle would be fought among Liverpool's society dinners and biscuit parties. From the moment the last shot was fired at Chickamauga Creek, I'd been Rankin's creature – the perfect dupe, the war-worn hero sent to raise charitable funds, from which he would be so easily parted.

"Senator Rankin, do join us." Still, Harrowby maintained this conceit of gentility. "We are taking tea – orange pekoe, fresh from the pot. And some jelly roll with the finest, *finest* raspberry preserve."

"I'll take something stronger, if you don't mind, Harrowby." Without awaiting a reply, Rankin took the brandy decanter and swilled a good quarter-pint measure into a crystal globe.

Odd, I thought, that these two conspirators should address each other by their surnames, while Harrowby conversed with me – the victim – on Christian name terms. As Rankin came to sit with us, there was an almost palpable tension between him and Harrowby.

The terriers arranged themselves, one by each of his cannon-black boots. "You probably won't believe this, de Brooke – or should I call you Hotchkiss – but I'm sorry we had to involve you in this. I won't pretend anything but the deepest contempt for you and your liberal ideas, but you're a damn good commander, much better employed killing Yankees in large numbers."

Harrowby had also fallen quiet, neither drinking his tea nor eating his cake.

"Fact is that my joint-investor here" – Rankin indicated Harrowby with a sweep of his bough-like arm – "has lost so heavily at faro that the business we lately obtained, as a vehicle to procure this ship, will be foreclosed by our creditors unless the vessel is delivered before Christmas. To pay off the shipbuilder we must complete a final instalment payment of some £30,000. We expected the bazaar to raise only half that, but with you to lead the charge, the event was successful beyond our most optimistic predictions."

Clearly, Harrowby's enormous gambling debts had drawn Rankin into a financial crisis which was the source of the friction between them. It was friction that I intended to use to my advantage.

All the same, I couldn't prevent a dose of sarcastic bile seeping into my tone. "How satisfying to know that the Confederacy will be defrauded by twice as much as had been anticipated, due to my efforts."

"Not defrauded, defended." Rankin swilled down half his brandy as if it was lemonade. "This ship of ours will, indeed, enable the South to prevail."

"What ship is she?"

"That cannot yet be revealed."

"And to whom will it be delivered?"

Rankin gave me a straight stare. "I assure you on my honour, de Brooke, this vessel will be used in the interest of the Confederate States of America."

Returning his gaze, I spoke with too much haste, but no regret. "I can't believe you have any honour."

I saw his shovel-shaped jaw tighten under my words and I took some pleasure from his anger. "You'll rue that slur, de Brooke, rue it deep and hard."

Finishing his brandy, he set the globe glass down on the low table between us. "For the time being, my position as a senator of the Confederacy means that I outrank you by some distance and I am now ordering that you surrender those monies."

I made a bitter chuckle. "You don't even outrank the meanest drummer boy, Rankin. You're a civilian. I take my orders from the officer commanding the Army of Northern Virginia. That would be Robert Lee."

Rankin's boot clubbed one of the terriers aside as his detonating temper drove him to his feet. "Don't imagine that can't be fixed!"

The manor's ancient timbers seemed to tremble under his tread as he marched from the room, the two dogs following with ears flat and tails tucked.

Harrowby looked at me solicitously. "He's right, Jubal. It will take time, but he will get the authority he requires."

"And you will blackmail me in the meantime, won't you, Arthur?"

He looked genuinely shamefaced. "Sad to say, I have no choice."

"I'll need time. The bank won't keep that amount of cash under the counter."

"Don't take too much, Jubal. For all our sakes." There was entreaty as well as threat in Harrowby's voice.

I left him then gazing forlornly, at his unfinished jelly roll, unable to stand another minute of the vicious charade that was being enacted and longing to be back in the field with real men whose loyalty and trust I could take for granted.

23

EXPERIENCES IN THE LIFE OF A SLAVE GIRL BY TRINITY GIDDINGS

Liverpool, England, December, 1863.

Five days after Josiah and I met Jigsaw-man, I received an urgent request, delivered by messenger, to attend Josiah's ship, HMS *Shearwater*, which was now lying in Prince's Dock.

As I approached the dockside I witnessed the strangest occurrence: leaving the ship were three white men wearing blackface in the manner of music hall minstrels who used burned cork to colour their skin and exaggerate their lips. Thought I was in the midst of some unearthly dream, swear to God. Blinked; looked again; yet still those minstrel boys remained before me, eyes agoggle in counterfeit complexions.

This child tried to imagine what might have got into Josiah's head to permit these people on board his ship? Not a week since, he expressed a forthright opinion that minstrels hampered the abolitionist cause by promoting the notion that Negroes were naturally cheery folk, entirely content in their lot on American plantations.

All logic deserted me when some two dozen more of those blacked-up minstrels appeared from the *Shearwater*, followed by a petty officer who directed them to a long wagon hitched to a team of six sturdy horses.

Only when I saw those boys humping dark-stained sacks from the cart did I figure out what was going on: they were loading coal into the ship's bunkers; their faces, hands hair, every part of them ingrained by coal-dust. The nature of their labour became all the more obvious when I realised that the coal yards lay on the opposite side of Bath Street, which ran parallel to the dockside.

Laughed, then, at my own credulity. What a humorous tale it would make for Josiah. But, almost instantly, I stopped chortling. They were filling the *Shearwater* with coal because she was making ready to leave Liverpool.

A lieutenant greeted me at the companionway and escorted me to Josiah's cabin, where I was told the captain would attend presently.

Looking about, I saw my friend's familiar apothecary's wares laid up in every available space. Sweet, earthy odours, minding me of that first voyage we shared across the ocean when I occupied Josiah's cabin. Long time ago. And yet this was a deception – I'd arrived in Great Britain not three months back. So much done happened to me in this foreign-familiar land that it gave the illusion of stretching time.

Wandered to Josiah's desk, where a document that I took to be his orders was set down in elaborate calligraphy that addressed itself to 'Commander Josiah Mill RN, of Her Britannic Majesty's Ship *Shearwater*'.

Read the opening line out loud: "Being in all respects ready for sea …"

"Read on, Trinity!" Josiah appeared in the door frame. "There's nothing secret about *Shearwater*'s mission."

I manufactured a dry chuckle. "All that spirally writing makes my eyes go dizzy."

Truth was I didn't wish to read his orders because those first few words told me more than I cared to know. Ship was ready for sea.

"I've been instructed to take *Shearwater* to the China station immediately," he said.

My friend done already told me China was his most likely destination, so I wasn't surprised by this news. No, not this child. Tearful-sorry, for sure. Yet what sort of friend would I be if I laid the dead weight of my distress on shoulders already overburdened?

Josiah was no fool, though, and sensed my anxiety. "I shan't be gone for ever."

"It will feel like forever."

"You have Lady Alice. And you're quickly making new friends. There's Jubal de Brooke. He seems to have taken a liking to you."

Threw Josiah a powerful angry glance. Why had he mentioned Soldier-boy? And why wasn't Josiah jealous?

"Jubal de Brooke is an enemy to black folk everywhere."

"He's an enemy to the Yankees. That isn't quite the same."

How Josiah vexed me with his notions of level-headedness. Pig-headedness was more fitten.

"I want you to find happiness, Trinity. Fulfilment." Stood opposite, placing his arms on my shoulders, hugged me tight and my spleen could not endure. "I want you to obtain all those many and marvellous things that lie within your grasp here in Britain."

"Like love and devotion?" I joshed.

Never doubted Josiah's devotion. But casting back, I began to study on that night we'd laid together.

"You realise you'll be deeply missed, Josiah."

"Now … now … Enough of this melancholy." In a trice, he whipped round and hastened across the cabin to produce a sheaf of papers from his desk. "I lately received important correspondence concerning the source of that bolt provided by Mr Leatherbarrow. This is why I asked you to come so promptly."

All ears, I watched him riffle through the handwritten pages till he found what he was looking for.

"The bolt comes from the factory of Haslam & Oglethorpe in Sheffield. The managing director, Mr Haslam, confirmed that the serial number stamped on the shank corresponds to a substantial order for such components from McConville's. Furthermore …" Josiah flipped through more pages of notes, then looked up at me with a faint smile. "The records show the Pasham & Edgeport Steam Navigation Company, which Mr Leatherbarrow says ordered the large ironclad from McConville's, was lately acquired in an unusual transaction. The entire share capital of Pasham & Edgeport was obtained by Imperial Industries & Company, for a consideration of some £200,000."

Josiah eyed me expectantly, as if something important should become apparent to me from this information. But this child's ignorance on commercial affairs was deeper than any ocean trench.

"Imperial Industries manufactures steam compound engines for textile mills but has, since the so-called 'cotton famine', broadened its activities to include the building of engines for ships. These have included blockade runners, which, as we know, are entirely legal. But no one suspected, until now, that

Imperial Industries has been engaged in the manufacture of the engines for an entirely illegal Confederate ironclad."

Regarded my friend with an expression of stifled excitement. "That's wonderful news, Josiah, but I've never heard of this Imperial Industries concern."

Josiah tossed the report on his desk. "You've heard of the company's majority shareholder, though – Lord Arthur Harrowby."

"He's the new friend of the big Massa, ain't he?"

"Let's not jump ahead now, Trinity. We need absolute proof this time, before –"

"I know, I know … but I can't wait to see Rankin in leg irons, on his way to some noxious prison. My dream would be complete if the British were to transport that unspeakable villain to Botany Bay."

24

RECOLLECTIONS OF A CONFEDERATE GENERAL BY JUBAL DE BROOKE

Liverpool, England, December, 1863.

The next day I tracked down the one person in Liverpool who might be able to help – James Dunwoody Bulloch, chief Confederate agent in Europe.

I'd meant to approach him on his doorstep, but lost my nerve; then again at the end of Wellington Street and at various points after that. The reason for my hesitation was that I didn't quite know how much to reveal, or whether to trust him at all.

I was accustomed to the loneliness of command, but now found myself locked in a peculiar type of solitude. Though I longed to share my dilemma with the people I'd come to know and trust, this wasn't possible because any or all may be implicated – knowingly or not. My isolation had been compounded by quitting Dunstead Manor, which I had come to regard as a home, for quarters at the Wellington Hotel on Dale Street.

As I pondered these issues, a chorus of voices rose up from the Mariner's Church nearby, accompanied by organ music. It was just two weeks before Christmas Day and the congregation was singing *Hark the Herald Angels Sing.*

At the heart of my predicament were two sets of circumstances that I couldn't believe were unconnected. Firstly, the McConvilles were on the brink of ruin due to the late payment of substantial monies by a shipping line that had ordered a large merchant vessel, the *Himalaya.* Secondly, I was being blackmailed because Harrowby and Rankin needed funds for a ship – allegedly vital to the Confederate interest – for which final settlement was overdue, placing Harrowby's company also at risk of collapse.

Could it be that this ship – whether the *Himalaya* or another vessel – had been ordered from the McConville yards? That Harrowby's debts meant he couldn't pay McConville's who, in turn, were unable to satisfy their own creditors? The apparent solution – some £28,000 proceeding from the Liberty Bazaar – lay in my hands.

What to do?

If there was a connection between Harrowby's business and the difficulties at McConville's, how much did Sarah know? Was she privy to the blackmail conspiracy? Her recent behaviour certainly suggested desperation that I knew to be related to business finance.

Yesterday, any question of Sarah's loyalty would have been unthinkable.

Yet exactly the same could be said of Arthur Harrowby. His treachery had cut me deep for, despite his many shortcomings, I'd regarded him as a firm friend.

Could I turn that money over to him and Rankin? Notwithstanding what I'd told Rankin about taking orders only from General Lee, I could, if called to account, reasonably assert that I'd parted with the funds under the instructions of a senior member of the Confederate government. Moreover, if Harrowby went ahead with his threat, my father would be the principal victim. Elderly and frail, I doubted he'd survive the scandal. The blackmailers had effectively put a gun to my father's head and my actions alone would determine whether the trigger was pulled.

Weighed against this was my duty as an officer, sent here to muster aid for hungry wives, widows and children of Confederate soldiers fallen in battle or taken prisoner by the Yankees. How could I possibly explain my craven dereliction to the widow and children of Sergeant Papajohn, along with hundreds of thousands of others, equally destitute, equally deserving?

I'd been covertly following Bulloch from his home in Wellington Street some one half-hour ago trying to pluck up the nerve to approach him. As the purchasing agent in Europe for the Confederate States Navy, Bulloch was heavily involved in the procurement of British-built warships for the South. I'd met him briefly some two months ago, and knew him to be a decent man, despite the clandestine nature of his work.

By the time we reached George's Dock, however, I'd become weary of vacillation and, discarding restraint, stepped towards him.

Before I could speak, he turned to face me wearing a baleful smile. He was an energetic-looking man in his late thirties with a balding pate that made him appear somewhat older. Dense whiskers covered his jowls and upper lip, though not his jaw, embellishing his rounded countenance with a distinctive aitch-shaped beard.

"I wish I could say I was surprised to see you, General de

Brooke," he said. "And I must tell you, at once, this is not the place to discuss the matters I suspect you wish to discuss."

His insight brought a furrow to my brow. "How did you know my approach was anything other than social?"

His attentive eyes gleamed with a hint of mischief. "I'd been aware of your presence in Wellington Street before I opened the front door of my house. It seemed unlikely that you'd followed me for the best part of one mile simply to pass the time of day."

He must have noticed my astounded expression, for he made a good-humoured chuckle. "You must understand, General, that I'd be remiss in my duties if I was not spying on the Yankees, or indeed, being spied upon myself. To enjoy any degree of success in my work, I must be acutely aware of what is happening around me."

Feeling rather foolish, I complemented him on his vigilance.

"We should continue this conversation someplace else."

"Where?"

"Here." He slipped a folded sheet of paper into my breast pocket. "Tomorrow at three o'clock."

*

I'd never seen the like of the whalebone shed, an arched construction built from the ribs of whales, brought to Liverpool as a result of the port's association with the 'Greenland trade'. The pale bones rose in four pairs from the damp earth like sabre-teeth, each tapering inward to meet the tip of its counterpart, some twenty feet above the ground. Timber beams ran horizontally from the front to the back of the building, with crooked timbers forming a roof. The only items stored there were a rickety donkey cart and a pile of rodent-nibbled sacks that might once have contained grain.

The shed was situated on rough ground off Blenheim Street, and I'd come here on Bulloch's instructions following our terse conversation the previous morning at George's Dock.

"Good day, General de Brooke."

Surprised by the quietness of his tread, I swung round to see Bulloch standing amid an intersection of shadows cast by the huge whale ribs.

I shook his extended hand. "For sure, you've chosen an unusual location, Mr Bulloch."

"You must forgive my brusqueness yesterday, General, but Liverpool waterfront is no place to conduct a confidential discussion."

There followed an awkward hiatus in which I struggled for the correct words to introduce my topic.

Sensing my problem, Bulloch made an accommodating shrug. "Before we continue, General, let us both agree that this conversation never took place. In other words, nothing that passes between us can be attributed to the other. In such a way we can express ourselves more liberally."

"I'm grateful, Mr Bulloch. I've come to you because I understand something of your role for our government here in Liverpool – that it's your business to monitor the building of ships on the Mersey that may become available to the Confederacy."

The amicable smile remained amid his aitch-shaped whiskers. "That is not something I'm able to discuss, General."

I smiled back, beginning to understand his implicit code: by not denying my assertion he was, in effect, confirming it. It seemed this conversation was going to be about what was not said, rather than what was.

"I seek your advice regarding a ship that certain parties,

known to both you and I, have assured me is critically important to the Confederacy. I have been asked to divert significant funds to complete the purchase of this vessel from a yard on the Mersey. Among my main concerns, in deciding whether to comply with this request, is the nature and purpose of a ship that I know nothing about."

Bulloch made a helpless shrug. "I pride myself on my diligence, General, but your information is so vague that it's exceedingly difficult to offer assistance."

"Forgive me, Mr Bulloch." Again, I felt naïve. "I've clearly presumed too much about your knowledge of what happens on the Mersey."

"That great river encompasses five miles of quays, docks, shipyards and landing stages on each bank." He used the tip of his boot to describe the broadening estuary on the muddy ground, drawing a rough circle that indicated Liverpool and another that I understood to represent Birkenhead. "Add them together and you have nearly ten miles of waterfront – a busy, hectic, bewildering and often dangerous place to do business."

"And yet, your achievements are considerable, Mr Bulloch," I said.

My companion made a self-deprecating expression. "I'm fortunate to have had some measure of success, General. But the scale of the Mersey shipping trade is a mixed blessing. On the one hand it means I can get business done unobserved; on the other it means other interests – perhaps including the parties you refer to – are able to profit from private ventures that can frustrate my own plans, whether intentionally or not."

I decided to take a risk. "This ship may be a merchantman named the *Himalaya* and may have been ordered from McConville's at Birkenhead."

Bulloch raised a dense eyebrow at that. "Forgive me,

General, but I thought you were well acquainted with the owners of that particular yard."

"Indeed I am, but my room for manoeuvre is restricted because much of my information was given in confidence." I shrugged, feeling rather shabby at divulging this to a man I knew hardly at all, except by reputation. "Moreover, the link between the *Himalaya* and the ship for which I've been asked to provide funds is entirely speculative."

Stubbing the tip of his boot in the circle that represented Birkenhead, he looked at me with a vexed expression. "I must tell you, General, that I have no knowledge of the *Himalaya*, which is, in itself, disconcerting. I'd expect to be aware of such a major undertaking, even if it is a merchantman. Having said this, I've seen large vessels built for the Confederacy that our enemies were not aware of until they were slipping their moorings. And I presume the parties involved have the resources to conceal their activities."

Anxious not to appear artless yet again, I was reluctant to ask my next question; yet I had to know the answer. "Have you heard any rumours of the building of a ship powerful enough to win the war for the South?"

I flinched as he laughed – though, I noticed, not mockingly. "After the loss of the Laird rams only a few months ago, any such rumours should be rejected as fanciful yarns."

These 'Laird rams' were powerful, armoured warships with guns mounted in revolving turrets and bows with sharp underwater spikes designed to be rammed into the hulls of their prey. I'd read in the newspapers that they'd been seized by the British authorities that September gone, under extreme pressure from the United States minister in London.

"I say fanciful, and yet ..." Bulloch paused, tugging his side whiskers, as if trying to tease some elusive realisation from inside his head. "If there had been another ironclad venture in progress, this would be a damn clever time to bring it to fruition. Everyone – the Yankees and the British – would dismiss it out of hand. Exactly as I just did."

I looked at him with a grim smile. "Then I need you to suspend your judgement, sir, for the scheme I am about to unfold requires the considerable use of imagination to fully fathom."

25

EXPERIENCES IN THE LIFE OF A SLAVE GIRL BY TRINITY GIDDINGS

Liverpool, England, December, 1863.

Want to see the stupidest critter God ever made? Turn your gaze on this child.

I arrived back at Lady Alice's house fitten to scream in frustration, though, in truth, I should never have gotten my hopes up. Josiah and I lately attended the offices of Little Big Man in the Custom House, and then Thomas Haines Dudley at the US Consulate. We'd acquainted each with the intelligence delivered by that Jigsaw-man and the evidence from the Sheffield foundry where those iron bolts done been made.

Never trusted that shrimpy politician since I saw him pandering to the Confederate supporters at that garden party. My distrust proved well-founded. Little Big Man refused outright to take any action after what he described as the 'ineffable calamity' at Applegarth's. When Josiah explained that this was precisely what the conspirators planned, Little Big Man laughed to scorn him, declaring he'd not tolerate another 'syllable of slander' on the names of Lord Harrowby or the McConvilles.

Mr Dudley gave us a more sympathetic hearing, but the outcome was no different: he couldn't take action on the grounds of an iron bolt and the say-so of Jigsaw-man who, Josiah was forced to concede, had no shortage of axes nor grinding wheels in regard to his former employer.

As the front door closed behind me, I thanked the Lord that Lady Alice was not at home. Now that might sound downright ungrateful, but it was like this: Lady Alice was not one to let matters rest. She'd huff and puff and there'd be letters to the prime minister and the foreign secretary and the devil to pay if they didn't agree instantly to her demands.

I'd been studying on such thoughts some while when the front door bell jingled and I heard the footman attend to the caller.

Short time later there came a tap on my door and I opened it to see the footman holding out a brown paper package which he said was addressed to me.

I could barely muster the energy to take it from him, but as I did so, the sight of my name scrawled in Jigsaw-man's spidery hand sent my pulse scurrying. When the door was closed, I tore away the wrapping paper.

Before me was a Bible, bound in leather and secured by a metal clasp. With it, a short note from Jigsaw-man.

Read thus: *If ever I possessed religious faith I have lately lost all, though I know you have not. You may draw strength from the passages in Job 41, commencing 'Can'st thou draw out Leviathan?'*

Of course, I knew the book of Job and understood the references to Leviathan. He was a big old sea beast that made the deeps boil and could not be defeated by the weapons of men.

Opening the Good Book, I all but dropped it in horror – swear to God!

Its pages had been cut away to form a deep cavity.

Was this desecration a product of Jigsaw-man's vanished faith?

Then I noticed something wedged in the hollow. Cautiously extracting it, I found a heavy object wrapped up in waxed paper. Opened out, this revealed an iron key and roughly sketched map of India Works on the Great Float West at Birkenhead, which I knew to be the principal shipbuilding yard of McConvilles. On this map, Jigsaw-man done drawn the main gates and dry docks and also an arrow indicating side-gates. In the Great Float he'd pencilled a slender oval labelled 'Leviathan', which no doubt represented the *Himalaya*. According to the map, she was moored adjacent to the dockside.

The key, now cold and heavy in my hand, could only have been provided to open those side-gates.

*

India Works was so quiet you might imagine it done been shut down. Sadly, not so. The absence of activity was due to the fact I'd gone there on the Sabbath. I trusted that the Lord would forgive me, for I had once more donned my disguise as a mariner and was about to trespass on private land.

Standing at the end of Ilchester Road, I looked across the railway tracks to the high brick wall skirting the works. No sign of life, save for an occasional bawdy song issuing from a terrace of shabby houses on Bucleuch Street. Bleak December morning; cold slaps of wind stung my cheeks; pale-bellied clouds grew dark where they met the watery horizon, minding me of puddle-stained skirts.

With a brisk glance around to make sure I was unobserved, I crossed the rail tracks and headed down the side of the brick wall, some twenty feet tall, that surrounded the works. Put me in mind of the great wall skirting the borough jail in Great Howard Street.

Directly ahead of me was an old mortar mill with bottle-shaped kilns and, on the opposite bank of the Great Float, a copper store and petroleum shed.

The side-gates were somewhat bigger than I'd expected: stout timber portals wide enough to admit rail tracks. The padlock, too, was substantial – a rusty iron slab with a metal shutter covering the keyhole. Jigsaw-man's key fitted snugly enough, but wouldn't turn in that rusty slot. No matter how hard I gripped and twisted, the lock refused to budge.

Cussed under my breath. The longer I was there, the greater the risk of getting caught. Then what? I'd prevailed on my friends too greatly already and couldn't count on them coming to my rescue again. The image of the borough jail returned to my mind.

Why wouldn't that damned key work?

Scrape of metal on stone sent me whirling round. The key tumbled from my grasp, tinkling on the cobbles, though in my ears it sounded louder than the bell at the Big House that tolled when a slave escaped.

My eyes scanned the scene every which way – so fast I could barely focus. But there was nothing save a discarded tin can, rolling in the wind along the street cobbles.

Picking up the key, I spat on it to aid lubrication. Not ladylike, yet it had the required effect. Squeaking and groaning, the padlock's mechanisms slowly shifted until it fell open.

Removing the lock, I pushed against one of the two large gates and was powerful gratified when it opened.

With a rush of excitement, I slipped through the aperture to find myself in a short tunnel with an arched roof. Moved with some caution into its gloomy clasp, nostrils filled with sour odours of cold stone and damp wood.

Another set of gates appeared at the far end – also padlocked. This I hadn't been anticipating and my spirits plummeted. Tried the key; no use. Too big even to fit in the keyhole.

At that moment my temper got stolen away. Tossing aside the key, I balled my fists and banged and banged on the hard timbers.

Not sure when I became aware of another presence in that tunnel. Whatever I heard behind me was no tin can – I could tell that much.

Heartbeat skittered; breathing snagged. Couldn't turn. I tried, but every muscle done locked. What trickery was this? Jigsaw-man in league with Stakes Rights Rankin?

"You might do better with this."

Josiah was standing there beside me. In his hand, he held a hacksaw.

Glad though I was to see him, I couldn't keep a scolding note from my voice. "You scared me witless, Josiah."

"Would you rather I hadn't come?"

"How did you know to find me here?"

"I received a note from Mr Leatherbarrow."

Josiah looked at me with a curious frown. "Now tell me how *you* came to be here?"

When I'd done explaining, he gave me a querulous look, then raised the hacksaw and set about the padlock.

Took a good while, but taking turns with the blade, we at last cut through the lock. Inner gates squawked as Josiah prised them open.

As we stepped into the shipyard proper, he caught my arm. "We should beware of the watchmen. I suspect that there are at least two of them."

This was something I hadn't figured on and I was suddenly even more grateful for Josiah's presence. Girl gets caught trespassing by a watch-keeper, no telling what might happen.

Place seemed so much bigger inside than out. Row after row of substantial ships in various stages of construction: tall-masted schooners; stubby coastal vessels; iron-hulled steam packets; yes, and sleek blockade runners also. Everywhere, cranes and derricks, heavy lifting gear, scaffolding and small steam locomotives.

Anxiously, we glanced around the yard, but there were no signs of those watchmen.

Believing that providence had at last smiled on us, I followed my friend from the gatehouse, towards the great vessel moored to the dockside. We moved cautiously, darting between stacked wooden crates and stockpiles of timber and iron beams.

That this ship was the *Himalaya*, I had no doubt. End to end, her sleek black hull must have spanned 350 feet, maybe more. As a merchant vessel she'd be a graceful giant; gird her flanks with armour plate and you'd have a powerful mighty monster.

"Now I know why Jigsaw-man referred to those passages in the Good Book about Leviathan," I said.

Josiah gazed at the ship with a grim countenance. " 'Out of his mouth go burning lamps, and sparks of fire leap out. Out of his nostrils goeth smoke, as out of a seething pot or cauldron ... Upon earth there is not his like, who is made without fear.' " His polished tones gave the words a sharper edge of foreboding.

We moved towards the vessel. Less than halfway across

the yard, the toecap of my boot struck a discarded iron bolt, sending it skittering and chinking across the ground. Josiah's expression was someplace between a cringe and a scowl.

We pressed on. Tried to watch where I was treading, yet my eyes were constantly drawn to the gatehouse.

A blurry movement near that prison-like wall brought me to a halt. One of those watchmen? I hesitated, anticipating a cry of alarm, even a gunshot.

Josiah frowned. "What's wrong?"

"I think I saw something move, over by the wall."

His gaze followed mine, sweeping this way and that.

Both jumped backward as a grey shape shifted among the shadows.

Then we heard a familiar mewl and saw a large seagull go flapping into the air. Josiah made a sheepish smile. "Shipyards are a favourite haunt of those scavenging pests."

We hastened to the rear of the ship, where we found a broad companionway slanting up from the dockside to the quarterdeck.

As we stepped on board I experienced an odd sense of familiarity combined with strangeness. Although considerably larger, the layout of the upper deck was similar to that of both HMS *Vigilant* and Josiah's new command, the *Shearwater*. Yet this vessel was queerly empty of guns and nautical paraphernalia. Gave me an unsettling feeling that this was not a new vessel, but some ghost ship, abandoned by a desperate crew. Wind shivered the rigging, producing a low droning sound. Faint creakings lifted over the sides where the great vessel strained against her mooring ropes.

"I've never seen these on a merchantman." Josiah's excited voice shook me from my reflections. He was indicating semi-circular rail tracks that formed lace-like patterns along the deck. I knew from my time on board the *Vigilant* that these iron racers were used for swivelling big guns so they could be aimed at the enemy.

Brief flicker of light on the fringe of my vision made me turn to the gatehouse.

Probably nothing.

Surely nothing.

But where were those watchmen? Now this may sound downright muddle-headed, but I found myself wishing I could see them – then at least we'd know how to avoid them.

"Trinity, look you here." Squatting near the ship's side, Josiah used the tip of his pocket knife to draw a vertical line that displaced a tarry substance, like a ploughshare turning earth. When he reached a certain point, he turned the knife horizontal and drew a similar line; then another vertical and a final horizontal until he'd revealed a large rectangle.

"It's a gun port." Josiah said. "They'll have caulked them all with oakum and painted over the seams so as to present a flush appearance."

As he continued to probe the side of the vessel, I moved toward to the forecastle.

Passing the forward hatch, I heard another noise – this time like a distant rock-slide. Doubtless the wind soughing in the sails.

But there were no sails.

Something else then, not physical? Scolded myself for entertaining such superstition. This was no ghost ship, but a product of scientific engineering.

Bundling up my wits, I pressed on, walking quickly up to the ship's tapering bows. Leaning over the side, I gazed down at the soupy water – and there I saw Leviathan. Yes I did!

The sharp ramming beak was submerged a few feet below the surface, minding me of some old alligator astalk in the shallows. If further evidence was needed that the *Himalaya* was a man-of-war, this was it.

"Josiah, cast your eyes on this!"

I wasn't too concerned when he didn't reply. Must've stayed back on the quarterdeck, even gone below. He'd be pursuing his investigations on the lower decks, peering into holds and bunkers and boiler rooms and suchlike.

Began to make my way back.

Taking a lungful of air, I fixed to call Josiah's name, but then thought of those unseen watchmen and carried on in silence. Josiah would be waiting exactly where I'd left him, not ten minutes ago.

My friend was there all right. But not alone.

Standing on either side of him were two burly constables. This child's soul sank still further when I saw that Josiah done been handcuffed. Born free, raised as an officer of Queen Victoria's navy, he now had the aspect of a chattel slave on the auction block.

Casting around for blame, I could look no further than myself. No one else had brought my friend to this appalling pass.

Feelings of guilt, though, would have to wait. Right now, my duty to Josiah was to escape and expose the true nature of this diabolical enterprise.

Peering along the hull, I made out two more constables right aft and a further pair on the dockside near the companionway. With them were the two watchmen. No wonder we'd failed to see them – they'd been all this while alerting the authorities.

Moving back to the prow, I examined the thick mooring rope that ran from the bow to an iron bollard on the dockside. It would be a tricky business, but I reckoned I could lower myself along the mooring line and reach the jetty.

Easing myself quietly over the ship's side, I wrapped my arms around the mooring line, then flung my legs overboard, curling them round the rope. I'd planned to slide down to the dockside, but the rope wasn't as taut as it seemed and I went plunging toward the water. Muscles burned as the rope stiffened just a few feet from the surface. For a time, I couldn't move. Breath came in sharp, painful sobs. The water beneath me was still and stagnant. Big old rat went paddling by, spiky coat glistening in the dismal light. One slip and I'd surely drown, or die from swallowing that poisonous water. Yet I'd no choice but to proceed with my plan. Slowly, I started to work my way down the rope, moving first my arms, then my feet. The span from ship to shore couldn't have exceeded fifteen feet, but it seemed without end as the mooring line's coarse fibres pricked my fingers and scratched my face.

Nonetheless, I was making progress, shifting bit by bit closer to safety. Swift glance along the hull showed the constables and two watchmen still standing by the companionway.

At last, I lowered my feet and let myself drop onto the jetty.

The gatehouse seemed unattended. If I could find a way back through that side entrance, I'd be able to find Lady Alice and raise the alarm.

"You there!"

Words penetrated my ears like a hornet sting. A constable was bearing down on me from the doorway of a small workshop further along the jetty.

I bolted toward a stack of big wooden crates, but my shoes skidded on the loose gravel. I went tumbling on all fours, grazing hands and knees in a painful sprawl. Over rasping sucks of breath, I heard the fast-approaching crunch of boots.

Scrambling to my feet, I set off again toward the crates.

"You there, stop!"

His voice sounded devilish close. Panicky glance over my shoulder showed he was less than fifty yards behind and gaining fast – eyes wild, mouth agape, boots mashing the ground into a gritty cloud.

Lungs scorched as I closed on the stack of crates. Drawing nearer, there was a small aperture, like a door into a walled city. I darted towards it, turning my body side-on so I could squeeze through the narrow gap. Once inside, I found myself in a boxwood maze, threaded by narrow pathways. Quickly losing all sense of direction, I scurried left and right, again and again, until I careered into a dead-end. All but crashed into the wall that sealed it off.

I sank to the ground, heart pummelling as if some small critter got trapped in my rib cage and was trying to thump his way out.

Any moment now, I expected that constable to come in after me.

But he didn't. I strained for the sound of his approach. Nothing.

After some while, I recovered a little strength and took stock of my surroundings. It would be foolish to go back out the way I'd just come in, and there was no way forward. But there was a way upward. Mostly, the crates were stacked two or three deep. Yet half way along this dead-end passage, one box stood alone. Although it was five feet high, I was able to lever myself up by climbing on the battens nailed to its front. Once up, I realised a number of other crates had also been left one-deep. They formed a gloomy gorge between the rows of high-piled boxes. It zigzagged every which way, eventually bringing me to the edge of the stack.

Peering over the side, the shipyard was still and quiet. I was perhaps one hundred yards from the gatehouse and a careful look to either side revealed the way was clear. Maybe the constable was on the far side of these crates. So long as he wasn't here, I didn't much care.

Letting myself down to the ground as quietly as possible, I set off towards a large iron tank, some halfway to the gatehouse. Moving slowly, resisting the compulsion to run, I came up to the tank and concealed myself behind it. Another look round. Still no sign of the constable. I didn't fool myself that he given up his search, but dared to hope that my situation was looking brighter.

Treading carefully on the stony ground, anxious not to kick or crush any object that might attract attention, I set off again for the gatehouse.

Closer, closer still … thirty yards … twenty … I could see the flaking green paintwork and the rusted hinges on the big doors.

Freedom beckoned.

Hope began to rise.

Then tumbled with a crash.

Felt the noise, rather than heard it: familiar clink of iron chain, scrape of boots on gravel. Turning, I saw the constable appear from behind a pile of steel rods, barely fifteen feet away. In one hand he held a truncheon, in the other a pair of iron cuffs.

26

Recollections of a Confederate General by Jubal de Brooke

Liverpool, England, December, 1863.

Sarah McConville graced me with a warm smile and fond embrace as I was shown into the drawing room. She was dressed as if for some lavish occasion, though I knew from a previous conversation that she had no such commitments that day.

"What do you think, Jubal?" She stepped back, enabling me to see the dress of luxuriant silk.

"You look very lovely, my dear," I murmured, preferring not to imagine how much she'd paid for that mountain of frothy fabric while her family's business gathered pace in the general direction of hell. Yet I couldn't help but reflect that this profligacy was so very unlike the woman I'd come so to admire.

"It arrived this very morning, direct from Tipston's in Regent Street – that is *the* Regent Street, the one in London.

Mrs Marjoribanks recommends Tipston's most highly. She knows so much about these matters."

There was an awkward silence before I managed to say, "I gather your father is not at home this morning?"

"You're the very devil of a chap, Jubal!" Taking my hand in hers, she urged me towards the stairs. "Come along, then, we can dress again later."

When I refused to move, she turned to me with an arch smile. Yet the frank honesty that had drawn me to her from the outset seemed to have been replaced by unappealing forwardness. "I see. You want me here in the drawing room? Very saucy, if I may make so bold – but then you are the bold one, are you not?"

Presenting me with her back, she flicked intricate spirals of blonde hair from her bare shoulders. "Hurry – unfasten me."

Instead, I took her by the shoulders and turned her to face me. Still, there seemed to be no awareness that this was anything but the occasion of one lover calling on another.

"I'm not here for pleasure, Sarah," I said, "but a matter of grave importance. I want to speak to you alone, which was why I inquired about your father's absence."

Her features arranged themselves into an agreeable smile and I noticed that her hair had been elaborately arranged in coils and ringlets.

"You are a crabby fellow today, Jubal. A drink, perhaps to elevate your humour?"

"It is not yet eleven o'clock." Her behaviour was such that I suspected she might already have been drinking.

"No matter, we are free spirits, are we not? Libertarians both."

"You should know that I went to see Jimmy Bulloch yesterday." She shot me a look of surprise.

"A delightful man, is he not?"

"The meeting was not a social one."

"Then what?" She moved nimbly to a crystal decanter, removing its heavy stopper.

Pouring herself a substantial measure of brandy, Sarah looked at me with an expression of vague boredom. "I shall have a drink, even if you shan't."

"Bulloch knows nothing of the *Himalaya*."

She jammed the stopper back in the decanter so hard I thought the glass would shatter. "Why should he? It's not his business."

"It's his job to buy ships for the South, is it not? It's exactly and entirely his damned business."

"How dare you raise your voice to me, Jubal." Her eyes gleamed fiercely above the small horizon of her brandy globe. "And how do you know about the *Himalaya*? My father's been talking to you, hasn't he?"

"Your father deserves better from you, Sarah." By now I'd obtained control of my temper. "I deserve better."

"And you shall have better, my dear Jubal." Sipping the liquor, she set down the glass and approached me with extended arms. "Come, let us go to my chamber."

I took her hands in mine but held her back from the embrace she intended. "The *Himalaya* is a warship, isn't she? Built in secret behind Bulloch's back for States Rights Rankin and Arthur Harrowby."

"Yes, she is. She is a warship. And a very fine one." Sarah's demeanour had veered from one of ebullience to chilly defiance. "Not a ship afloat to match her except the *Warrior* class."

"Why did you agree to build her? You must have known your father wouldn't countenance it? That it was unlawful?"

"I'm building her for the Confederacy, Jubal. For you!"

"You laid her keel two years ago, Sarah, before you knew I existed."

"Well, then, I did it for your cause – it's the same as doing it for you." She smiled and tried to thrust herself forward, lips pursed to kiss mine.

Gripping her hands more tightly, I forced her back. "You did it for money."

"You're crushing my hands, Jubal!"

Releasing my grip, I took refuge from her advances behind a chair.

"I needed that money in a way you and your like couldn't begin to imagine."

"How can that be so when you and your father own one of the most prosperous shipyards on the Mersey?"

"Shipyards can fail. Any business can fail." Her tone had become more reasonable. "With the profits from the *Himalaya* invested in bonds, I need never worry about returning to the slums of Scotland Road."

"And yet here you are, having brought your father's business from great success to the edge of insolvency."

"It's not my fault, Jubal, none of it. How was I to know that Arthur's fondness for the faro tables would lead him into such debt?"

I couldn't prevent sour mirth escaping my throat. "So Arthur couldn't pay for the ship and still you proceeded on capital borrowed from the bank. When they started to talk about foreclosure, you and Arthur put your heads together with Rankin and produced me – the perfect solution to your financial problems."

She frowned. "I did no such thing."

"Don't treat me like a fool, Sarah."

"Please explain, Jubal, how any of this business is connected to you?" Her unaffected anger took me aback.

Was it possible that she was ignorant of the blackmail plot?

Deciding to test her, I explained the entire story, all the while watching her expression for indications of complicity. None were apparent.

"I don't care if you're not blue-blooded, Jubal." There was fresh excitement in her tone. "Nor whether your grandfather was an earl or a lackey. What matters now is that we can both of us achieve great wealth for ourselves and keep our good names."

"How so?"

"Simply by your handing over the monies from the Liberty Bazaar. You would be following orders issued by a member of the Confederate government – no blame could attach – and our profit would be enormous." Her eyes glistened. "If the *Himalaya* succeeds in breaking the Union blockade – as I'm sure she will – there will be more lucrative orders, more profit. We would become rich beyond measure. This is not a calamity, but a glorious opportunity."

"It isn't so simple, Sarah."

"But of course it is. Your choice could not be clearer. You must give Arthur and Senator Rankin that money. If you do, your future and mine will be assured. If you do not, we shall be ruined, both."

"What of honour? Of law? More important still, what would I say to the destitute widows and children of those boys who have fallen in battle?"

"When the war is won, when the South has her independence, restitution can be made."

"It would be too late. These people need relief now, not in six months or a year. There is no restitution from the grave."

"This is a matter of survival, Jubal – yours and mine."

"And to the devil with principle and decency?"

"I can tell you've spent some good while in my father's sanctimonious presence."

Her remark was perplexing. "I haven't seen your father today, nor any day this week."

For the first time, since I arrived, she acquired a worried look. "We exchanged angry words and he left the house in a temper, calling for the brougham. I presumed he'd gone to see you; that you were here in consequence."

She looked around anxiously, as if for clues.

"I guess he'll have gone to the waterfront for some fresh air." I spoke reassuringly, as she seemed on the edge of tears.

Pulling herself together, her voice came in anxious sputters. "You shall obtain those funds, Jubal. We shall complete the ship. We shall drive out the wicked spectre of poverty."

"There is no wicked spectre, Sarah. It is in your mind only." Leaning forward, I took the glass of liquor from her. She surrendered it without demur, like a child relieved of a toy that had lost all fascination.

"I'll not go back. Never. Better dead."

"Back where?" I reached out to her, but now she backed away from me.

"Never never."

"You mean Scotland Road? You should abandon such silly thoughts, Sarah."

Retreating to the fireplace, she placed her head in her hands, kneading her scalp as if to placate some wriggling demon within.

"Sarah, you must collect yourself."

"Go to your bankers, Jubal. Fetch those monies." When she turned back to me, I saw that various artificial hair pieces had started to come loose – an arrangement of ringlets slipped forward over her brow, giving the impression that her hairline was advancing over her face; a pile of coiled tresses had fallen to one side, like a bird's nest dislodged from a thicket.

Her eyes, too, had a wild aspect. "Go. Go now. Do not tarry."

Unable to calm or reason with her, I did as she demanded, thinking to return later in the day.

Soon after I'd left the house, a cab drew up outside and from it stepped a dapper young man attired in a Brunswick green frock coat. He seemed vaguely familiar.

Only that morning, I'd have pondered on his arrival, perhaps felt a prod of jealousy – at the very least, curiosity. Now, I felt nothing but guilty relief to be gone from that house.

Climbing into my carriage, I bade the driver take me to the waterfront. I, too, would benefit from a dose of clear air; and perhaps find Thomas McConville, whose disappearance had distressed his daughter.

As my coach turned the corner into Mount Pleasant, I recalled the identity of Sarah's visitor: he was Erasmus Pickering, the banker she'd importuned at Lady Chalcross' garden party. This was evidently why she'd spent all that time preparing herself. I cringed at the impression she'd make if she received him, with her hair – like her thoughts – in such a tangle.

Yet I had distractions of my own. In particular, what I was going to do with £28,000 entrusted to my safekeeping.

27

EXPERIENCES IN THE LIFE OF A SLAVE GIRL BY TRINITY GIDDINGS

Liverpool, England, December, 1863.

"Game's up, lad." The constable gave me a fearsome look. "It'll go badly for you if you give me trouble." Almost laughable that he considered me capable of resistance. Dead-beat and dismayed, I held out my arms and let him shackle my wrists.

As he steered me towards a large commercial building at the far end of the shipyard, the cold metal cuffs chafed my skin and the jingle of iron chains spoke to me in a language none but a chattel slave could comprehend.

This sense of defeat became all the more hurtful when I was taken into a clerks' office and found Josiah, similarly bound.

Standing beside him was the chief constable, who threw me a harsh look. "You would be Miss Giddings?"

Since he had clearly obtained this information from Josiah, I confirmed it with a surly nod.

"You have been arrested for trespass," he told me. "However, in light of your friend's claim to be a naval officer and you being a foreigner, we've requested the magistrate to attend."

"What will happen then?" I asked.

Chief constable regarded me with a condescending expression. "The magistrate will decide what to do with the pair of you."

"We must be patient, Trinity." There was a hint of warning in Josiah's tone that suggested further conversation with our captors was not desirable.

Josiah was only too correct about the need for patience. Sitting in those stuffy confines, we soon became tired of exchanging stoical shrugs and reassuring smiles. Big clock on the wall showed nearly two hours had gone by before that magistrate arrived.

His name was Sir Lionel Jervis and he was a narrow-faced fellow in his late middle years with frosty hair and harsh eyes. When he entered the office, we were ordered to stand and it soon became clear that Sir Lionel was treating this little office as a court of law.

First thing he did was instruct the constables to remove our handcuffs. This was hardly the chiefest of my present concerns, but went some way to restoring my dignity.

Next, the magistrate addressed Josiah. As a serving naval officer, there was a question of legal jurisdiction, so Sir Lionel done sent a telegram to the Admiralty and received a reply ordering Josiah to report immediately to London.

Josiah nodded grimly, said nothing.

Turning to me, Sir Lionel made a rheumy expression. "I will state immediately, Miss Giddings, that I find your current condition most regrettable. I have always been a friend to abolitionism, but by breaking the law you do that noble cause a great disservice."

Now that angered me. I wanted to tell him to look with his own eyes at the evidence of law breaking that lay in the shape of the *Himalaya*, not one hundred yards away in the Great Float. Stole a quick glance at Josiah, but he seemed to read my thoughts and shook his head.

Sir Lionel's voice became gravelly. "I have spoken on this matter with your sponsor, Lady Alice Featherfax, who has agreed to stand surety in the sum of £20. The condition I attach to your bail is that you reside with Lady Alice in Falkner Square, until further notice."

Of course, I was powerful relieved to discover that he wasn't going to put me in jail, yet I was also anxious to know when my trial would take place.

"That depends on the shipyard owners." Magistrate gave me a sharp stare. "We will discover presently whether they wish charges to be brought."

*

Four days later, I learnt that the bail conditions had been lifted in a note from Josiah. Eager to find out why, I set off by carriage for the little shop in Vernon Street.

Josiah was waiting at the shop door. Without a word, he took my hand as I stepped from the carriage and led me into the shop. Its warm redolence of teasel root and celandine, Queen Anne's lace and milk thistle acted as a welcome antidote to the pungent whiffs out on the street.

In the parlour, Josiah poured out two cups of tea and bade me sit facing him at the hearth.

"So, tell me what's happened," I demanded, impatiently.

He finished stirring his tea and looked up with a wan smile.

"The nub of it is that the McConvilles do not wish to pursue a prosecution. This is hardly surprising as a court hearing would halt their conspiracy and expose their activities to public examination."

Looked down at the amber tea in my cup. "Our position isn't so good, is it?"

When he didn't reply, I looked up, anxiously. "What is to become of you, Josiah?"

"Normally there would be a court martial, but this would be acutely embarrassing for the government and their Lordships of the Admiralty are determined that this will not happen."

More bad news to come, this child could tell that much. Yet I waited, allowing Josiah to tell me in his own time.

"I've received orders to take *Shearwater* to Cape Town, thence to the China station via Madras. I am directed to leave on the next available tide."

Looked at him quizzically: had I heard him correctly?

In my confusion, I forgot to hold onto my tea cup and felt it slide between my fingers. Fine porcelain shattered, hot orange liquid spattering the polished wooden floor.

Neither of us moved. I'd known for some weeks that Josiah would be leaving for China. But not right now, like this.

Once more, my friend Josiah surprised me. "I shan't go. I'll refuse to obey my orders and force a court martial."

I looked at him, appalled. "But you would surely ruin your career."

Small shrug from Josiah. "It must be done."

Gazed down at the spilled tea pooling round the wrecked china. Thoughts skittered every which way. After some while, I gave him a spiky look. "No, Josiah, it must not be done. By the time your court martial could be held, the *Himalaya* would have long since quit these shores. You'd achieve nothing but the destruction of your ambitions – all you've dreamed of since you were a child."

"That is of small consequence – "

I came to my feet indignantly. "Your duty is to show the world how black folk can succeed at anything they desire – which includes the very important duty of commanding one of Her Majesty's ships."

Knocked by my vehemence, he looked up at me, blinking. "But I can't leave you here, alone."

"And I can't let you toss away all you've worked for." Didn't flinch, no not once. "Besides, you were ready to leave me in Liverpool before this *Himalaya* business blew up. You said I should find happiness and fulfilment in Great Britain, did you not?"

Josiah stood up, took my hands in his. "You should know that Sir Eustace Baggott is making moves to have you deported to the United States."

Laughed to scorn Little Big Man. "We can still prevent the *Himalaya* from leaving Liverpool."

There was a curious humour in his voice. "I might be forgiven for thinking you want rid of me, Trinity."

"You would not be forgiven for thinking that, Josiah." At that juncture my resolve wilted some. Turned my face to disguise the moisture in my eyes.

It was like this: never in my life had I loved a man so much as Josiah; yet if this love was to be worthy, I could not let him destroy himself. Been studying, also, on the nature of our bond; seen, at last, that Josiah had always been more a father to me than a lover. Time this child grew up, learned to stand on her own feet.

Yet despite all these righteous thoughts, I was powerful scared.

Standing by the window overlooking the sunless canyon of Vernon Street, I felt his hands on my shoulders, turning me round to face him. Resisted at first, then succumbed.

"There's no shame in tears, Trinity."

"I do so want you to stay, Josiah."

"I know."

"But you will obey those orders, won't you?"

"I'll think on it," he said.

*

Josiah went a piece further than thinking on it: he sailed away, with not so much as a goodbye kiss.

Courier arrived soon after dawn with a note that said little, but delivered a mighty punch. In his elegant, sloping hand, Josiah announced that he'd decided to act on my entreaty and was, at that moment, taking the *Shearwater* to sea. Asked my forgiveness for parting in this way, but hoped I'd understand that a farewell on the dockside would be still more painful, and requested that I stay at home in Falkner Square. The note closed with an expression of deep affection, and a curiously optimistic confidence that justice would be done.

Not for the first time, I ignored his wishes and took a cab to the waterfront, my head whirling with anger and anguish. Yet even as the cab clattered and bounced on the damp cobblestones, I struggled to reconcile my sentiments. Had Josiah not done precisely what I'd demanded of him? Was it not true that a parting on the dockside would have achieved nothing but greater hurt for the both of us?

Such questions soon proved by the bye. When the cab pulled up near George's Pier, the *Shearwater* was already steering towards the central channel of the Mersey.

I looked on, helpless, as she vanished amid the multitude of vessels thronging the river.

Yet again, I felt so very lonesome. Stood there a good while, as if Josiah might change his mind and the *Shearwater* would re-emerge from the early morning haze.

"A fine ship, is she not?" The voice was a whispery croak.

Looked round, a mite irritated by this intrusion, to see a frail old boy with milky, unfocused eyes and a mauve slit of a mouth. Whittled out features draped in papery skin gave the impression he'd tumbled from a coffin.

But such thoughts were uncharitable. "Do you mean the *Shearwater*?"

"I do indeed."

Smiled kindly at this poorly little fellow; perhaps he had a son in Josiah's crew and was here to see him off. "Do you have someone on board who is dear to you?"

Old boy's dry laugh sounded like a wooden spoon being run across the ridges of a washboard. "No one save the ship herself."

Got the impression he was scorning me. "How do you figure that?"

"I built her." Purple mouth stretched in the merest smile.

Disturbing inklings began to stir in the back of my head – sense of things stacking up in a way they shouldn't.

"I'm Thomas McConville." He extended a narrow hand. "I'm pleased to make your acquaintance, Miss Giddings."

"Should I be pleased to make yours, Mr McConville?" Puzzlement, fear, suspicion began jostling for attention as this child tried to make sense of the encounter.

"I believe you will be, if you will hear me out."

Gave him a chilly look. "In view of what has lately transpired, Mr McConville, why do you imagine I should want to listen to anything you have to say?"

"Because Commander Mill did."

That shook me.

"You spoke to Josiah?"

"Shortly before he left. The truth is that I convinced him to do so – though I do confess he drove a hard bargain."

No wind in my sails now, not a puff. Had I not persuaded Josiah to follow his orders? And what was this talk about making bargains?

"Josiah would sooner deal with the devil than a rakehell such as States Rights Rankin."

Slight hint of humour in those swampy eyes. "Quite right too. It was precisely to avoid having to deal with Rankin that I set various wheels in motion, not the least of which was approaching Commander Mill."

I blinked, seeing this fellow in a very different light. Thomas McConville was no feeble old turkey, I could tell that much.

As if reading my mind, he dipped into his pilot coat and took out a large document file wrapped up in oilskin. "These are the design plans and contract between the Pasham & Edgeport Steam Navigation Company and my shipyard. They contain the detailed information you require to have the vessel seized and all commercial activity surrounding her suspended."

Squinted, striving to readjust my thoughts. One half of me suspected another trap; the other half told me this was too downright peculiar to be anything other than what it seemed.

"Why are you doing this, Mr McConville?"

His sharp-sloping shoulders lifted in a small shrug. "A rare coincidence of conscience and self-interest, Miss Giddings. You know, of course, that my company has been constructing blockade runners for the South for some time. You may disapprove morally, but I'm sure you agree that in legal terms these vessels are entirely proper." Stony resonance entered his crackly voice as he went on. "Building warships for the Confederacy is another matter. Warships are illegal and immoral and I won't be a party to any such enterprise."

I frowned, more out of confusion than criticism. "Forgive me, Mr McConville, but hasn't your shipyard given over some two years to the building of precisely such a vessel?"

"Yes, indeed – though without my knowledge or consent. The deterioration of my health has been gradual and the running of the shipyard has passed increasingly to my daughter, whose attitude to commercial risk has become more and more wayward. I say this as an admission, not an abnegation of responsibility."

Rheumy eyes gazed forlornly over my shoulder at the watery highway of the Mersey. "Had I been available to counsel and assist Sarah, this damned project would never have been sanctioned. I'm afraid I failed her when she most needed a father's hand."

"You cannot be blamed for the condition of your health, Mr McConville." Not sure why I said that to him, to this man who, until moments earlier, I'd considered to be my implacable enemy.

Old boy shivered in the strengthening wind. Thought it might blow him off his feet, but he stayed upright. "Of course, I can only deal with circumstances as I find them. When I discovered by accident the ruinous nature of this *Himalaya* project, I was appalled. The shipyard is in enormous peril – and with it the livelihoods of many thousands of workmen – because Sarah borrowed from the bank in expectation of payment from Pasham & Edgeport which has not been forthcoming."

He paused, wheezy gasps filling the silence between us, as

he strove to fill those depleted lungs with enough strength to continue. "So, conscience, yes; but also self-interest in the welfare of my daughter and the future of the business that I laid up from nought."

"How can you serve either by giving me these documents?"

Old boy made another rattling chuckle. "Even if the *Himalaya* venture succeeded in lifting the Federal blockade, the shipyard would lose orders because there would be no demand for blockade runners, which are our most profitable business activity. No, what I need to save the shipyard is a buyer for the *Himalaya*, able to pay her full value and guarantee payment so the bank will drop its foreclosure action."

I regarded this wily old boy with rising fascination – perhaps even a touch of admiration. "I presume you have identified such a buyer, Mr McConville."

"It's quite simple, really, Miss Giddings. You will take the designs and contract for the *Himalaya* to the United States consul. Mr Dudley will waste no time in ensuring the British government seizes the vessel, as the Laird rams were seized, and the shipyard will recover all losses by selling the ship to the Royal Navy, as the Laird ships were sold."

Lord, there was no shortage of devious folk: no not in Liverpool. And yet, I'd laid up a respect for this sickly old man and his determination to do right, as he saw it.

"You mentioned that Josiah drove a hard bargain."

"Understandably, Commander Mill was reluctant to accept my disclosure at first sight. In return for quitting Liverpool, he demanded a sworn affidavit from me setting forth the role of my company in the *Himalaya* affair. If I failed to supply you with the documents in sufficient time to prevent the ship from falling into Confederate hands, this affidavit could be used by Commander Mill, effectively to destroy the shipyard."

So Josiah had done a deal with Thomas McConville before he left port. No wonder his note conveyed such confidence that justice would be done.

"Why did you want rid of Josiah? Why not give these plans and contracts directly to him?"

"Commander Mill has embarrassed certain parties at the Admiralty once too often. If they were to agree to abandon a court martial, they insisted that he quit these shores immediately. You, on the other hand, are not under their authority."

"You persuaded them against the court martial?"

That old boy gave me a knowing look. "I haven't spent these thirty years building ships for the Royal Navy without becoming well enough acquainted with influential individuals to call in a favour or two. It was merely a question of opening their eyes to the embarrassing folly of a public trial."

Thinking of Josiah, I couldn't help but chuckle some. "Far from wanting to avoid a court martial, Josiah welcomed one."

"I knew his reputation and feared as much, which was why I went to see him." Old boy's quaggy eyes brightened a shade and he regarded me fondly. "I'm immensely grateful to you, Miss Giddings, in that you'd already done the hard work. The commander explained this to me when we'd completed our agreement."

He pressed the oilskin-wrapped documents into my hands. "Take these immediately to the United States Consulate. Mr Dudley will know what to do."

Old boy returned to his carriage, moving with small, painful steps.

"Mr McConville!"

Slowly, he peered back at me.

"I do wish you well."

He just managed to touch the brim of his derby hat, though

I doubted he had sufficient strength to lift it. "And I you, Miss Giddings."

*

With fierce, fresh hope burning in my veins, I clutched the oilskin-wrapped documents tight to my breast and returned directly to the cab that had waited by George's Baths, some fifty yards distant.

I instructed the driver to take me to the United States Consulate in Water Street and the cab moved off, leaving the gunmetal Mersey behind. Perched on the deep blue seat, excited fitten to burst, this child imagined Thomas Haines Dudley's mule-face breaking into a reluctant smile as he examined the evidence we'd all been hunting for. At last, I could settle into some kind of normal life, here in my adopted country.

Strange how the memory tricks you, for I could have sworn that seat done been covered in green plush. But Mr McConville's revelations had been truly astounding. No matter that I'd been mistaken on such a trifle.

My only regret was that Josiah wasn't here to witness our victory, for his part in it was no less than anyone's. I considered, too, driving first back to Falkner Square so that Lady Alice might attend the US Consulate, also. But Mr McConville done been quite correct in instructing me to deliver those documents without delay. Alice and I could celebrate later, perhaps with a glass of champagne.

The cab paused at the entrance to Water Street and I began fishing in my purse for some coins to pay the fare. Glancing through the window, I saw the pale stone of the Tower Buildings where the consulate was located.

"How much?" I asked.

"Right smart more 'n you got, girl."

Blurry movement in the window frame. I looked round to see Fat-boy standing on the foot plate. Before I could move, he'd thrust himself into the cab. Smell of whiskey and onions carrying on his breath; great pillows of flesh pressing me against the back of the cab; and something sharp and painful in my ribs.

"One wrong move, girl, I'll open you like a catfish."

Looked down and saw a knife-blade gleaming in the small space between us.

"I'll take that, Missy."

A hand reached down through the driver's hatch and grabbed the oilskin wallet from my gasp. It seemed appallingly clear now that these kidnappers done been watching my meeting with Thomas McConville very closely.

Caught a glimpse of Blessing Dubois at the reins before the hatch slammed shut.

Then the cab was racing hellward along Water Street and all my dreams of a fresh and fulfilling life gone with it.

28

RECOLLECTIONS OF A CONFEDERATE GENERAL BY JUBAL DE BROOKE
Liverpool, England, December, 1863.

U nable to sustain my anger with Sarah, I found myself quitting the rooms I'd taken at the Wellington Hotel in Dale Street and returning to the McConvilles' town house in Abercromby Square.

Some five hours had passed since our heated exchange and on reflection, I felt I'd been too harsh with her. I hoped to apologise and set matters right.

In the event, Sarah was not at home, but her father was.

In the drawing room, McConville offered me a glass of brandy which I accepted gratefully.

His voice was an alloy of agitation and concern. "Much as I'm glad to see you, my dear Jubal, I had hoped to see Sarah walk through that door. She left some several hours since without telling the servants where she was going. I sent to the shipyard, but she has not been seen there all day. I even dispatched my footman to the home of that incorrigible tattler Mrs Marjoribanks, but she, for once, had no 'intelligence' to report."

Sensing that the time for tact was gone, I decided on a direct approach. "Thomas, I know you and Sarah quarrelled this morning on the subject of the *Himalaya*. She told me you'd parted on bad terms and was worried about your welfare – as I was."

"You are a considerate friend, Jubal." That thin, waspish smile teased his lips. "Did she also explain the nature of the *Himalaya*?"

I met his glaucous gaze. "I know the vessel is an ironclad warship meant for the Confederate Navy, and that Harrowby and Rankin are behind it."

"Damn Arthur and damn Rankin. But more than either, damn me." If my friend had possessed the strength he would have hollered those words; as it happened, they stumbled from his damaged lungs like wounded boys from a battlefield.

"Thomas, this situation is neither your fault nor of your making." I laid two hands on his shoulders, urging him to take a seat. I'd never touched him in that manner before and was shocked by the flimsiness of his body. "Sarah is a mature woman, experienced in commercial affairs and aware of cause and consequence. The time for excusing her, for reassigning her blame to yourself, is finished."

He refused to look at me. "Whatever happens next, those scoundrels Harrowby and Rankin will not lay hands on that ironclad, and nor will my business go to the wall."

Kneeling beside him, I spoke gently, as if to a frightened soldier. "What have you done, Thomas?"

He looked at me now, a strange defiance dancing in the blurry eyes. "I've given the design plans to Trinity Giddings.

Aye, and the contract implicating Harrowby and Rankin. But not before I spoke to an old associate at the Admiralty and made damned sure the navy will give us a good price for the *Himalaya*."

Despite the loss to my cause, I couldn't prevent a fond and admiring smile for this decrepit, yet boundlessly clever old fellow. Not only had he done the right thing, he'd saved his business and made a tidy profit into the bargain.

I felt a surge of joy, too, as I realised that his action had removed the need for me to subvert funds from the widows and orphans towards the purchase of the *Himalaya*.

Moreover, I had a strange sense of satisfaction that Trinity Giddings would finally triumph over Rankin and obtain public vindication for her actions.

Finishing my brandy, I set the glass down on the mantelpiece and gave him a stern look. "There's something you should know about me, Thomas. I, too, am caught up in this conspiracy. I'm not the man you thought I was."

When I'd done explaining the story of my grandfather's imposture and Harrowby and Rankin's blackmail plot, my friend made a pained expression. "Jubal, you are *exactly* the man I thought you were."

The sound of the doorbell ended our conversation.

We waited, with rising apprehension, as the footman went to the door.

Any hope that Sarah had come home vanished when the footman entered the drawing room with a message from the watchman at the India Works.

I was barely able to contain my impatience as my friend took out his spectacles and read the note.

At last, he gave me a grim look. "There's been a serious accident at the shipyard."

"Is anyone injured there?"

Crumpling the note in his fist, he gestured to the door. "The watchman hasn't said. We must go there immediately."

The brougham was drawn up at the front door and McConville and I clambered in. We set off at a canter along Mount Pleasant, but the evening was drawing in and the streets became increasingly choked with carriages and omnibuses. We moved like driftwood in a slow-moving stream into Church Street. My friend fidgeted incessantly with the pewter handle of his walking stick as the carriage skirted Derby Square and headed along James Street. The traffic on the water front was still more congested and we found ourselves stationary amid an angry dispute over right-of-way between two equally stubborn cab drivers.

"We'd be faster on foot," McConville said, flinging open the carriage door.

In spite of his infirmity, we hurried along the sidewalk. In the gas-lit gloom, I glimpsed the wares of street hawkers: eels wriggling in shallow bowls; pails of rancid-smelling fish-gut; a tub of freshly hacked pigs' feet; a rail of plucked geese, the texture of their skin disturbingly human. A long-limbed man, encumbered by chains and heavy iron collars, loomed in the sickly weaving gaslight. For an instant I imagined his goods to be bonds for slaves, then heard his hawker's call and realised he was selling restraints for guard dogs. Faint figures loomed from the thickening dusk. I barged them aside, leaving behind a wake of curses and profanities.

Somehow McConville had kept pace with me and we shuffled in a slow-shifting queue for the Woodside ferry.

Pushing ourselves into the overcrowded boat, we waited in silence as it steered for the opposite bank. The crossing was uncomfortable and seemingly interminable. My vision filled with gaudy splashes of boats' lights on the dark Mersey; nostrils with the tarry reek of coal-smoke; ears with the urgent churn of the paddle wheels.

I could think only of Sarah.

She would be safe: of course she would.

But what if she wasn't?

Why hadn't the watchman been more specific? Damn the man, damn him.

We took a cab from the landing stage at Woodside, arriving at the shipyard gates after a frustrating grind through Birkenhead.

The elderly watchman was awaiting our arrival. Lifting his cloth cap to McConville, his words came in an anxious rush: "There's been a terrible accident on board the *Himalaya*, sir. Physician's with her now."

"Her? You mean my daughter?"

The watchman nodded.

"What happened?"

"Thought the yard was empty, sir. Suddenly there was this cry from the *Himalaya*. I went to look. Found her on the lower deck, sir. Unconscious. Seems she'd fallen through the main hatch. Called the physician straight away, sir."

Turning to me, McConville pointed with his walking stick to the long black bulk of the *Himalaya*. "Please go there directly, Jubal. I'll follow as quickly as I can."

Sprinting across the yard, I hastened up the companionway onto the ship. I found the main hatch described by the watchman and started to descend a series of steep steps into the sour-smelling gut of the vessel. My way was lit by oil lamps, their lemony flames reflecting from sharp, hard surfaces. At the foot of the third set of steps, I found myself facing a great brass chronometer on the lower deck.

"Over here."

The voice came from behind me and I turned to see the physician kneeling beside Sarah. She was lying on the deck. His lantern threw a pallid wash across her face, which seemed remarkably peaceful.

I stooped into the small cone of light. "How is she?"

The physician gave me a sombre look and shook his head.

I took Sarah's hand which she'd balled into a fist and squeezed it.

"Sarah, my dear ..."

"I'm so sorry, Jubal ..." Her voice was a faint whisper. I leaned closer.

"Nothing to be sorry for, Sarah, nothing at all ..."

"N-never ... going ... back ... " She was barely breathing.

"Of course you're not, my dear. You're safe now." I gripped her hand more tightly. "Your father has made everything right. He will be here very shortly."

The briefest flicker of a smile, then her hand went limp and I watched the light seep from her eyes. Although I'd seen so many die in battle, this was especially hard to bear.

"Do you know how this happened?" I asked the doctor, feeling somewhat in a daze.

"I'd surmise that she tripped in the poor light. Unfortunately, all the deck hatches had been left open so there was nothing to break her fall."

Still gripping Sarah's hand, I raised it to my lips, but stopped when I caught sight of some cotton threads between her fingers. Prising them open, I found in her palm a heavy brass button stitched to a fragment of dark green cloth.

Sarah could not have been alone when she fell.

29

Experiences in the Life of a Slave Girl by Trinity Giddings

Liverpool, England, December, 1863.

The cab rattled lickety-split over the street cobbles while Fat-boy kept the tip of his blade pressed hard against the flesh below my rib cage.

After some short distance, he fished a raw onion from his pocket and crunched into it with his spade-like teeth. Hard to tell which was the more unpleasant, knife or onion. Fumes attacked my eyes, making them sting and fill with water. Tears went running down one cheek, then the other.

This made Fat-boy chuckle and he called up to Blessing Dubois, sitting in the driver's seat. "Poor little missy's weeping like a babe."

"I am not weeping. It's your disgusting onion making my eyes water."

This child's irritation seemed only to increase Fat-boy's amusement. "Well, if you ain't weeping now, you will be when our Massa's done with you."

Gave him a piercing stare. "Know what truly makes me want to cry?"

His grin merely widened. "Now what might that be?"

"Why, the sight of you two boys lickspittling to that hell-hound Rankin."

"You think you're right smart better'n me and Blessing, don't you, girl?" Fat-boy chuckled, but when he spoke again there was menace as well as mockery in his voice. "You'd better watch that mouth of yours."

"Don't you have any conscience? Don't you want our people to be free?"

Fat-boy put on a teasing expression. "Freedom? Now what's that? Why, I'll tell you what. It's a bunch of dreamy notions thought up by Yankees and Limeys with no honest work to do. Does freedom put a roof over your head, food in your belly?"

Strove in vain to douse my exasperation. "But here in Britain you can be free – you *are* free."

The point of that blade pinched a mite deeper. "Don't patronise me, little missy. Blessing and me, we been places: we done things you couldn't imagine. Our Massa trusts us, see. With trust we get rewards. Who needs freedom?"

"What about the rest of your kin – millions of souls toiling in bondage?"

"Let 'em toil."

"While you perform tricks for your Massa? You're no better than those little dogs – worse. Leastways they've got the excuse of being dumb animals."

Must've packed a powerful dose of bile in my tone for I pricked right through that Fat-boy's bubble of mirth, replacing it with bald rage. Tossing the onion through the cab window, he drew back his fist.

"You better not do that, Clement!" Blessing Dubois hollered down through the driver's hatch. "You put a mark on her, Massa won't take kindly."

Fat-boy lowered his fist. "You're right, Blessing. She ain't worth it."

Smile returned as he pushed his quilted cheek close to mine. "See, our Massa wants a clean slate to put his own marks on."

*

This child never truly hated a man as much as States Rights Rankin, who was presently sitting before me in the drawing room of Dunstead Manor. By Rankin's feet sat those two pesky Jack Russell terriers I'd outsmarted by tossing strips of liver onto the floor at the Liberty Bazaar.

Was that my measure? Getting the better of two little dogs?

Quick glance around the room confirmed we were alone. I'd half expected Lord Harrowby to be there, since this was his home. I reflected, too, that Jubal de Brooke had been staying at the manor, as Harrowby's guest, and hoped he might be present.

"Do you intend this silence to frighten me?" I spoke boldly enough, though in truth I was powerful anxious. With Josiah having sailed away and my whereabouts unknown to Lady Alice, I was helpless. Maybe if Soldier-boy was hereabouts I could get a message to him, for I was sure he wouldn't tolerate abduction and kidnap. Yet, taking account of the events that done already occurred that day, how could I be certain of anything?

"Your misguided British friends have taught you insolence aplenty." Mouth moved, man didn't. "I shall rectify that when I take you back to Society Hill."

Now that did scare me. Worse, he saw the fear register on my face.

"See that sheet of paper?" His boulder of a head inclined slightly, indicating a legal-looking document lying on the small table near his chair. "It's a contract of sale that completes a transaction between your former Massa, Zebulon Giddings, and your new one." Thin smile appeared in his countenance, like a fissure running across a cliff face. "That would be me."

Recouping myself quickly, I cut my eyes on him. "We both know that document has no legal power outside the Confederacy."

"That is of small consequence since we will shortly be back in South Carolina. A blockade runner is leaving Liverpool, bound for Charleston, tomorrow. You and I will be on it, though I'm afraid your return voyage will not include the use of officers' quarters."

Panicky thoughts went spinning round my head. Not till that moment did I realise the extent of his scheming. For all my escapades, I'd be returned to bondage in far crueller circumstances than I'd left. It was a sickening prospect.

"I even had your name changed," he said. "You shall be called Trinity Rankin. How does that suit?"

"Slave name, like any other." I pretended indifference. "Why should I care?"

But I did care. The name of my late mistress, Missy Antonia, had always carried happy associations. In those far-off days when she'd announced her intention to free me, I'd planned to keep it.

"Anyway, I'll never go back. I'd sooner throw myself over the side of your blockade runner."

Rankin's barrel-shaped chest heaved up and down as he chuckled. "You think I'd spend eight hundred dollars acquiring property without forethought to its safekeeping?"

This child gawped at that. Not referring to me as property, which was familiar language to any chattel slave. No, what stole my breath away was the big sums of time and money he'd invested in catching me. "I should be flattered that one slave girl deserves so much of a big Massa's attention."

"False modesty does you no credit. Your story has been published in every newspaper in Britain and France, not to mention the damned Union. It's important that your adventures are given an appropriate conclusion for all the world to see."

"Plenty other escaped slaves have told their tales." Now I was curious as well as frightened. "What's so different about mine?"

Big Massa scratched his spade-shaped chin, pretending to be thinking things through. "Well, let me see. Firstly, we have your widely publicised escape from a Society Hill plantation that is not only owned by my neighbour, but also lies at the heart of my political constituency. Next, there's the exceedingly prominent role you played alongside that abolitionist witch, Lady Alice Featherfax, in frustrating and embarrassing the organisers of the Liberty Bazaar, with whom I am closely associated."

He paused a moment, sucking long, slow breaths as if his heart done been beating too fast and he was trying to slow it down. "Yet perhaps what makes you especially deserving of my consideration is the episode in St George's Hall where you made me seem like a damned fool in front of the cream of European society." Rankin glanced down at the two white terriers still sitting by his feet. "Didn't she, Josie? Didn't she, Nap? You hear me? You paying attention, you two?"

Rising, he kicked first one dog, then the other. They squealed as they went skimming across the wooden floor.

"Raised 'em from ten-week-old pups. Trained 'em myself.

Loved 'em, loved 'em deep. But a dog that ain't its Massa's is less than useless." He didn't look up, though his voice crackled.

He took out a big six-shooter pistol and aimed it at one of the dogs. "Your fault now that they have to die."

"Any dog will chase after fresh meat. No matter what …"

Metallic click as he thumbed back the pistol's hammer. "I cannot tolerate disloyalty – in any creature I own."

"They don't deserve punishment for doing what comes natural."

He gave me a sideways look and for an instant I thought I glimpsed real regret in those alligator eyes. "You think I *want* to do this?"

"Why else?"

"They have to be shown who their Massa is. Dogs and slaves alike. They have to be shown."

"Why not show mercy? You have that power."

"No I don't." Big Massa gave me a helpless look that I'd never thought to see in that boulder-tumble of a face. "When I was much younger I once showed mercy to a runaway. No branding, no beating, just a few days behind bars. But then he ran again and my little brother got in his way. Only ten, but that didn't stop him being strangled to stop his hollering. My own brother murdered. All because of my so-called mercy. That runaway never did get caught, and I swore on my daddy's Bible I'd never show such weakness again."

He turned and looked back at the dog and when he spoke again, the granite tone returned to his voice. "I'm the Massa or I'm nothing at all."

He pulled the trigger. Hard bang, soft whelp. One of the terriers lay dead, splay of blood staining the fine carpet.

The other dog set up a furious barking.

"Cease that noise! Quiet, damn you!" Fleck of spittle

sprayed from big Massa's mouth.

Little dog paid no heed.

Another pistol shot.

Barking stopped.

My voice was dripping with sarcasm. "I guess that makes you feel real powerful, *Massa*?"

His tone was icy. "Just so as you know what I'm capable of, girl."

Couldn't keep the loathing from my voice. "I know from my brother Benjamin what you're capable of."

He considered this a moment as if a lamp got lit somewhere in his head. "Ah yes, Benjamin … Fine boy, as I recall. But like you, somewhat mentally deranged. And I see now why you hate me so much."

"Damned straight. And I'll never submit to bondage, not ever."

"Of course you won't." His smile was almost kindly. "When we return to Society Hill, you will be allowed to run away again – only this time you won't escape the jaws of those big hungry hounds."

*

They took me down into a cellar where a narrow bed and two chairs were lit by a solitary grease lamp; straw scattered on the stone floor; pot in one corner for a toilet. Low ceiling trapped odours of sour stone and lamp-black. On one chair lay a copy of John Milton's *Paradise Lost*, which happened to be among my favourite poems. Rankin's callous taunt, I wondered? Leastways I had something to occupy my mind.

Some while later, the door opened and a slender figure descended the stairs into the cellar. Only met Lord Harrowby once, yet I recognised him instantly. Even in his starched shirt sleeves and white britches, he conveyed a peacocky self-regard that minded me of Lord Byron.

"Miss Giddings, it is my sincerest, *sincerest* wish that you are not too distressed by this somewhat unseemly turn of events."

This child looked at him coolly. "By which you mean my unlawful abduction?"

"I see you've been reading *Paradise Lost*." Harrowby nodded in the direction of the poem, which lay open on the bed. "I gather from my niece, Alice, that you appreciate his work immensely and thought to comfort you."

Since there was nothing to be gained by riling him, I said: "Thank you. That was considerate."

"I have brought some sweetmeats." He indicated various confections symmetrically arranged on a dainty silver salver he was carrying. "There are sugared almonds and gingerbread wafers, macaroons, and some marzipan fancies. I must confess to an ineffably, *ineffably* sweet tooth."

Seemed this richcrat planned on sharing a small feast of cake and candy with me, but, compared with my confrontation with Rankin, this didn't appear such a bad alternative.

"May I sit?" His courtly etiquette was downright absurd in the circumstances, yet I had no choice but to play along. When we were both seated, he placed the sweetmeats on the bed nearby and bade me help myself.

I took a sugared almond; he a marzipan fancy.

Pushing it into the side of his mouth, he spoke with soft urgency. "Miss Giddings, you must know that I'm a reluctant conspirator in this unpleasantness, forced to desperate measures by the threat of financial calamity. If the *Himalaya* is not completed, I shall be declared bankrupt. Nonetheless, I am vehemently, *vehemently* opposed to slavery and it is not my wish that you should return to bondage."

His smile was disarming, though I knew from Lady Alice that he was a slippery schemer. All the same, I sensed some genuine sympathy and figured on exploiting it to discover the whereabouts of Soldier-boy. If he really did want to be my friend, now was the time to prove it.

"Is Jubal de Brooke still staying here as your guest?"

Tried not to sound too interested but struggled to hide my disappointment when Harrowby shook his head.

There was a note of profound weariness in his voice. "Sadly we have fallen out. Jubal has taken rooms in a hotel in Liverpool. However, I still hope he can be persuaded to act reasonably. As you are aware he, too, will be ruined unless he co-operates."

Now this was something – yes it was! This richcrat clearly believed I knew more than I did, doubtless due to misguided presumptions about my conversation with Thomas McConville, witnessed but not overheard by Fat-boy and Blessing Dubois.

"He's stubborn all right," I said, which was nothing less than God's truth.

"Would you care for a marzipan fancy?"

Little cakes looked a piece too sickly for my taste, but I took one nonetheless and was nicely surprised by its subtle taste and texture.

"Jubal thinks very highly of you, Miss Giddings. I do not mean to raise your hopes unduly, yet I pray his collaboration will result in an agreement with the senator that will allow you to keep your liberty."

I looked up sharply. "How so?"

"Jubal has a powerful bargaining chip, but he must be persuaded to use it."

"Then why doesn't he?"

"Because he wrongly believes handing over the cash from the Liberty Bazaar to obtain the *Himalaya* would betray the destitute families for whom it was intended. Yet if he was to insist that his co-operation was conditional on your freedom, the senator would have no alternative but to agree."

Giddy elation was soon replaced by suspicion that this was part of some deeper subterfuge to use me as bait for enticing Soldier-boy to hand over those monies.

"Jubal doesn't know I'm here, does he?"

Richcrat made a despairing shrug. "He refuses to receive me."

"A man of principle, then?"

"Would you care for the last gingerbread wafer?"

"Thank you, no."

"May I? They're my favourites."

"Please, take it."

But he didn't take the gingerbread wafer. Instead, he gazed at me with a look of forlorn whimsy. "Jubal is the man I wish I was but never managed to be. His ancestors in England might be less blue-blooded than he believed when he arrived, but that's done nothing, *nothing* to diminish him. Quite the opposite."

"Will you not eat that gingerbread wafer?" Of course I wasn't remotely interested in that morsel, but wanted a little time to consider what I'd learned.

Soldier-boy had custody of a great deal of money – I'd read newspaper reports that the Liberty Bazaar done raised £28,000 – and was refusing to hand this cash over to Harrowby and Rankin. Harrowby's talk of ancestors who weren't richcrats at all, combined with his disclosure that Jubal would be ruined also if he didn't play along, could mean only that Jubal was being blackmailed.

Almost laughed at that. Not from spite, you understand, but the powerful irony that Jubal de Brooke and this child done been manipulated all along by the same wicked enemy. Now, it appeared, our mutual foe was preparing to crush us both. Yet withal, Rankin minded me of a big old pike-fish whose jaws were being held open by a stick that he couldn't shift. Until he laid hands on those monies, he couldn't bite anyone.

A further encouraging thought occurred. "Your scheme to obtain the *Himalaya* is wrecked, isn't it? Jubal won't part with the cash, but also Mr McConville is refusing to sell the ship to anyone save the Royal Navy."

Richcrat took that gingerbread wafer, chewing on it ruminatively. "I do envy your idealism, Miss Giddings. But it is as Sir Robert Walpole once said: 'All men have their price'. Lamentably, he was correct."

Queer how scraps of knowledge sometimes spring from the deeps of your mind. See, Missy Antonia done taught me some British colonial history and I knew something of Walpole, Britain's first prime minister.

"Sir Robert didn't say that at all. He actually said: 'All *those* men have their price.' And he was referring to the band of ornery rascals conspiring against him."

Richcrat raised one eyebrow. "Alice was right, you are remarkably, *remarkably* well schooled."

I pressed my advantage. "Those conspirators might have recruited you and Rankin, but they would never have included Jubal de Brooke or Thomas McConville."

Surprisingly, Harrowby gave me a look of fondness that I believed was neither patronising nor affected. "You're entirely correct, Miss Giddings: I am not a virtuous fellow – though once I was. Nonetheless, I believe Jubal will hand over the monies because his elderly father would die of shame if the truth got out. Meanwhile Thomas, also an honourable chap, will see matters very differently when Rankin threatens him and all he holds dear."

"Man judges others by his own short measure: he'd better get ready for a shock." Laughed to scorn him. But my laughter was mirthless, my scorn hollow as I considered the poor chances of making my escape.

30

RECOLLECTIONS OF A CONFEDERATE GENERAL BY JUBAL DE BROOKE

Liverpool, England, December, 1863.

Through the frost-rimed window of my room in the Wellington Hotel, I watched a band of Christmas carollers in Dale Street. They carried a lantern hooked to a pole and held aloft so its radiance cast evenly on their song books. Faint strains of *Once in Royal David's City* carried up to my window. The street was a giddy wash of radiance from gas lamps and shop windows laid up with festive wares. Occasional drapes of snow rippled the inky night.

In other circumstances this would have been a happy scene. As it was, Sarah lay cold in the mortuary while her father was too shocked even to begin grieving. I, too, struggled to accept that she was gone; that this was not an aberration; that she was not waiting back at the house ready to embrace me with tender urgency, or scold me for disdaining Mrs Marjoribanks.

Barely six hours had passed since I'd found her on the

lower deck of the *Himalaya*, clutching that brass button. I was convinced this meant someone had been with her, that she'd torn the button from the other person's garment at the moment she'd fallen thirty feet to her death. Of course, this did not exclude the possibility of a tragic accident, but it did raise suspicions. I'd told Thomas McConville about the button and he'd agreed that I should inform the constables. The chief constable had agreed that an investigation was warranted, but where to start without suspects or witnesses?

Perhaps I was casting around for a scapegoat when much of the blame for what had happened could be laid at my door. Who was to say where that button had come from? One of her own garments, perhaps? She may well have been wandering around the ship in a distracted state of mind and tumbled from that dark, cluttered deck into the open hold. I'd known for a good while that Sarah was on the rim of hysteria and I should have taken better care of her … Yet, what might I have done that her father could not? For sure, I'd known Sarah had been anxious these last few weeks and this had resulted in uncharacteristic behaviour. Instead of responding with frustration and anger, I should have shown compassion and understanding. But, of course, it was too late for that and I was overwhelmed with a tide of guilt and regret …

In my distracted state, I wasn't certain when Sarah entered the room.

Her head was tilted at a sharp angle. One of her legs might also have been damaged, for she walked across the floorboards with a heavy limp, to sit opposite me in an armchair. A drop of blood gleamed at the corner of her mouth and her complexion was waxen. This, though, was no ghost.

"I'm so sorry, Sarah."

She didn't speak, nor even react.

"Can you forgive me?"

The air behind her obtained a misty texture that began to stir and weave itself into human shapes. I saw Turnbull, the liveryman from Harrisonburg who had been killed at First Manassas; and Bobbie Patterson, the streetcar driver from Washington DC, laid open like a tin colander at Gettysburg. And I saw Sergeant Papajohn, the comrade I'd fixed for the grave at Chickamauga Creek.

I was hallucinating again, yet this time I had a crucial advantage: I knew what was happening.

"Do you need forgiveness?" The question came not from Sarah, or those fallen boys, but from someplace inside my own head. "Can you hold yourself to account for every death? You cannot carry guilt that isn't rightly yours."

In that instant, I recognised the nature of my malady, and confronted it. When I looked again, the armchair was empty, the misty human shapes had vanished. This was not a victory – how could it be, amid so much loss? Yet it was the start of recovery. Of this I was certain.

*

Some good while later, a soft rap on the door roused me from my introspection. Taking a few moments to compose myself, I crossed the room to open it.

Before me, a portly Negro stood in the hotel corridor. He was a gaudily clad fellow wearing a yellow velveteen frock coat and pork-pie hat.

"Good evening, General de Brooke, sir." He raised the hat and made a smile that displayed two even decks of teeth. "My name is Clement Mureau. I've been requested to call on you by Senator Rankin and Lord Harrowby."

"I have nothing to discuss with either."

"I'm instructed to request, General sir, that you attend Dunstead Manor at eleven thirty o'clock tomorrow morning, bringing with you specific monies."

"Well, you've followed your instructions, Mr Mureau, so I'll bid you good night."

I started to close the door but he jammed it open with the side of his boot.

"Begging the General's pardon, but is that to say you won't be attending, sir?"

"There would be no point. As I told you, I have nothing to say to either the senator or Lord Harrowby. Now please remove your foot from my door."

His foot remained. "In that case, I'm also instructed to tell you, General sir, that a certain party – namely a runaway slave girl for whom Senator Rankin believes you have a particular regard – is currently present at the manor."

I do admit to being more stupefied than angered. "Are you saying Trinity Giddings is being held hostage?"

"I'm not instructed to tell you that, General, sir."

"I see…" I relaxed my pressure on the door and reluctantly invited him into my room. Although he was clearly nothing more than a messenger, there were things that needed saying that I didn't want overheard by passers-by in the hotel corridor.

"Miss Giddings' presence at Dunstead Manor must mean she's been taken there against her will," I said. "And since she'd lately been given custody of certain warship designs, I can only deduce that these have fallen into the hands of the senator and Lord Harrowby."

Mureau stood in my room, holding the little pork-pie hat against his vast chest. His expression of practised unscrupulousness struck an almost comic contrast to my back-

and-forth pacing.

"That being the case, they must be aware that Thomas McConville is refusing to sell this warship to them. So they can have no possible use for these funds in relation to the procurement of this warship."

I was reasoning aloud rather than addressing Mureau, and was therefore surprised when he responded. "That ain't necessarily so, General sir."

"What do you mean?"

"I don't know any more than I just told you, sir." Mureau sounded genuinely abject. "It's just what got told to me by the senator: that the deal for the big battle boat might yet go ahead. Only way to find out more, sir, is to attend the manor tomorrow morning, like the senator requests."

*

My approach sent two crows clapping into the bright winter sky over Dunstead Manor, wings glinting in the sunlight as they drifted across the parkland, white and stiff with frost.

I'd paid off the cab on the main road and walked up the quarter-mile driveway carrying my sturdy leather holdall. The unusual nature of my request had prompted an inquisitive expression from the bank manager, but he maintained a diplomatic silence as a clerk filled the holdall.

As I walked, one of my new boots continued to chafe the side of my foot, while the stiff leather squeaked with each step as if I was treading on some small critter. I'd put on the unworn boots without forethought and not become aware of the problem until it was too late to return to the hotel to change them.

Clement Mureau waited by the manor house door and

escorted me to the great hall where Rankin and Harrowby were waiting.

As I followed him through the lobby, every step sent a fresh poke of pain through my left foot, while the squeak of the new leather scraped my nerves.

My hosts were waiting at the far end of Harrowby's long banqueting table. Rankin instructed Mureau to leave and I placed my holdall on the table.

"I'm pleased you are here, Jubal," Harrowby said.

"Regrettably, I cannot say the same, Arthur."

My next words were directed at both Harrowby and Rankin. "Before we proceed any further, I want to see Trinity Giddings."

The senator scowled, but his incipient protest was stifled by Harrowby.

"I shall fetch her at once."

Disappearing into the scullery, he returned a few moments later with Trinity at his side. I was mightily relieved that she appeared unharmed, if a trifle dishevelled.

"Are you all right?"

"Thank you, yes." She made a small smile. "Save, of course, for being held captive."

Rankin's voice intruded. "Very well, you've seen her, de Brooke. Now hand over the cash."

"But you no longer have need of it." I said. "You must know the *Himalaya* will never become a Confederate ship because Thomas McConville will not sell her to you."

"You underestimate us, sir …"

"I doubt it. Next to you, Robespierre was a dabbler."

"Give me that bag, damn you."

"Not without knowing what you mean to do with it."

Rankin sounded increasingly exasperated. "We can deal with

Thomas McConville and still acquire the *Himalaya*."

"Exactly how do you propose to deal with Thomas? When last I spoke to him on this matter he was quite adamant that the ship would be sold to the British navy."

Rankin's breath streamed from flared nostrils, giving him the aspect of an enraged bull. Plainly, he didn't want to reveal his intentions, but realised he had no choice if he was to obtain the holdall. "In view of his poor health and recent bereavement, removing McConville would be simple. With his daughter's tragic demise, the shipyard would be wound up and its assets pass to the bank."

"Have you parted company with your senses, Rankin?" I failed to keep the note of disbelief from my voice.

"Quite the reverse. I've reached an agreement with Erasmus Pickering, the bank's director. If the shipyard is declared insolvent, we will acquire the *Himalaya* as part of the distribution of its assets."

The mention of that name ignited a time-fuse deep in my memory. It burned slowly at first, barely alight, then the spark took hold and went fizzing through my mind, illuminating forgotten detail with alarming clarity. I recalled that brass button with the shred of Brunswick green cloth I'd found in Sarah's hand; the arrival of Erasmus Pickering at the house in Abercromby Square, moments after I'd left her that last time; Pickering striding along the pavement; Pickering stepping up to the door; Pickering in his Brunswick green frock coat with those smart brass buttons.

I looked at Rankin with renewed astonishment. "Pickering – he killed Sarah, didn't he?"

"That's a wild accusation, de Brooke."

"Yet nothing less than the truth. You put him up to it, didn't you?"

Rankin's shrug was disturbingly vague.

"If you want this holdall, Rankin, you'd better give me a proper answer."

"You've got it wrong, de Brooke." His manner was relaxed, almost affable. "Pickering approached *me*."

"Yet you did nothing to dissuade him?"

"From a course of action that would directly benefit the Confederacy?"

I strove to marshal my thoughts. Following Sarah's death, it would hardly be suspicious if Thomas was to expire sooner rather than later. As he now had no heir, the insolvent shipyard would be shut down and control of its affairs passed to Pickering as the bank's director. He would then be in a position to lay up enormous profits from the sale of the shipyard's assets, including the *Himalaya*.

I turned to Harrowby and saw him quail at my aghast expression. "I could believe anything of this man. But *you*, Arthur?"

"I knew nothing of Pickering's plan, Jubal. I would not have countenanced it." That Harrowby, usually the most loquacious of individuals, could find no more than two short sentences suggested he was telling the truth.

"This lunacy must end here," I said.

Tugging the holdall from the table, I looked at Trinity, standing with Harrowby, behind Rankin. "Miss Giddings and I are leaving."

She started to move towards me, but Harrowby caught her arm.

In the same instant, I saw Rankin reach into his frock coat and pull out a small Derringer pistol.

"If you believe I'll let you stroll off with the cash and this creature, it's you who needs a head-doctor. Fact is, de Brooke, they're both my property now."

I glanced again at Harrowby. "Has decency completely deserted you, Arthur?"

"I'm so very, *very* sorry, Jubal." He, too, produced a pistol – a Remington Army Model six-shooter that was far more lethal than Rankin's single-shot miniature.

What I did next hinged on a conviction that Harrowby would not shoot, whereas Rankin would.

The space separating Rankin and me was perhaps twenty paces. I'd take each one slowly, pausing for a few seconds before the next, with the objective of inducing him to fire off his single round at the greatest possible range. At twenty paces his stunted pistol would be wildly inaccurate; at ten, the risk of his hitting me would double; at five, well, it would be difficult to miss – yet, by that time, I'd be upon him.

"You'd better be a sure shot, Rankin, otherwise I'll take away that pop-gun and march you to the constables myself."

Step one ... step two. My left foot smarted where the boot abraded the flesh. In the same movement, the squawk of unsupple leather scratched my eardrums.

"Stop right there, de Brooke!" There was rising anxiety in Rankin's voice.

"Killing helpless slaves is one thing, Rankin. Murdering a frail old man – well, that would probably take a fraction more nerve. But the question you must answer in the next few seconds is this: do you have it in your coward's hide to pull that trigger and lay open a general of the Confederacy?"

I took another three slow steps. Each one scoured the tender skin on my foot and brought another aggravating oink from the boot.

"You can't win, de Brooke." Rankin's affected laughter was unconvincing, yet not as close to panic as I'd hoped. "Even if you reach me, I'm twice as big as you and a whole lot stronger."

I kept my tone measured, almost casual. "If you'd ever fought a battle, Rankin, you'd know that none of that matters. Speed is all that counts."

I continued my advance, pausing between strides, hoping he'd fire that one round before I got too close, praying it would fly over my head or wide of my chest. But, dammit, my foot was agonisingly sore, my nerves mauled by the high-pitched creak of new boot-leather.

"You'd best stop, de Brooke. Stop, I say, or I will shoot!"

An extra layer of alarm in his voice pushed the pain in my foot from the front of my mind, at least until my next step.

"There must be a way of resolving these issues, Jubal," Harrowby said. His loss of nerve was crucial to the success of my plan, because his revolver was far more dangerous than Rankin's Derringer. Yet Harrowby didn't sound especially anxious.

Another step closer ... another. More foot-pain. More boot-noise – an iron gate swinging on a rusty hinge. Was I the only one in that room who could hear it?

"Jubal, for pity's sake!" This was more encouraging from Harrowby – half an octave higher and perceptibly more agitated.

There was a mechanical click as Rankin cocked the Derringer's hammer.

"I'll blast you to hell, de Brooke. On my oath I will!"

Yet still he didn't shoot.

At a distance of ten paces, I was desperate for him to pull that trigger. Any closer and the side of a barn would present a more difficult target. I tried again to taunt him. "You're all talk, aren't you, Rankin? If you weren't a spineless rogue you'd have shot me before now."

Twelve paces … thirteen …

The air was hammered from my lungs.

I doubled up, choking for air, stumbling sideways. For a few seconds I clung to the edge of the table. A warm seeping sensation in my abdomen told me I was bleeding. I slid to the floor.

Down on all fours, I watched blood spatter and pool on the stone flags. How curious that the only source of pain was my left foot. But at least that damned boot-squeak had stopped.

There was a different smell, too, a reminiscent one. Scorched powder.

And Rankin's voice, forcing itself to be heard above the distant yet deafening fizz in my ears: "Not much of a hero now, are you, General?"

31

EXPERIENCES IN THE LIFE OF A SLAVE GIRL BY TRINITY GIDDINGS

Liverpool, England, December, 1863.

Soldier-boy was moonstruck; but I'd known that long before he began his suicidal advance on States Rights Rankin. You wade through a cold stream in britches and shoes just for a dance, you got to be borderline crazy.

I expected Rankin to pull that trigger any moment as Soldier-boy went on facing him down, taunting and insulting and ridiculing.

Did Jubal want to die?

Never seen such audacious nerve, though I guessed he must have ... Boy lives through all those battles, he's bound to leave something of his soul behind. Maybe he thought he was back at Chancellorsville or Gettysburg. Minded myself that he'd fought those battles against President Lincoln's armies, against the cause of black folks' liberty. Yet Josiah done been right when he told me Soldier-boy was not our people's enemy.

Right now, he was on my side and I his. From what I could tell, he'd come to that creaky old manor house entirely on my account, and I'd be lying if I said I wasn't grateful.

I was aware, too, of Lord Harrowby's presence close behind me. With that long-barrelled six-shooter, he could have shot Jubal there and then.

So why didn't he? I knew from Lady Alice that Harrowby and Soldier-boy done become good friends – a fact confirmed from Harrowby's own mouth when he'd shown me kindness and sweetmeats.

No, this child wasn't surprised that Harrowby didn't open fire. But when Rankin's shot rang out and Jubal tumbled down and I thought only to panic, I was surprised to feel something curved and smooth and heavy being pressed into my hand.

It was the grip of the revolver.

Richcrat addressed me in a throaty hiss. "You must get Jubal to a physician. Do whatever you have to."

Vanished in a trice, leaving me with that pistol.

I tried to raise it but was shocked by its heaviness.

Jubal was crouching on hands and knees, blood spilling freely onto the floor. Rankin towered over him, hefting the Derringer over his head, fixing to smash it down like a club.

Drew back the hammer of the six-shooter, looked down the barrel, but it wavered and quivered in my grip, suddenly twice the weight, burning the muscles in my arm.

Rankin said something to Soldier-boy that I couldn't quite hear, words of mockery and malice about Jubal not being much of a hero right now.

I'd thought to aim for Rankin's heart, but it was all I could do to keep the revolver from dropping to my side. If I didn't shoot that instant, I'd be too late. Finger fumbled round the trigger guard; eyes blurred and smarted as I tried not to blink.

Rankin's club-arm came down.

Pistol jumped in my grip as if it done come alive. The bullet took Rankin between the shoulder blades, passing through his chest, throwing out crimson spume.

Big Massa swivelled drunkenly, turned to face me wearing a look of deep bewilderment. Opened his mouth to speak, but all that came out was a croak.

Should I have shown mercy? Lord forgive me, but I was utterly depleted of that Christian quality.

The pistol was oddly weightless as I pulled back the hammer and fired again. This time a chunk of his shoulder lifted out. Force of the bullet spun him in a semi-circle and made one arm flip up, as if he was performing a Virginia reel.

Somehow, big Massa stayed on his feet.

My final bullet took away the side of his head and that enormous frame slowly toppled, sprawling across the table before slithering to the floor.

The gun became weighty again, sweating hot stinky fumes like a toiling beast.

Shot a man dead. How did I feel? Hard to say. No giddy rush of revenge. Big Massa was just an obstacle that had to be moved aside for the sake of those dear to me, just as I'd shift a rock that was stopping up a stream and preventing the water from reaching folk who needed to drink.

In truth, this child felt nothing save powerful weary numbness ... until my fool of a brain minded me that Jubal would surely die unless I got a physician very soon.

He was still down on hands and knees, blood oozing from his stomach, puddling on the dinted stone floor. Placing the revolver on the table, I ran to his side.

"You hear me, Jubal?"

Wheezy words stumbled from his mouth. "Is that

you, Trinity?"

"Yes," I said. "Yes, it's me."

*

Never been on a hospital ward before: beds set out in regimented lines under cones of waxy gaslight; uneasy quietness burdened with odours of chlorine and iodine, camphor and the odd waft of excrement.

The nurse showed me to Soldier-boy's bedside.

He looked up at me from a mound of pillows, fashioned a weary grin. "I believe I must thank you for my life."

Sitting on the chair near his bed, I returned the smile. "Well, since you got shot on my account I reckon it's me should be thanking you. But let's not quibble."

"The surgeon tells me I'm very lucky. The bullet went straight through my waist without touching anything vital. But there's a great deal of damage to the abdominal muscles. I'll need a stick to walk for a good long while; never fight another battle."

No more battles was not necessarily bad news, though this was not a fitten occasion to say so.

After the shooting, I'd searched the manor house in hopes of enlisting help from Harrowby's servants, but the place was deserted – Fat-boy and Blessing Dubois had also vanished. So I'd flagged down a cab on the main road and brought Soldier-boy directly to the infirmary in Brownlow Street. Physician said he'd have died from loss of blood if we'd arrived any later.

"Are you comfortable?"

"Thank you, yes. All the more so for seeing you." His features strained as he tried to adjust his posture, then gave up with a frustrated snort.

"You must lie back and rest."

"You must tell me what happened."

"When you're stronger."

"Now, Trinity. Please."

When I'd done telling, he regarded me sternly.

"What you did took great courage."

"It's not courage when you have no choice."

"You could have run – as Arthur did."

"You shouldn't be too angry with him. He didn't have to give me the gun." Lord knew why I was defending that richcrat dandy.

Soldier-boy paused, as if studying on the present situation. "The world will hardly be a worse place for not having Rankin in it, but the authorities will want to question both of us about what happened."

"You think there'll be trouble?"

He shook his head. "You acted to prevent a murder. My account will corroborate yours, and Arthur – the only other witness – is on the run."

"Where will he go?"

"Abroad, I think, until the furore subsides." He made a dry chuckle and I sensed that, despite everything, he was still fond of Lord Harrowby. "He'll no doubt review the prospect of returning to Britain from the faro tables of some swish Parisian salon."

"He told me about the plot to blackmail you." I looked away, embarrassed to possess this shabby knowledge. "I'm so sorry, Jubal."

Soldier-boy kept his eyes on mine. "I can't pretend it wasn't a shock. But, the only true way to judge a person is by their actions. Questions of pedigree are better left to the breeders of dogs and horses."

Reaching under my chair, I produced his leather holdall, which I'd made sure to bring in the cab. Girl goes around carrying £28,000, she'd better make sure she keeps it safe. "I thought you'd be anxious as to the whereabouts of this."

Far from expressing gratitude or relief, Soldier-boy's earnest tone done been replaced by an attitude of mild amusement. "You haven't looked inside, have you?"

"It's not my property." I spoke tartly, somewhat irritated by his airy manner.

"Your trustworthiness does you credit, Trinity." Sensing my annoyance, he addressed me more soberly. "But please look inside the bag."

Baffled, I hefted the holdall onto my lap and unfastened the brass buckles. My puzzlement deepened as I found myself looking not at a fortune in bank bills but many small bundles of newsprint.

"Persuading the bank manager to fill it with old newspaper was considerably more difficult than getting him to stuff it with cash."

"He does run a bank, not a news-stand." Looked up from the bag. "Why did you bring it to the manor house?"

"A ruse. They wouldn't have allowed me in without it."

"But if you had no intention of submitting to the threat of blackmail, why did you come at all?"

Pale blue eyes fastened on mine. "Is that not obvious?"

Penny finally dropped. I realised this man done risked everything to save me.

"They knew you'd come for me, didn't they?"

He gave a small smile. "They used you as bait, but in the end *you* trapped *them*."

"We trapped them."

He reached across and held my hand and we sat there companionably for some time, with no need for words.

A nurse carrying a copper bedpan stumbled and it fell clattering on the floor, spilling its pungent contents. Nurse cussed, began mopping.

When I turned back, I saw Jubal done slid back into unconsciousness.

32

RECOLLECTIONS OF A CONFEDERATE GENERAL BY JUBAL DE BROOKE

Liverpool, England, January, 1864.

Sarah was laid to rest two weeks after her death. We stood by the lip of the grave in St James' Cemetery in Liverpool as the clergyman concluded the liturgy. It was a cold January morning, though not so cold as to freeze the ground and keep the grave-diggers from their work. A cape of overcast cloud threatened rain, but none came.

We mourners formed a queue behind Thomas McConville, who tossed a handful of earth onto the casket before retreating to the cortège on the avenue a few yards away.

After a short while, I joined him.

"How is your wound, Jubal?" He looked at me with a concerned expression.

"There's a little discomfort, but no pain." I touched my side, still bandaged, but now without stitches which meant I could walk using a stick. "And how are you, Thomas?"

"Well enough for this business." He made a wheezy chuckle. "There are plenty here who reckoned they'd be burying two McConvilles today."

"You're one of the toughest men I've known." This wasn't flattery: my friend had summoned considerable energy and presence of mind to manage his daughter's funeral arrangements.

"There are times when I wish I wasn't so damned resilient." He spoke with an air of wistfulness. "A great part of me is ready to quit this world, but I have a stubborn streak that seems intent on keeping me here. The physician tells me I shall be waking up of a morning for a while yet."

"That pleases me immensely, Thomas."

He turned to watch the line of mourners file past Sarah's grave, each depositing a small amount of earth on the coffin. "I received a letter this morning from the Admiralty."

"Good news, I hope?"

"I suppose it is. Their Lordships have confirmed that they'll purchase the *Himalaya* for the sum I require, which will return the shipyard to profitability."

He sounded indifferent to these encouraging developments and I found his attitude confusing.

"Why didn't Sarah come to me?" He looked at me sharply. "If she'd come to me, rather than going to that idiot Pickering, she wouldn't be lying in yonder grave, nor he facing the gallows."

"You mustn't reproach yourself, Thomas." I touched his forearm. "I believe Sarah approached Pickering because she was reluctant to burden you with shipyard business. She took some wrong turns, as we all do, but no doubt with the best of intentions and – "

"You'd better mind what you're saying, Jubal."

I gave my friend a baffled look.

"Mrs Marjoribanks is approaching – not a word of this shipyard business to her, unless you want it known in every corner of Liverpool within the hour."

This would, indeed, be a memorable day: after nearly four months in Liverpool I was finally going to meet the city's most accomplished gossip. Glancing over my shoulder, I saw a petite young woman with dark hair and engaging eyes coming towards us and felt somewhat wrong-footed because I'd been anticipating an elderly harridan.

After McConville had introduced me to Mrs Marjoribanks, she spoke some kind words about Sarah in a surprisingly melodic voice.

It would be uncharitable to suggest that Mrs Marjoribanks had attended the funeral for any other purpose than to pay her respects to Sarah. Nonetheless, I obtained a sense of rising excitement in her tone as she glanced from McConville to me. "Has either of you gentlemen heard from Lord Harrowby?"

Watching us shake our heads, she launched into her own tidings with gusto. "Your lack of information is to be expected, for I received intelligence only yesterday that Lord Harrowby has been seen at the residence of our mutual friend, Countess Giavoglio, in Milan. Further, it is my firm understanding that he is to return to Britain within the month to defend his reputation and resume his business activities, having received a substantial cash investment from commercial interests in Italy."

I maintained an indifferent gaze, though this was merely a pretence to deny Mrs Marjoribanks the satisfaction of having surprised me.

Yet even as I congratulated myself on keeping these feelings hidden, Mrs Marjoribanks outflanked me with a manoeuvre that defied indifference. "Regrettable news, is it not, that Miss Giddings is quitting Liverpool?"

I'd somehow evaded serious injury on the battlefield, but this was exactly how I imagined I'd feel when my luck ran out: numb shock and a curious sense of time marching to a different beat. "Where is she going?"

Mrs Marjoribanks' face was very close to mine, though I wasn't aware of having moved towards her. "When is she leaving?"

A number of mourners turned towards me.

With an apprehensive expression, Mrs Marjoribanks stepped back. "Why, my understanding is that Miss Giddings is preparing to take ship for the United States – even as we speak. According to my information …"

I didn't hear the rest of her sentence for I was hurrying along the cemetery's central avenue in the direction of Upper Parliament Street.

I'd visited Lady Alice Featherfax's house only a few days previously to thank Trinity for coming to see me at the infirmary. Although attentive and concerned for my welfare, she'd appeared distracted. Now I knew why.

Even as I hastened towards Falkner Square, I couldn't decide what I'd do when I got there. Of course I had powerful feelings for Trinity. The trouble was I wasn't sure where I expected them to lead. I'd presumed there would be plenty of time to find out. How wrong I'd been.

Dodging the carriages as I crossed Sandon Street, I approached the problem from a different direction. If I couldn't figure out what I did want, I certainly knew what I *didn't*. I hadn't risked everything when I'd faced Rankin at Dunstead Manor so Trinity could sail away as if none of it had happened. That we should part with so many unanswered questions was unthinkable.

*

Lady Alice received me in the drawing room.

"*Bonjour, Général.* Though I suspect there is little *bon* about the nature of your call."

"I'm no longer a general, Lady Alice," I said. "I've resigned my commission."

This was not entirely true. I'd written to offer my resignation, but it hadn't yet been accepted. Nonetheless I doubted there would be anyone in Richmond sorry to see the last of me. Anxious to avoid another scandal, Sir Eustace Baggott had arranged for the events at Dunstead Manor to be passed off as a shooting accident. For its part, the Confederacy would be only too keen to avoid the embarrassment of a public trial that would have revealed how a Rebel general had been wounded by a Confederate senator, who was subsequently killed by an escaped slave girl.

Lady Alice regarded me with a querulous expression. "Well, *Mr* de Brooke, what have you to say for yourself?"

"I must see Trinity at once."

"She is not here."

"So Mrs Marjoribanks' intelligence is correct?"

With annoying insouciance, Lady Alice moved across the room to examine a large King James Bible that was lying open on her writing bureau. "That rather depends on what Mrs Marjoribanks has told you."

"She says Trinity is quitting Liverpool this very day, bound for the United States."

Lady Alice looked at me with a judgmental stare. "That is quite right. Trinity is taking a steamer to New York."

"Will you tell me her reason for leaving?"

"You!" Her eyes glinted. "You are her reason."

"I'd rather hoped I might be among her reasons for staying."

"That might have been so if you'd chosen to express your feelings for her more directly." Lady Alice's anger had subsided into stifled frustration.

My own voice was fuelled with exasperation. "It was for Trinity that I made a spectacle of myself that day at Grassendale; for her that I placed myself at no small hazard in the encounter with Senator Rankin. How much more directly can a fellow express himself?"

None of this passed muster with Lady Alice. "Men often believe actions speak louder than words, Mr de Brooke; but an earnestly spoken sentiment is far more likely to impress a lady of Trinity's sensibilities."

I threw up my hands in a gesture of agitation. "The situation is complicated. I thought there would be time enough to consider the best tactics."

She looked at me with Old Testament severity. "Trinity's happiness is at issue here, not some military objective. You must uncomplicate your situation and you must do it *rapidamente*."

"To do that, I need your help."

"Do you consider that you deserve it?"

This woman was infuriating, but I could not afford to lose my patience with her. "Does Trinity deserve otherwise?"

This last salvo appeared to have found a chink in Lady Alice's armour. "Very well, then …"

"Tell me where I can find Trinity."

Lady Alice turned away, as if pondering the question, then shut the Bible with a thunderous clap. "She is boarding the SS *Arabian*, presently moored at Prince's Dock. My brougham is waiting outside. You arrived just as I was preparing to leave for the dockside to see her off, but in view of what you have said, I think it better that you go instead."

The drive to the waterfront was excruciatingly slow. Traffic on Duke Street was halted by a herd of cattle being driven across the road. Leaning from the carriage window, I watched people on the sidewalk moving more quickly. Were it not for the wound in my side, I'd have jumped out and run.

When, at last, we arrived at Prince's Parade, I made for the towering masts of the Arabian. I'd expected to see Trinity standing by the companionway, awaiting Lady Alice. I even pictured the puzzled look on her face when she saw me.

Instead, I was confronted by a churning crowd of several hundred souls on a dockside with not one square foot of unoccupied space.

33

EXPERIENCES IN THE LIFE OF A SLAVE GIRL BY TRINITY GIDDINGS

Liverpool, England, January, 1864.

Prince's Parade thronged with folk readying themselves for long voyages and painful absences. Spiky tang of horse-sweat and greasy whiff of coal-smoke spoke of one journey's end and another's beginning.

This child had no wish to leave Liverpool. Yet I had to clear my head of that Soldier-boy or lose what little wit that still remained. No doubt Jubal did have some fondness for me, and also a modicum of respect. In another time, things might have turned out differently. But it was like this: slave girl gets too much above herself, she's got an awful long way to tumble. Now that may strike you as faint-hearted, even plain cowardly. Truth was that I had too little faith and too much pride.

Lady Alice done listened to my woes with great sympathy; even offered to approach Jubal, setting them out. Yet what would that have achieved, save to trade my dignity for his pity?

Lady Alice also entreated me to say goodbye to him, but that would have been downright awkward. Back a boy into a corner and he'll likely tell you what he thinks he ought to say in place of what he really believes.

So we went to see Thomas Haines Dudley at the United States Consulate, who kindly arranged my passage to New York, where provision would be made for my immediate needs. What I would do in the future was a matter for providence.

The ship that would carry me back across the Atlantic, the *Arabian*, now lay at the dockside. She was a handsome steamer with spacious accommodation for passengers – though not on the same scale as the *Himalaya*, due to be acquired by the Royal Navy from that wily old boy, Thomas McConville. In this respect, I'd finished the task which I believe the Lord brought me here to complete, so my decision to quit Liverpool was logical as well as practical.

The *Arabian* sounded her steam-whistle, signalling that she was preparing to cast off.

I looked round for Lady Alice, who'd promised to come to the landing stage to wave goodbye.

Many passengers were already moving along the companionways. Others had already boarded and were calling to loved ones from the tall sides.

Panicky sensations fizzed in my chest. Soon I'd be alone again, not one soul known to me in New York City. Did I truly want to leave behind all those friends I'd made in Liverpool? Yet it wasn't a matter of wanting to leave, but needing to.

I did so want to say goodbye to Alice, but where the devil was she? I glanced round the milling dockside, but my vision was obstructed by a man who'd appeared directly in front of me. It took me a moment to realise it was Soldier-boy himself.

"Lady Alice sends her apologies. I came in her place."

What he'd said didn't make any sense. Fixed him with a scolding stare. "This is hardly an occasion for silliness, Jubal."

"No, Trinity, it is not."

"And yet you say Alice sent you here?"

His breeziness collapsed in an expression of bewilderment. "In a manner of speaking, she did. But I'm here of my own choosing."

"Why *are* you here, Jubal?"

Soldier-boy said nothing. Mouth shifted, words stayed put.

Had he come to say a complicated goodbye – of the kind I'd tried so hard to avoid? Or was there more bound up in his speechlessness than I done trusted myself to imagine? Maybe. But every which way you looked at this, those words could only come from him.

I asked my question again: "What are you doing here, Jubal?"

More clumsy hush. Dockside bustle raced away, leaving us like small objects viewed from the wrong end of a telescope. No one but Jubal and me in that pinhead universe. Minded the time we danced the *varsovienne* after he'd crossed that stream at Grassendale. Then, as now, we stood on the same earth as the folk all around, yet were in the gaze of a different star.

At last, he said: "You mustn't go to New York, Trinity."

"Why must I not?"

"If you stayed in Liverpool, you'd be happier."

"Happiness is a luxury for fools and richcrats."

More silence. Lord, Soldier-boy was keen on his silences that day.

I decided to force the issue. "Anyway, why would I be happier?"

There was an artlessness about his manner that minded me more of a gawky youth than a military commander. "I'd see to it," he said, at length.

305

"What leads you to suppose you could do such a thing, or that I'd want you to?"

"Everything we know about each other; and everything we've yet to discover."

"And what do you know about me?" I'd become aware that this was more of an interrogation than a conversation. Yet I had to press him, else we'd never have got anywhere.

Curiously, my bellicose manner seemed to bring him out from behind his defences. He began to speak with a little more confidence – I even detected a faint hint of the humour that had apparently deserted him. "I'll tell you one thing I know, Trinity: you can deal easily with all manner of hardship and adversity, but the idea of happiness is frightening. Should I tell you why?"

"I think you'd better, Jubal."

He regarded me directly. "For you, Trinity, happiness is an uncertain venture into a foreign land – a daunting prospect even for the bravest soul."

Had to admire his boldness. And though I didn't entirely care for what I was hearing, I let him continue without interruption. Girl waits this long for a boy to find words, she might as well get her money's worth.

"Consider the consequences if you get on board that steamer. We'd never meet again – and that's a prospect that certainly scares me."

"Am I to understand that you harbour feelings for me, Jubal?" I spoke tartly, but he appeared to sense that I was also teasing him.

"Would I be here else?"

"Might I inquire, then, as to when these feelings became apparent to you?"

"When does a trickle become a stream? A stream, a river?"

Small shrug, brave smile, then he said: "Is my affection so misplaced?"

I gazed at him very sternly. "You are dear to me also, Jubal, but I fear this may not be enough to overcome the very great obstacle that divides us."

"Which obstacle would that be, Trinity?"

"Your world and mine and the distance between."

"Distance has nothing to do with closeness. And besides, I no longer have a world, descended as I am from a common thief and shameless trickster."

I allowed myself to chuckle at that.

Jubal laughed too, but then his voice obtained abrupt tension. "Trinity, I have to know if there can be a future for you and me."

What to say? He was right: I done never experienced the sort of happiness white folk often took for granted. For this reason, I was afraid to cross the threshold lying before me for fear I might trip over and come to grief. Yet, why had I gone through that hole in the peach orchard fence before first fowl crow? Why had I ventured down the Great Pee Dee River, and crossed the Atlantic Ocean, if not for the want of happiness? When I forced myself to study on the question, I had to concede that nothing of any great worth was to be achieved without the acceptance of hazard and the commitment of faith.

Look I gave him was both flinty and tender. "If we're ready to make our peace, find our truth, yes, there can always be a future."

He smiled. "They'll be scandalised back home."

I smiled back. "I do hope so."

*

Walking arm in arm into that chilly afternoon, thronged with voyagers and mariners, I studied on our prospects. Chattel slave, lately up from bondage, and a Rebel general who'd fight no more battles? Many would laugh to scorn us, or worse. Yet, by turns and backtracks, I was certain we'd find what we sought, and more.

Now that was something … yes, it was.

Author's note

Historians agree that events in Liverpool and Birkenhead in 1863 could have radically redirected the course of the American Civil War. Unstinting efforts were made by the slave-holding Confederacy to acquire Mersey-built ironclad warships sufficiently powerful to break the Union navy's suffocating blockade of southern ports. Equally determined steps were taken by the North to stop this happening. If the blockade had been lifted, the South could have exported cotton to British textile mills, financing the shipment of vital war materials to supply its forces. Had the South achieved this aim, it might have won the American civil war.

In an age when 'Liverpool went Dixie', supporters of the Confederacy staged a successful bazaar in the city's St George's Hall in October, 1864, raising £20,000 for wounded Rebel soldiers and their families, but it could quite plausibly have taken place a year earlier, as it does in this work of fiction.

Doing the research was a diverse and rewarding exercise. Excellent books by historians including Richard Blackett and James M McPherson cast illuminating light on the period – as do the slave narratives, especially Harriet Jacobs' *Incidents in the Life of a Slave Girl*.

I found fascinating insights into mid-19th century Liverpool in contemporary novels such as Herman Melville's *Redburn: His First Voyage*, and articles by local journalist Hugh Shimmin, editor and owner of the wonderfully named *Porcupine* newspaper. Shimmin's street-level accounts vividly depict the destitute and chaotic lives of Liverpool's lower classes, including compelling reports of dogfights, bare-knuckle boxing, and grog dens.

Perhaps the most absorbing aspect of researching Liverpool in this period is that many important locations remain accessible. St George's Hall is as magnificent now as it was 150 years ago; the town houses of Falkner Square and Abercromby Square have lost none of their sedate elegance ; and the office building in Rumford Place, once occupied by 'Fraser Trenholm & Company', is much the same as when it was the unofficial 'Confederate embassy'.

The vast infrastructure of Liverpool Docks – where much of the narrative is set – has been preserved as part of a World Heritage Site. It requires very little imagination to transport yourself back in time to the tumultuous days when Liverpool was, as UNESCO's official citation describes it, "the supreme example of a commercial port at the time of Britain's greatest global influence."

Liverpool benefited enormously from the people who poured into the city from around the world in the 19th century, bringing a raft of new ideas, musical styles and cultures. Their influence later helped create the Liverpool of the Swinging Sixties, a hothouse of creative innovation from which the sound of the Beatles and the Mersey Beat famously emerged. Rather than exporting warships, Liverpudlians ultimately changed America with their music and messages of peace.

The championing of black music and blues musicians by the Beatles helped to combat racism, which still blights the South and other parts of the USA. In 2008, Liverpool became European Capital of Culture in recognition of its importance as a major international city. Today, Liverpool can look back on its history with mixed emotions, but can never be accused of not having made a difference – in Britain, America and the world at large. It is fascinating to contemplate what the next chapter will bring for this vibrant, ever-changing metropolis.

David Chadwick

For more great reading go to:

<u>www.aurorametro.com</u>

Select historical fiction to enjoy:

The Physician of Sanlucar by Jonathan Falla
978-1-906582-38-8

Kipling and Trix by Mary Hamer
978-1-906582-34-0

Pomegranate Sky by Louise Soraya Black
978-1-906582-10-4

The River's Song by Suchen Christine Lim
978-1-906582-98-2

The Evolutionist; the strange tale of Alfred Russel Wallace
by Avi Sirlin
978-1-906582-53-1

The Leipzig Affair by Fiona Rintoul
978-1-906582-97-5

Tracks, Racing the Sun by Sandro Martini
978-1-906582-43-2